To w... a great wr... from Penny

THE
PELICAN
MOTEL

PENNY GUMBERT

 FriesenPress

Suite 300 - 990 Fort St
Victoria, BC, V8V 3K2
Canada

www.friesenpress.com

ISBN
978-1-4602-8888-7 (Hardcover)
978-1-4602-8889-4 (Paperback)
978-1-4602-8890-0 (eBook)

1. FICTION

Distributed to the trade by The Ingram Book Company

For Mom & Dad, both bibliophiles,
my favorite kind of people

And to my husband John, a snowbird at heart

TABLE OF CONTENTS

*The problem with temptation
is that you may never get another chance.*

Laurence J. Peter,
formulator of The Peter Principle

...but what if you *do*?

THE PELICAN MOTEL

CHAPTER ONE

When you go looking for rescue, you end up trapped in your own weakness.

Deb Caletti

What was she to do? Run and hide? Not with her arthritis. Outwit her guards? Could she? Call for reinforcements? No, she was alone. It takes someone strong to march all by herself into her eighties, best foot forward. Hard to do when you've a hump in your back and a lump in your throat, and all the more difficult for Esmerelda who was in the middle of a cat and mouse game. Is this how rodents feel? Puny and powerless, eating whatever's at hand? Esmerelda was the mouse, but one with no appetite – for food or anything else. Her fork picked at the meal, never actually spearing anything. Would they notice? To look busy she switched the fork to her left hand and picked up the silver knife. It felt so heavy. She cut off a piece of cutlet, then hid it under some lettuce while the fork came to her mouth. She pretended to chew and felt like Harpo Marx, masticating and rolling her eyes at the flavors. She giggled, then stopped. Better be careful. They might take note and report her to the doctor.

She had no taste for anything these days. She sighed, put down her cutlery and patted her lips with the napkin. A streak of burgundy lipstick stained the damask. Would it be a permanent stain? It was one of a set of twelve she and her husband David had purchased in Spain. Why were they using her keepsake linens? Had they asked her permission? Would she remember if they had?

Rain was hitting the window, desperate to get in, insistent and annoying. Tap, tap, tap. Rap, rappity rap. Rain, rain, go away, she mumbled to herself, and take me with you! She'd love to break out but how would an old lady make a run for it? Oil up the wheels of her walker and roll like hell? At two miles an hour? That might get her to the driveway before one of them came to retrieve her.

It was one of those early spring days when it was just as likely to sleet as to rain. She'd always loved to walk, no matter the weather, but she was rarely outside these days because Bruce and Jenny insisted she might slip and fall and break something or, worse still, get lost. Get lost? She knew her way around these roads, all the way to the golf course two miles away. She had walked it every day for fifteen years, until the knee problem. Someone should go with you, Esmerelda, Bruce would admonish. His ingratiating voice echoed in her ear. Always pleasant and thoughtful, Bruce. Too damned pleasant and too bloody thoughtful. And the man had an irritating habit of reminding her of her sister Susan who had never been someone she wanted to think about, especially now she was dead. When Bruce moved in Esmerelda's free will had moved out. How had that happened?

She stopped pretending to eat and concentrated on remembering the course of events. Only two days after Harry her physical thera- pist left for Florida Bruce's smiling face had appeared at the window, accompanied by a tap, tap, tap, just like the annoying rain; then a mimed 'hello!' through the pane until his glasses fell off his nose and he had to scurry around in the garden to find them. When he took time to clean them Esmerelda was able to fortify herself before going to the front door. Why was he here? She thought she'd got rid of him for good.

"You're back?" she'd asked, opening the door. "I thought you had business....."

"Just for a few days. Esmerelda. I felt so bad leaving. My guilty conscience, I guess." Esmerelda raised her eyebrows at that. "Guilt at leaving you, I mean, in the hands of a stranger. I wanted to come back before now."

Glad you didn't, thought Esmy. Instead, she said, "I was quite fine. Harry, the physical therapist did a grand job."

"Are you sure? You're....ambulatory again? That was a bad tumble you took." Who would have thought an old lady could survive a fall down sixteen stairs?

"I'm hunky dory," laughed Esmy and did a little twist of the hips. It was true. Bruce had worked miracles in more ways than physical. She'd tried to make sure Bruce knew that. "As good as new. Well, not new, I guess. But pretty much so. I thought I wrote and told you so?"

"I could hardly believe it. Had to see for myself, Esmerelda. No headaches? No other health issues?" He'd stepped inside the house, baggage and all, before she could say no.

"You're staying? Where's Jenny?"

"She's not with me on this trip. It's just a short business spree. I was passing through so I thought I'd take the opportunity to see with my own eyes that you're coping."

"More than coping, Bruce. I feel wonderful." Even now, sitting here months later watching her meal congeal, she could remember how great things had been back then. The physical therapy had restored her health and mobility and Harry's influence had enriched her life in ways she never thought possible. When had it all gone wrong? When she'd opened the door that day to Bruce? She should have sent him packing. Why hadn't she? Esmerelda snapped the napkin in her lap, remembering her foolhardiness. She recalled Bruce smiling ingratiatingly. Had she been fooled? His forehead was dotted with beads of sweat for some reason, though it wasn't warm, and even cooler inside the house.

Harry had liked the place cool too, like her, especially when he was working. He knew his job. He believed it was essential to develop the right exercise program for each individual. That took trial and error and, if she were patient – they'd laughed at that – he'd do some experimenting. She'd told him to go for it! His strategy was to isolate a specific muscle group for each exercise. It had worked. Together they'd devised just the regime she needed to heal her knee and develop more muscle tone in her legs. With her life long habit of walking everywhere, he said she'd ensured a strong physical base for recovery. That was why she'd been able to proclaim "I'm more than wonderful, in fact!" to Bruce that day last autumn. Standing up to Bruce had made her knees lock, something Harry had told her to watch out for. So she'd relaxed her stance, and her attitude too, unfortunately. "Well, it is nice of you to drop by."

Looking back now she knew letting Bruce back into the house that day had been a mistake. Why had she ever done it? Because he was family and that should count for something? "Just for a couple of days, Bruce?" she remembered asking. At his nod Esmerelda had acquiesced and let him stay, against her better judgment.

Two days stretched into a week. Then, before she knew it they were both there again. Jenny had arrived with her spicy cooking and her love affair with noise. They'd settled in and appeared smugly complacent about the future, right there in her home! Except when she told them all about Harry and his art gallery.

"But what about the library you were going to endow, Esmy? It was something we'd planned together. Remember?" Bruce had taken off his glasses and cleaned them. That was when she'd noticed he was using one of her husband's hankies. Where had he found it? Had he been going through the chiffonier? The nerve!

"Oh, there's enough for both the library and an art gallery. I wanted to do this for Harry. He managed to...." She'd stopped herself from giving any more explanations. Esmerelda had decided not to share with Bruce what Harry had done for her. Somehow she'd known to keep that to herself. "He's a very talented artist, and he got me painting too. I enjoy it. He deserves to have his own studio and gallery."

"That must take a lot of money to set someone up like that for life?" Glasses back on, they were perched so that Bruce had to look down his nose at Esmerelda.

"It's just a little annuity, Bruce." She'd had the courage to look into his eyes and say, "And it is my money, after all. Don't worry about our plans for the library. It'll happen too. Perhaps not on such a grand scale, though, as we first talked about."

Now it seemed as if they never left her alone. It drove her crazy. What could she do? As she sat there, folding and unfolding her napkin, she had a thought. Jenny was out of the room. Would she have time? Esmerelda reached over and picked up the phone. She had Harry's number memorized. She hadn't forgotten everything, no matter what people thought. When she heard his friendly voice she felt like crying, but checked herself. Time was of the essence. Who knew how long this call could last? Jenny might be back at any moment.

When Harry answered, she just started chattering. "Hi Harry! It's wonderful to hear your voice. Are you keeping well?"

"Esmerelda! Gosh, it's good to hear from you. How's the weather up there?"

"New England's acting like its namesake. Cold and drizzly. We seem to be living under a cloud these days. How is it in Florida?"

"Esmy, you really should have come down with me. Right now the sun is streaming through the windows. I can feel it on my back. Soothing, for sure. It's just what the doctor ordered, you know."

"Sounds delightful...."

"Why not change your mind, then? Come on down. I could meet you at the airport."

"No, no. Things are best this way."

"I don't want to nag you, but you could check out this place I've found. I think it's going to make a great gallery. I would value your opinion, you know."

"Harry, you know there's business I have to take care of."

"Okay, okay. I understand. How's that going?" Harry was the only one who knew her exciting plans. She couldn't admit to him she'd put the brakes on going ahead with them.

"Well, it's taking me some time. Harry, tell me about the gallery."

"I can't tell you how exciting this all is. If it hadn't been for you, I'd still be kneading backs."

"Ah, but you do it so well, Harry."

"Yeah," Harry chuckled, "but you said I paint even better!"

"You do, Harry. Have you been working?"

"On my portfolio? Yes, ma'am. Lots of great subjects down here, not to mention the sunsets. You wouldn't believe the colors! Some of my renditions look artificial – the contrasts are so blatant."

"I'm sure they're beautiful."

"I've been trying to produce a kaleidoscope effect. It's the way the light dances through the moisture in the clouds. Truly amazing. Not sure I've achieved it yet. Esmy, I can't tell you what this has done for me...."

"Yes, yes. Don't waste time thanking me again, please!"

"But you deserve...so much more!"

"Hey, I'm getting as much pleasure from this as you. Picture me as a patron in the Renaissance. I'm giving you your own Medici Palace."

"Well, I wouldn't exactly call this place I've checked out a palace, but it comes close in my mind. The interior walls have some kind of siding that's horizontal. It's just perfect for hanging my work. Strip lighting, too, that's adjustable. It's not on the main drag, but it's pretty close to the main shopping area, in one of the best shopping districts too. Esmy, I wish you'd consent to coming down for just a short time."

Travel? How could she, the way she was feeling? That's when Esmerelda lost her nerve, Perhaps she was dramatizing the situation. She didn't want for anything, really. She had the phone, her computer and library books. Someone was there to prepare her food and see to her pills. Esmerelda had never been one to complain and even now she wasn't sure she had cause. So, second thoughts silenced her real concerns. "I...don't think I could, Harry. I....not right now." Should she tell him? "You see, I've not been myself lately."

"Esmy, what's wrong?"

"Oh, Harry, I guess I just miss you." No. She still had some pride left. "I'm fine. Just being a bit maudlin. An old lady's allowed to be that once in awhile. Right?"

"I could come north, Esmy..."

"Don't you dare! You get on with setting up your new gallery. Send me pictures too. Email me them. Okay?"

"Speaking of email, have you set up a meeting with your....favorite correspondent?"

It would break her heart to admit she hadn't done what they'd planned together. "I'm intending to. Really, Harry, I am planning on that. I'm waiting until I feel a bit more....confident."

"No time like the present, Esmy. Isn't that what you kept telling me?"

"Okay, okay, Harry. I'm going to get right on it, soon as we hang up." She said her last goodbyes. Just in time too, because Jenny came back, clucking her tongue at how little Esmy had eaten, before whisking away her tray. Esmerelda suddenly was overwhelmed by loneliness. All her close friends had passed away. Relatives too, except for that smarmy Bruce who'd crawled out of the woodwork, the long lost kin she didn't want. She felt much more comfortable with Harry, sharing ideas with him, asking his advice. Heaven knows, she couldn't trust Bruce's opinion one iota. Fine state of affairs for someone in her position. Longevity, it sucked, thought Esmerelda.

Though she'd shied from her reasons for calling Harry she felt a little better. Esmerelda had a special feeling for the man, one she couldn't describe to anyone else, much less herself. In her more private moments she thought being a benefactor to Harry was an atonement for her actions years ago or should she say her inactions? Had her decision as a girl condoned bigotry and racism? At least now she'd done one thing to make reparations. Harry and she were on a plane of friendship...... almost like mother and son. The thought gave her pause. He could have been her son. He was the right age.

CHAPTER TWO

Once I make up my mind, I'm full of indecision.

Oscar Levant

Maudlin? That would be the last word to describe Esmerelda Graham. Harry found her phone call unsettling. After he hung up her words echoed in his brain. "I'll wait until I'm feeling a bit more confident." Why hadn't she gone ahead and made contact with her pen pal, or should he say her computer pal? She'd been planning to do just that as soon as she sent him off to Florida. Arranging a meeting with him was going to make her life come full circle. But she hadn't. Why not?

Had Bruce interfered? Harry had never met her grandnephew, but when he saw the effect of his conversations on Esmy a year ago he took a dislike to him. Esmy had inspired a fierce loyalty in Harry. Had Bruce returned? Invaded her privacy again?

Was his trip north a fool's journey? Might be better if it was. Maybe he was just imagining the worst, but once he'd made the decision there was no holding him back, as always. The old 'angels rush in where devils fear to tread' thing, the kind he was prone to, though he was sure no angel. Not the right color, some would think. Something just didn't seem right, going by Esmerelda's last phone call, and when the letter arrived from the lawyer Harry got more and more uneasy until finally he packed the car, flung in some CDs, maps and snacks. He'd face Bruce head on like a stubborn goat. Sure, he may be family, but that doesn't give someone permission to interfere in anyone's life. How many skulls would Harry have to butt to get Bruce to give up such a stupid scheme?

This wasn't the best time for Harry to be taking off, either. He had stuff pending back home. In fact, he'd left things in a mess. The story of his life lately. But a good mess. He had to make some decisions – the color of the gallery, inside and out, the security system would have to be in place and he'd started thinking about a little café on the adjoining patio. He could likely entertain having other artists' work on show too – some jewelry or pottery, perhaps even photography. Give customers lots to look at and spend time browsing. He needed to see to insurance. Most importantly, he was trying to get a studio up and running in the back and get some things done for the grand opening and he had lots of framing to do. Two other galleries had seen his work and had commissioned pieces for out-of-state stores. Esmerelda had hitched his wagon to a comet, it seemed. His very own guardian angel, and he was determined he'd repay the favor. Being so busy meant he'd not been good at keeping in touch with Esmy. He was sure feeling bad about it.

Try as he might, the monotony of driving had taken its toll, even along the coastal highway. He shouldn't have left it so late to start out. He was tired and The Pelican Motel had been the only motel hoping for business with its timid sign, stuttering the almost word – 'V_c__cy'. It was apparent the more reputable places didn't need his money. They'd turned off all their flashing lights. With his bad back he couldn't just pull over to the side of the road for a snooze. He'd never be able to walk in the morning, much less drive. Even now he could feel the spasms taking root. Ironic, really. He'd spent years helping people with their bad backs doing deep massages and ended up wrecking his own back. What he needed was a hard floor and two pillows, one for under his knees. He didn't really care about the seediness of the Pelican Motel. He wouldn't be sleeping in any flea-bitten bed, not with his back. A floor was just what the doctor ordered.

"You want a room for the night?" The desk clerk sounded incredulous. Strange. Maybe he thought Harry just needed it for an hour? He didn't even look at Harry when he asked the question. The clerk was focusing on his elbow, scratching a dry spot.

"Huh?" His blemish was distracting Harry too, who tried not to look at the drops of blood the fellow's fingernails had spawned on his skin. One red bubble hung, as if afraid to fall to the floor. Harry looked down and saw why. No place for anyone's lifeline, a dirty piece of tile carpet. It was tile made to look like a piece of Berber carpeting but, like the guy, it wasn't coming off as the real McCoy. This fellow couldn't even muster up the anger of a Basil Fawlty. Too laid back, or maybe he wasn't furious at his lot in life. He stopped scratching. Good job, 'cause his skin didn't look like it could take much more. Silence. Harry realized the clerk was watching him, waiting for an answer. Harry looked into his face. "Yeah, one night. That's right."

"Special on three for one." An eyebrow shot up in expectation.

"Pardon?" What was he offering? Some kind of kinky sex? Three for one? Harry could believe it, in a place like this.

"Stay three nights for the price of one," the clerk said, grinning.

"Oh. That's a good deal," Harry lied. "But I've got to keep moving. Sorry." This wouldn't be where he'd choose to spend an extra couple of nights. Along the A1A there are lots of nice spots and plenty to see. It's why he'd forsaken the faster route of I-95. Needed a bit of a breather in his mad rush to the north. He'd seen some intriguing places, too. Must be good fishing to boot, going by the number of boats being towed. Harry wished he could hang around for a visit. A cramp kneaded his innards. The greasy meal three hours ago had fueled him, but left his tank running on gas of the worst kind. He had to have a pit stop, if nothing else.

The desk clerk made a snorting sound. "Everyone's on the run these days, trying to outdo the next guy." Harry was taken aback. Was he a clairvoyant among his other talents? He hadn't moved from his spot behind the counter, was just standing there, tapping his pencil. Not impatiently. Harry recognized the rhythm. *Take Five*. The man was really into it, gripped by the compelling beat. Harry was too. He was mesmerized, rooted to the spot or maybe it was the sticky floor. He found myself asking, "How can you make money giving a room away for that price?"

The clerk gave a sheepish grin. "Well, it looks good if there's a car or two parked in the court. Makes the place look respectable." Both hands were moving now, all ten fingers, tapping to beat the band. The man was definitely marching to a different drummer.

"There are cars outside. Not just mine," Harry pointed out. "Three or four. And a pick-up truck."

Into the music as he was, the guy was still ready for a chat. "A decent car or two, I mean. Not just heaps of metal. The truck's mine. Other two *'vehicles'* belong to friends." He leaned into the word with his whole body. Veeee-hicles, accenting the first syllable to the accompaniment of two pairs of fingers stuck up in the air in matching victory signs. He was lying like Nixon and knew it. Hard to call those buckets of bolts veeee-hicles. "Well, to be strictly accurate, just one of them belongs to a friend. It won't go." His fingers landed on the counter so both palms could slap a feverish finale. A bowl filled with nuts jumped, sending the peanuts scattering over the pink Formica, jumping beans on the run. He used his arm to sweep them into a hand waiting at the edge of the counter, then offered them to Harry, who declined.

"Toothache," Harry muttered, pointing to his mouth. Idiot. Why did he point to his mouth? The guy knew about teeth and elbows and music and lots more. Harry would bet on it. Looked like he'd been around. The clerk shrugged and threw the nuts under the counter. Harry could hear them land in a bucket, or maybe a tin can.

"Here, I've something that'll take care of that." From below the counter he took out a gallon bottle of what looked like liquid mahogany, sloshed some into the little bowl that held the nuts and offered the drink to Harry. The pungent smell of alcohol whacked his nostrils as the guy took a swig himself from the bottle. Harry accepted, taking a little slurp. He'd never drunk from a bowl before. It felt good. A dribble escaped down Harry's chin. He licked it with a flick of his tongue. Smooth and strong. A goofy grin spread across Harry's face. A whisker of wild abandon tickled its way up from the bottom of his being. The guy smiled back at Harry. Nice fellow. Awfully generous, really. With that first sip, Harry's bowels started to unwind. He took another gulp, less hesitant this time. "The other piece of junk's been abandoned ever since the police showed up here one night. The fellow who drove it in took off without paying. He leapt out the back window of his room and never came back. What's the use? I mean, who can you trust? I never got paid for that room, you know."

"Does that happen a lot?"

"Nope. People I get in here are regular joes, like yourself. Salesmen who want to save a few bucks and just catch forty winks. Workers who don't want to waste their wages on hotels."

"What kind of workers?"

"There's always something going on in Florida. If it isn't clean-ing up after hurricanes, it's road construction, and there's always new surveys going up, like those gated communities. You wouldn't believe how fast one of those can shape up."

"I think I saw a couple of those. They look pretty private."

"They are. Most cater to the over 55 crowd. Guarantee no kids, no noise, no hassles. You'd never hear a basketball up against a garage door in one of those places."

"Sort of artificial, though?"

"Well, if you've lived your whole life putting up with hassles, it just might be nice to know you can get some peace and quiet at the end of your life."

"Guess so, but they must be like little ghost towns."

"Don't bet on it! Lots have huge recreation centers with heated pool, sauna and jacuzzis. Come complete with golf course. I saw one that had the sign posted that said pedestrians and golf carts have right of way over cars."

"Now, that sounds like a holiday haven."

"Some are. Of course, they have a lot of rules, like the no kid rule. No clotheslines, all cars put into garages. No parking on the street. No weird colors for your exteriors. There's one going up over on 98 right now. That one's brought lots of workers in."

"Those guys make much?"

"Guys just starting in construction can make $12-$15 bucks an hour."

"Not bad."

"It's hot, dirty and dusty and they work you all hours. Right now they're crying out for heavy machine operators to excavate, grade properties and pave them. And before they can do that they've got to clear the land, sometimes demolish old buildings, build parking lots. You name it, they'll do it – all in a manner of weeks."

"There's lots of road construction too, I see."

"Always is, it seems. Over here on this part of the coastal highway we're saved all that mess. They pretty well leave us alone."

"It's a nice spot you have here," Harry said. He stuck out his hand.

"My name's Gus." They shook hands. "Let's say twenty bucks. Cash."

CHAPTER THREE

One might well say that mankind is divisible into two great classes: hosts and guests.

Sir Max Beerbohm

Harry was right to feel uneasy. What he suspected – that Bruce had reappeared in Esmy's life – had occurred. There wasn't much to be said for Bruce, except he was persistent, especially in getting something he wanted. So he usually did. He had first appeared in Esmerelda's life two years before. At that time his visit had been just an annoying interruption in her routine, but in reality it was much more – a premonition of worse to come.

Esmy was spry for her age. The morning Bruce came into her life, long before the tumble down the cellar stairs, Esmerelda had just settled herself into her favorite position, legs crossed in a sitting posture, hands resting on her knees. Meditation requires quiet and Esmy usually did it in the mornings after the neighborhood quietened down, right after the children were sent off to school and people had gone to work. She preferred the contemplative path of meditation and picked for her subject that day a basil leaf from her kitchen counter herb collection that was prettily arranged in yellow pots. Color was important to Esmy. She hadn't minded her hair turning white because it meant she could wear bright colors now – purple and red and emerald and sapphire – to advantage.

That morning Esmerelda examined the deep green of the leaf before placing it on a white saucer on the floor. Green and white, the colors in her sunroom. In summer the decor matched the out-of-doors. In winter it was an oasis in a sea of white snowy mounds visible through the windows. She rubbed the leaf gently to release its fragrance. She couldn't help bringing her fingertips to her nostrils to inhale the aroma. One deep inhalation, then slowly she exhaled, relaxing her arms, her wrists, her fingers. With index fingers touching thumbs, she stared at the leaf, looked at the asymmetric edges and was astonished at the number of little indentations. A rough estimate, ten per edge meant altogether there'd have to be.... how many? As usual she had to put a brake on her thoughts. No words were to be used in the contemplation. It was always a temptation but she knew she should remind herself to just look and experience.

Esmy brought her mind back to task. Look. Examine the texture with your eyes. One side seemed softer. There she was again, assigning words, labels, descriptions. For some reason, it wasn't working that day. Perhaps she should go back to counting her breaths, what she usually did when her mind wouldn't behave. At least it would relax her. She got to eighty-seven when something interrupted her concentration. Eighty – in -eight – out, eighty – in – nine – out. The sound became louder. Damn. The insistent ring of the doorbell took its toll. Try as she might, she couldn't block it out. Meditation requires quiet. Esmy Graham finally had to succumb, uncross her legs and stumble to her feet. Getting up was a lot harder than getting down, she thought. Still, she knew she was pretty agile for a 72 year old.

"Esmerelda! I sure have looked forward to meeting you."

A large man stood peering at her through tortoise shell glasses. He looked like a giant owl, out of his element. Who was this man? "I'm sorry......?"

"It's Bruce. Bruce Forrest. Didn't you get my letter?"

Of course. Susan's grandson. Esmerelda's only living relative. He'd written to her a few months back. There had been an exchange of letters and emails since his first missive. None had sat well with her. A couple of them were still on her desk for some reason. Maybe because she still hadn't sorted out her unease at receiving them.

Hi, Esmy. She hadn't taken kindly to his use of the diminutive. *How are you? I hope this news won't be too much of a shock. My Grandma, Susan Nelson — your sister — passed away last month. She'd had a long fight with cancer, which she lost. I don't know if you know but I am her only grandchild. I went to live with her and Gramps when I was a teenager. She told me all about you.* I bet she did, thought Esmerelda. *I'm sorry to be the bearer of bad tidings but I thought you should know.*

She'd written back, thanking him for having thought to notify her. She'd been relieved she hadn't had to attend her sister's funeral. His second letter came only days later.

Dearest Esmy. Dearest? That was a bit presumptuous. *Grandma Susan used to talk a lot about you. I feel as if I know you.* How could that be? Her sister wasn't exactly a font of information about Esmerelda and what she'd made of her life. They hadn't spoken for decades. She could hardly imagine what Susan would have to say about her younger sister, other than shameful secrets. *I might be coming east for some business matters. May I drop by and pay my repsects?* Was it the spelling error or the request that had made Esmy recoil? She had no wish to meet Susan's grandson. Grandson — something she never could have. She was barren. David, Esmy's husband, balked when she used that word, said it was nonsense. He stated she was full of life and that was what was important. She had not acceded to Bruce's request.

Instead she'd noted his email address and sent back a short reply via the internet. A personal note would have seemed too inviting, she thought.

Hello, Bruce: I hope your trip goes well. My schedule in the next few weeks is rather full so I cannot entertain a visit right now. Best of luck with your business enterprises. Let's keep in touch, though, via email. She'd intended that as a salve to any feeling of rejection he might get from her refusal.

His response had been immediate this time. *Esmy! You amaze me! Using email at your age!!* All those exclamation marks were off-putting, in Esmy's mind. So was the reference to her age. *Of course, I understand. I know you're a busy woman. It's good to keep yurself occupied.* Another spelling error. *I won't impose. But anytime you feel like seeing me, I'd love to come by. Grandma Susan had some photo albums I think you should have.* I wonder if she kept any of my fall from grace? Bet not. There would be almost a whole year missing from those albums, thought Esmerelda.

She didn't know why he'd contacted her and continued to correspond so regularly. For sure, she didn't expect to see him on her doorstep. She had never issued an invitation. In fact, she had avoided it.

"Bruce? What a surprise!" What else could she have said? That was the truth. "It's nice to meet face to face." That part wasn't. "How are you?" Her sister and she had never got along, especially when Susan had sided with their father and made Esmerelda do something she'd always regretted. That was nearly sixty years ago, a whole lifetime. Now Susan was gone, and her father too, of course, and her only living blood relative was this young man standing on her doorstep. Even so, Esmerelda had felt no stirrings of familial affection.

"Just fine, other than being excited, and nervous, about meeting you."

"Oh!" Nervous? She could imagine all that her sister would have said about her through the years. "Do come in." She remembered feeling disconcerted to see him walk to the edge of the porch and pick up two suitcases she hadn't noticed. He grinned and waited for her to turn around and walk into the house first.

"After you, Esmerelda." Esmy bristled. Not a good start. She didn't like people using first names on an initial meeting.

"What brings you here?" A little abrupt. Esmerelda relented. "Would you like a cup of tea?"

"That would be mighty fine, Esmerelda. I have a thirst you wouldn't believe." He followed her into the kitchen after setting down his luggage in the foyer. "I had some car trouble so it's in the shop in town for repairs. Wouldn't you know it? My transmission died!"

"That sounds serious. How did you get here?" There wasn't a garage or car shop within three miles of her house. And why had he brought luggage?

"Well, I had them drop me off before towing the car back to the shop."

"Oh." His turning up on her doorstep was a shock. "I'm sorry about your grandmother, Bruce." Better get the topic of Susan out of the way first.

"Thank you. It was a peaceful end, considering how far the cancer had spread. I was relieved for her, actually."

Esmerelda's husband David had suffered from colon cancer. Her tone softened. "You must have been a comfort to her. I didn't even know she was ill." She felt she had to explain. "Your grandmother and I were never close. You know that we had...um...words, I guess you'd say. Years ago. Nothing ever got patched up."

"Yes, you wrote about that. I understand. My Grandma Susan, she sure could be stubborn. I know that. After my parents died...."

"Tell me about that, Bruce." Apparently her sister Susan had taken in her grandson after the death of her son and daughter-in-law in a freak accident.

"They were in the wrong place at the wrong time. A bomb goes off in a bank and everyone's life changes. Or ends. I went to live with Grandma and Grandpa when I was thirteen years old. Grandma was sure different from my Mom. I guess my mother spoiled me, but I never had an argument with anyone until I went to live with Grandma. Boy, she never gave an inch."

Esmerelda could believe it. The older daughter, Susan, could always get her own way. Their father doted on Susan, maybe she because she took after him. They were simpatico, agreed on everything. Mother had died giving birth to Esmerelda, perhaps another reason the younger daughter lost her father's favor. "Well, your grandmother took after our father. She was sure she knew what was best for everyone. So did my Dad. They were a formidable pair." Esmerelda often wondered if she herself resembled her mother in any way. Would they have understood each other?

"I know that but I wish you'd seen Grandma these last few years. She often talked about you. I think she missed you. She said someday I should....try to get in touch...." Esmerelda took the lid off the tea caddy and busied herself with making tea. A lump in her throat prevented words.

"Guess you're wondering why she thought I should get in touch?" asked Bruce.

"Well, I have to admit..."

"I think she didn't want me to be all by myself." Susan, still interfering with other people's lives, even from the grave. Arranging things, whether you wanted her to or not. Who asked her to interfere? How dare she ignore me for decades and then, when her grandson's left alone, expect me to be there for him? Was she ever there for me when I needed her in my corner? Esmerelda put a halt on these kinds of thoughts. It was a litany whose time was long past. Was it possible Susan had realized finally what it meant for Esmerelda to be a widow, living all alone, when it shouldn't have been that way? Maybe, at the end, Susan didn't want her to be lonely. Or was she being too generous as to Susan's motives? Was it wishful thinking that her sister had finally had regrets?

"Now you're on your own too, I thought I should have a look see and make sure you're okay."

Esmerelda turned to face him, giving him a careful appraisal. "You have your grandmother's eyes. The way one turns up at the corner. Blue too, with long lashes."

"And short sighted. Like Dad." Esmerelda had never met Bruce's father.

"Tell me about your mother and father."

"What do you want to know?"

"Were they happy?"

"As much as anyone, I guess. When I was in school full time Mom tried to open a book store, but it didn't last long. Grandma Susan told Dad he shouldn't have let her waste his money that way. That took the wind out of Mom's sails, I think. It takes a while for businesses to get up and running and Dad couldn't afford to be that patient. Mom finally gave up. Sometimes she went into Dad's office- he was an accountant- and worked as a receptionist for him. Grandma said that was much better than a woman running her own business."

She began to feel sad for her sister at that moment. Couldn't Susan have understood her daughter-in-law's dream? Did she get some perverted pleasure in thwarting every woman other than herself? Was she to be the only one to have a say in her destiny? Esmerelda concentrated on pouring boiling water into the teapot and took her time setting out milk and sugar and then sliced a half wedge of lemon she had on

a saucer on the counter. She'd woken up with a sore throat and had
made a hot lemon on awakening. Perhaps that was why it hurt her to
talk right now. Or was the old antagonism rearing its ugly head?

"And your grandparents? Susan and her husband? What was their
life like?"

Bruce said, "Grandpa doted on Grandma Susan. She pretty well
ran the house and Gramps liked it that way. She used to give him a list
on Mondays telling him what to do. He never minded. He said that
was how to stay in her good books. They played bridge on Thursday
nights, watched old movies on television on Saturday nights and
always went to the first mass on Sundays. Did pretty well everything
together. When Grandpa died Grandma was really lonely." Esmerelda
could imagine. One less person to boss around.

"But she had you!" Esmerelda spoke sharply. Her tone surprised
her grandnephew. She saw him wince. How could he have known his
grandmother had effectively guaranteed that Esmerelda would never
have anyone of her own flesh and blood? She wondered what kind
of grandmother Susan had been. She had to admit she was curious
about that, and went ahead and asked. Had the woman ordered and
arranged Bruce's life too?

"Yes, so I got out on my own as soon as I could. To college,
then work."

"What is your work?"

"I took a degree in library science."

"Library science? So you're a librarian?" Then why all the spelling mistakes?

Bruce adjusted his glasses and Esmy noticed a dent on the bridge
of his nose. "Well, I'd like to be. However, with all the cutbacks it
means technicians are doing the work of librarians. Used to be that
a good library would have several fully qualified librarians. Now, if
there's one full time, the library's lucky."

"And you? Do you have a library? To work in?"

"No, afraid not. I'm hoping things will change soon and municipalities will start to realize they need more than pencil pushers and date stampers in their libraries. In the meantime I'm doing a bit of traveling. Seeing these great United States. Keeping my options open, I guess you'd say."

Esmerelda had marveled at how some things can be inherited like a love of books. That was the only thing she and Susan had ever agreed upon, their tastes in literature. "Would you like a piece of rum cake?"

"Rum cake? That's new to me! I'd love some." Esmerelda went to the tin container on the counter. She lifted out the glass serving dish for the cake. Cinnamon brown with dots of raisins and iced with an almond flavored white icing. She'd made it the day before, not really knowing why. Just to prove she could do it? It had turned out well, moist and tasty. She'd used real rum too, in a note of defiance, rejecting the imitation rum flavoring in the cupboard. She knew the recipe by heart as she'd made it often for David, it being one of his favorites. It was nice to have someone to share it with. Bruce squinted at the plates she put on the tray in front of him.

"I think we'll have this in the sunroom." The man may be short-sighted, but he certainly was a sight for sore eyes, thought Esmerelda. Dusty blond hair, broad shoulders on a thin frame. A healthy specimen, for sure, but at the same time there was a vulnerability to him. He must take after his father in that way. His matriarch grandmother had had a backbone like a ramrod.

"Do you have a time frame? If nothing turns up, what will you do?"

"Oh, have my own radio show!" Bruce laughed.

"Pardon?"

"Just my little joke. Grandma used to say I liked the sound of my own voice. I've done a bit of acting. Guess all my reading has filled my head with characters, past and present." Esmerelda had set everything out on a tray. Bruce quickly picked it up and said, "Lead the way, ma'am." She walked into the sun porch and gestured to the tea trolley. After depositing the tray he waited until she'd taken her seat before he sat down.

He examined the woman. Esmerelda sat erect and confident, with just a hint of a dowager's hump. It was obvious Esmerelda hadn't been bowed by life. Her hair too showed a spirited rejection of the aging process. It was a flattering silvery white. Her face was unlined and her movements were fluid other than a little stiffness in her hands, affecting her management of the tea things. Bruce had waited years to meet Grandma Susan's sister, the object of much disdain in many years of conversations with his grandmother.

That was the beginning of a long visit. It took just weeks for Esmerelda to come to resent Bruce and his intrusion into her life, once so peaceful, yet full and rewarding. Bruce had done more than just disrupted her routines. Why hadn't Esmerelda remembered that the second time around? Why, after Harry, the physical therapist, had left for Florida had she not closed the door on Bruce when he'd returned to her doorstep. You can't teach an old dog?

CHAPTER FOUR

Whenever I think of the past it brings back so many memories.

Steven Wright

"Can't I use my credit card? My boss...." Gus shook his head. He knew Harry didn't need a receipt to hand into any accounting department. He sensed Harry wasn't on any business trip, but had decided the fellow was going north to finish up some old business, maybe something he should have seen to before? Harry had his own thoughts. He knew he was being typical, better late than never. Why had he let Esmy send him packing? He wasn't sure she would like him interfering, but after her phone call he had a gut feeling, a sinking in the pit of his stomach that was pulling him in after it. Was something wrong? Was it suspicion, or just plain old guilt? Harry knew he should have made a return visit before now. Together he and Esmy had locked onto a plan that would serve them both well. She deserved it after all she'd done for him, and he knew she'd welcome him even if she were offended at his butting in. She was that kind of lady.

Harry wasn't her friend for what he could get out of it, no matter what anyone thought. He really liked the woman. They'd hit it off from the beginning when he walked in the door with his exercise table and she greeted him with the words, "My doctor must think you're a magician. Do you honestly think some physical therapy is going to make a new woman out of me? I bet you...." She looked around the foyer and finally her finger painted to a little work of art, the kind Harry had only seen in museums or art galleries. His eyes took in the glory of Renoir. She continued, "....that picture up there that you'll give up in defeat." A Renoir print in a private home, just hanging on the wall, like any old family memento. He recognized it. *Standing Bather.*

Harry murmured, "That young woman always seemed sad to me, as if she didn't want to get dressed and go out."

"You think that too?" asked Esmerelda. She looked back at the sketch and murmured, "That's how it strikes me too, almost as if she's in mourning."

"Perhaps she knows her husband is cheating on her."

"Do you know what I think?" Esmerelda paused. "She...she has just....had to shower.. and realizes she isn't pregnant, after all."

"You could be right! That would explain the slump of her shoulders, the hand near her stomach." They were to have many conversations like that in the weeks to come. Esmy collected art and Harry's secret passion was painting. In his time with her he hadn't done all that much – just his job, really, getting her up and walking again after the bad fall – but she didn't share that opinion. She said he'd saved her life, literally. Given it meaning. Him, Harry Somer, who had never made a difference in anyone's life, even his Mom's.

His mother named him after Harry Belafonte. Before his dad died she was really into music. She fancied herself the second Lena Horne. With her mixed parentage and her voice, she could have been too. Dad encouraged her. He'd drive her to auditions and if she was lucky enough to get a job he'd pick her up every night after her gig. Good job, too, because Mom was a looker. When Harry was younger his father would plop him in the back seat of the car and they'd go get her. Harry usually was asleep until Mom jumped into the car, chattering like a magpie. She'd have the stale smell of tobacco mixed in with the Lily of the Valley perfume Dad gave her every year. She'd give his father a big kiss on the lips before regaling him with the evening's action. They were real lovebirds.

Mom always said Harry took after Dad and not her. He liked to draw buildings and design houses unlike any she'd ever seen. He made a living driving a bus but at nights, after he got home and ate his dinner, he'd bring out his sketch pads and start doodling. Come to think of it that might be why he never minded being a bus driver. He got to look at all the architecture on his routes, from the corner store to the skyscraper at the corner of Seventh and Windsor. On Sundays he sometimes took Harry downtown and pointed out all the buildings he thought had interesting features. It might be a carved door or some brass hardware. When he spotted a unique cornerstone it made his day. Harry inherited his eye for detail from Dad. When he was a little older he'd have his own notebooks and work alongside his father, but he preferred sketching nature – birds and trees, even leaves lying on the pavement.

When his Dad had a massive coronary sitting at the steering wheel of his bus – he must have had a premonition because he'd pulled it to the side of the road, surprising all his passengers – his Mom lost her zest for life. She didn't take any more jobs at night, giving it all up to be a cashier at the supermarket down the street. She got serious. Harry too. At night there'd be no drawing lessons, just homework on the kitchen table with Mom helping him try to understand the mechanics of math. She always said his Dad would have been a better teacher. Harry gave up the dream of being an artist. It didn't seem right anymore.

Harry was an oddball in high school. None of his teachers could pigeonhole him. He wasn't a brain, but sometimes he had flashes of insight, though they never lasted long. He always seemed to be worrying, mostly about Mom. He knew he had to wear the pants in the family but he didn't know how. Kids weren't sure how to take him because he wasn't into homework or sports. He'd inherited a good voice, but was too shy to join the choir.

It was his physical education teacher who suggested he study to be a physiotherapist. He knew Harry's marks in the academics weren't going to get him into university. With his upper body strength the teacher said Harry would be perfect for the job. It would get him into a line of work that could support him and his mother. By that time she was suffering from emphysema. She'd never been able to kick the habit of smoking after all those jobs in nightclubs. She was wasting away. After his father died Harry knew she was lonely. He just wasn't enough for her.

But he'd been able to help Esmerelda, and she sure helped him too and she promised she would again if Harry ever needed it. She was a feisty old girl, as independent as they come. Maybe Harry shouldn't be running to her rescue?

The motel clerk was right. Harry didn't need a receipt to hand over to any boss for accounts payable. Harry didn't know why he said that. Perhaps he was embarrassed at not having much money on him. He'd never had much. Now that he didn't have to worry about money he still didn't keep much cash on hand. Old habits die hard. Harry passed a twenty over to the desk clerk who slipped it into his wallet. No cash registers here.

"I keep asking the cops to drag that piece of crap away." Harry had asked him about a wreck of a car he'd parked beside. He took another swig from the bottle, wiping up a dribble from the rim with his index finger, then rubbing the moisture into a rash on his elbow.

As good a disinfectant as any, Harry guessed and noticed clotted blood. "It's a real clunker. But all they says is it's not their business. What I say is, why should I pay to have it dragged away? So it just sits there. Something's got into the upholstery, so I leave the windows open." He was rapping out some reggae now.

"Good idea." Better in the car than one of the rooms. "So, you don't get much business, Gus?" The tension in Harry's spine eased along with the cramps in my stomach.

Gus seemed miffed. "Not much business?" Stuffing his thumbs into a couple of belt loops he stood tall and loomed over Harry. "Now, why do you say that...? Oh, you mean what I said about it'll be good to have a nice car like yours parked outside?" His body resumed an at-ease position. This time he was flexing his fingers, intertwined and above his head. A panther unwinding. "I'll be straight with you. I don't hardly get any business really." He yawned noisily. Now he had his money, he was really opening up. "Don't know why. You see all those other places along this stretch of road?" His hands were gesturing left, then right. "Roofs off? Windows still needing fixing? Well, my place came through the hurricanes pretty well. Hardly any damage at all."

Harry had to agree with the fellow. The place was still standing. Intact. Well, not exactly intact. That wasn't the best word to describe The Pelican Motel, but he had to admit it was all there in one piece, looking like something out of the thirties. The roofing companies and contractors were doing a record business – going through the roof, I guess you could say – up and down the coast, after the hurricanes hit Florida head-on, four of them, one after another. The government had organized hearings to see how they were going to straighten out the mess. Not just the physical stuff, either. The insurance companies were fighting over details like deductibles and dates and which damages they were responsible for. First effects perhaps,

they admitted, but surely not the subsequent damage from a weakening of the structures? But no one had had time to breathe, never mind
repair, before another hellish wind came raging in off the Atlantic. It
wasn't just the insurance companies who were crying foul. So were
the residents, and businesses too, who had to carry on as best they
could. The Pelican Motel didn't appear to have any after-effects. What
hadn't fallen down at The Pelican Motel never would, cemented
together by years of dirt and decay. It was the kind of structure you'd
see in another two decades, or four, folding into itself. It would never
drop down in defeat.

Some things can endure the test of time, like Esmerelda. Her
grandnephew, or whatever he wanted to call himself, was going to
find that out, if Harry had any say in the matter. Maybe Bruce already
had, but he sure wasn't giving an inch. Harry was going to help him
out with that. He'd take great pleasure in seeing defeat on the guy's
face when he faced reality. Would Harry make it in time, damn it?
Harry missed Esmerelda. He should have been in touch sooner but
things kept getting in the way. Harry could kick himself. At the very
worst he better make sure things ended up the way she wanted.

"I saw a lot of dumpsters coming down this way, still being filled
with debris. Storage units too."

"Yup. For people to keep their furniture in while their houses are
being repaired. Just plain junk is lying around too. And there's been
some looting. Some people don't rent those storage cubes. They just
cover up their belongings with plastic sheeting. Would you believe
it? Listen, businesses are paying those people to use tarps advertising
their logos! I wonder what smart ass thought of that! I can't believe
how many people are making money out of this disaster."

"Those dumpsters seem to be on every other driveway. And it
happened months ago, didn't it? Is it taking that long to get things
taken care of?"

"Not for everyone. You wouldn't believe some of the things that have happened. Fellow over in Lakeland got enough insurance money – right away – to renovate the entire interior!"

"While some haven't got a penny?"

"You got it in one. Of course, some of those people will never get insurance again. That makes owning a house a pretty risky proposition when you're living in hurricane country."

"It's a wonder they have enough building supplies to meet all the demands."

"Sometimes they don't. One lady had her roof half done and they ran out of the grey colored shingles. They had to shovel off what they'd done and start again with another color. That isn't unusual."

"I can just imagine the landfill sites. Where do they put it all?"

"Who knows? There have been some dismal stories too. The Bok Sanctuary at Lake Wales lost nearly a quarter of its old oaks. The debris in their park was four feet deep."

"Yeah?"

"I heard the gardener say it would keep having an effect. They were counting on the shade of those trees to protect other plants. And the goldfish were scooped up out of the ponds and thrown for miles. Lots and lots of damage. Their volunteers had their work cut out for them. It was amazing the carillon stayed intact."

"Carillon?"

"Yup. It's in a marble tower and has over 60 bronze bells. Some of them are huge. It's an awesome sight, that carillon. It was a good job those bells stayed in place. I wouldn't want one of them flying through the air."

That carillon might make a good picture. "This must have been a really dangerous place during the hurricanes. Guess you and the Pelican Motel were lucky!"

"My lucky day, eh? Like when I inherited this place." Inherited it? Talk about coincidences.

He piqued Harry's curiosity. "This place is yours? You inherited it? When was that?" A door slammed behind Harry. He knocked over his empty glass. It was the middle of the night, after all. Who was up and about? He swiveled his head and felt his back creak in protest. He was looking at what looked like a walking cadaver.

CHAPTER FIVE

A day without sunshine is like, you know, night.

Steve Martin

"Feeling skittish, mister?" The woman was alive, but thin as a rail and dressed in mule slippers and a quilted bed jacket. Harry could tell she was skinny because her pelvis was poking through the sheer nylon nightie like the wings of a skinny chicken. "Hi there, Annie. Can't sleep?" asked Gus.

"Aw, you know how it is, Gus. Drank too much last night. You gotta stop me like I asked. I keep telling you, for God's sake." A mutt at her feet whined, then licked the big toe sticking out of one of her slippers. The woman flicked the dog off her foot.

"Now, Annie, you know there's no stopping you when you get like that." She shrugged, pulled out a pack of cigarettes and a lighter from a plastic fanny pack and lit up. Her inhalation was long and noisy. A death rattle. She shoved the package in Harry's direction.

"No, thanks," Harry said.

"Who the hell are you, mister? And put your eyeballs back into your head."

"Now, Annie. Don't you go talking to one of my customers like that."

"Customer! You ain't had a customer since.... since when, Gus? A month ago?"

"Never you mind her, mister. Her memory's about as bad as her lungs."

"You got some water for Little Bertie here?" Gus took a bowl from under the counter and poured in some water from a kettle behind him. Then he retrieved a glass from the same place and poured Annie a shot, a little one. "Here you go, old thing. Hair of the dog."

"Don't you go calling me old thing, for God's sakes!"

"Well, well, Miss Annie. I do apologize for taking liberties. And maybe I was talking to Little Bertie?"

The woman's temper died down as fast as it had flared. "My little mutt's no old thing. Just a pup, like you, Gus, you sweet talker, you." With that she glanced at Harry. "You look like you'd be a sweet talker too. You're one fine looking man."

Harry didn't know what to say except, "Hi, Annie. You can call me Harry."

"Black don't crack, eh?" laughed the woman.

He couldn't take offense. Looking at this wrinkled old woman he had to hope the adage was true. He gave her a smile.

She returned a slight nod of the head in acknowledgment. "This guy's a honey, you know?" she said, glancing at the desk clerk. She took short sips of the drink, all the while eyeing the visitor as she sat down on a naugahyde divan in a corner of the foyer. Harry couldn't take his eyes off her. She bent both legs and put her hands out in front like she was going to ski downhill. Then she dropped her rear into the cushions behind her. Old as she was, and with both hands full, she still didn't spill a drop. Relieved, she sighed — more of a wheeze, really — leaned back and crossed her legs. Her knobby knees looked like shells that had been out in the sun too long, all ridged and chalky white. It took one jump for Little Bertie to land right next to her. He nestled into her thigh. Little comfort there. The woman's hands rested on her lap as she took turns sipping and smoking. Right, left. Right, left. The dog fell asleep immediately, undisturbed by the regular rhythm of an elbow jabbing him in the spine. Showed all you needed was a spot of your own and a good friend.

It made Harry more determined to be a better friend and get north to do his bit for Esmy. All she wanted was a place to herself and she needed someone like him to help her. His friend Esmy deserved no less. Gus turned back to him, raised his eyebrows in question, holding out the bottle. Harry nodded.

"Thanks," Harry said, lifting his glass. He turned so he could keep one eye on the woman and still carry on his conversation with Gus. He didn't want to appear rude. One thing his mother had drilled into him – be a gentleman, just like his Dad. It's one of the things Esmeralda likes about him, his manners. She was the first person since his mother who hadn't typecast Harry. Everyone pigeonholed him, and they all had the perfect solution for his life. His gym teacher took one look at his physique and thought he knew what was best. He never even suspected Harry had a creative streak. Took one look at his shoulders and signed him up for the wrestling team, but Harry quit after the first practice. Women were the same. They thought he was just a dumb lummox of a guy they could boss around. He was a man of few words, not because of shyness, but because he had nothing to say. Even the teachers at the training clinic never expected he'd be a success at the job because of his quiet demeanor. They likely thought he wouldn't get himself out there to be hired. It was only when Sarah, the head trainer saw his sketches of tendons and joints that they started to take him seriously. He understood the exercises because he'd studied the physical structure of the body to help him draw people better in his pictures. He always had to prove himself to people except for his parents – and Esmerelda. His mother died last year, finally, after a long, tiring battle with her health. If it hadn't been for Esmy........

Gus went on. "As I was saying I inherited this joint a year ago from my Uncle Rod."

"Rod was a honey, too," said Annie.

"Inherited Annie here, along with the motel. Didn't I?" He took an ashtray over to her and slipped it under the hand with the cigarette. Its ash had been hanging precariously for a minute now. The divan must be her spot. The upholstery was dotted with little burn holes.

"Don't get cheeky again, Gus."

"Annie lives here long-term. Pays by the month. She and two others."

"Don't you mention them in front of me, Gus!"

Gus looked at Harry and grinned. "Misty and Huntz. They're a couple who...."

"No way those two are married! Living in sin!"

Gus gave a half smile. You could tell he'd heard this tirade before. "They're a couple who have room 10. Making it into a little home, really."

"She plays her music too loud."

"It's okay, Harry. Their stereo went on the blink two days ago. They won't be bothering you." Harry wasn't concerned. He knew he was never going to get any sleep tonight. Not much night left, really. He seemed to be in some kind of stupor in the twilight zone of a Floridian night, seasonably sultry. He didn't feel like moving a muscle.

"Huh! That's why it's been nice and quiet. That Misty only thinks of herself," muttered Annie.

"Besides, they've gone south to do some fishing," added Gus. "You like fishing, Harry?"

"Never really tried it. Maybe I should." After he sorted things out he might have some time, and the money. Sure hope that lawyer knows what he's talking about. He was staking everything on the guy's advice. Esmeralda's soft spot for him needed to be backed by facts. He knew that. From the first time she laid eyes on him, Esmy and he had hit it off. When he took her side against Bruce, that sealed it. The first time he did it, he'd had to snatch the phone from her hand. He remembered the look of surprise on her face. But he'd seen her crumpling face, the shaky hands, the foot tapping nervously. He remembered too the tone of Bruce's voice at the other end of the line.

"Hello. Is this Bruce Forrest? This is Harry Somer, Esmerelda Graham's physical therapist. You seem to have upset the lady." Esmy's hands continued to shake. With Harry's free hand he motioned her to sit down in the chair next to him. She did and grabbed his hand.

"Upset her? How on earth…?" Harry didn't like Bruce's wheedling tone of innocence. Who did he think he was kidding?

"It seems you're not taking no for an answer. I'd like to know the question, Bruce."

"The question? All I did was ask if she needed me to come back for a bit. To help out."

"She's got me right now, Mr. Forrest. I guess she thinks that's enough."

"How much longer do you think her therapy will take, Harry?"

"Why?"

"So I can arrange business matters. If she's going to need me, I want to be available for her."

"Let's just say the therapy is working. It's hard to say when it will be finished. I'm leaving that for Mrs. Graham to decide." Esmy nodded her head briskly.

"That leaves me up in the air….."

Esmy stood up and took the receiver from his hand. "Bruce. You see? I want you to get on with your life. I'm healing just fine. Don't worry about me. You don't need to come back at all. But let's keep in touch. Okay?" With that, she hung up the phone.

Undue influence, Bruce called it. Well, he was wrong. It wasn't Harry that had dreams of being some fat cat living off the toil of others. When Esmy insisted he move down to Florida and get his gallery going had Bruce taken the opportunity to move in on her again? While the cat's away? Was he back – against her wishes? Would Harry be able to prove it? Had she become vulnerable again?

"There's an old Chinese saying, Harry," Gus said, interrupting the man's thoughts.

"Yeah?" Harry had to stop rehashing events in his mind and start doing something about it.

"The time you spend fishing isn't subtracted from what time you've been given. It's a bonus."

"Nice thought, that." An intriguing idea, for sure. He couldn't help asking, "Does the same hold true for other good stuff?"

"Like what?"

"I don't know. Fine wine? A good woman? Things like that?"

"Nope." The guy was sure. "Just fishing."

Harry had stopped listening. A good woman. That made him think of Sarah who'd discovered his secret hobby of sketching. He'd admired her for more than her support. She'd let him do some sketches of her. He'd framed the best one when he graduated and given it to her. She'd even made sure Harry signed the picture. The lady believed in him. He'd given it to her as something to remember him by. He knew he'd never forget her. He'd used those drawings to paint a couple of life drawings in oils and they were powerful pieces.

Gus seemed to be in a reverie of his own too. Maybe about fishing. They were both were silent.

Until Annie spoke up. "That Huntz ain't all bad. He brought back a little table for me the other day. With a drawer. It's where I put my secret things."

"What secret things, Annie? You holding out on me?" Gus looked at me and grinned.

"Never you mind! You get all my money as it is."

"All your money?" Gus lowered his voice and explained. "She gets her room for a third of what it would cost her at one of those subsidized housing places. Don't you be thinking I'd rob a little old lady." Harry shook his head. If the woman had money to buy booze she had enough, was what he'd say. If she asked. She'd fallen asleep, the empty glass still clutched in her hand. Her cigarette had gone out. The dog opened one eye and glared at Harry. It's okay, fellow. "My Uncle Rod took her in when her hubby died back in 1995. The two were simple people, never finished high school. Got together when they were sent to a sheltered workshop. Inseparable, the pair of them. When it closed – it lost its funding from the government – Uncle Rod gave them both a job doing some care-taking around here. Cleaning up, doing small repairs. Now, don't laugh, Harry. I can see you're skeptical. The Pelican Motel did have better days."

"No, no. I'm not laughing. Times have been tough, for everyone."

"Uncle Rod always had a soft spot for strays. A disaffected Democrat, my Uncle Rod. He said each person had to do his bit to help out 'cause you couldn't count on the State, or the Feds for that matter. Annie and Bertie had no insurance, of course. Nothing. Not like Uncle Rod. Smart as a whip, that man. Knew what he wanted out of life and made sure he got it. He had insurance, even some investments, along with this place. Didn't forget others either, while still living the good life. He said he had all he needed, a roof over his head, enough to eat and his self-respect. And enough to run his boat. Spent most of his time fishing. That's why he called The Pelican Motel his piece of Paradise."

Harry had to laugh at that. "A lot of people think that way down here, even after the hurricanes. I saw a sign a few miles back scrawled in black marker on a piece of battered dock, I guess. It was stuck on a post by the side of the road. The words? 'It's Still Paradise!'"

Gus grinned. "Rightfully so. I respect Uncle Rod's feelings about this place. Luckily he left me the wherewithal to keep it open. I had nothing better going for me up north. The cold was getting to me too. I'm thinking I'll stay here for good. Been six months now and I'm still here. Get the odd rental, or long-term stay. Buys me groceries. Besides, if I closed I don't know what old Annie would do. I got her that little dog a few weeks back. A stray too, just like her. Couldn't stand to see the woman moping about. She needed some company. Been drinking less since the mutt came into her life. She named it after her husband. He was Big Bertie, a brute of a guy, but gentle as they come."

"Guess you have a soft spot, too?"

"Aw, no." But he seemed pleased at Harry's words and held out the bottle again. Little did Harry know this big guy with the soft spot for little old ladies would hold the key to Esmy's dilemma.

CHAPTER SIX

Actors are con men and con men are actors.

Edward Burns

Not only did Bruce Forrest take a seat in Esmerelda's sun porch the first time they met, he became a permanent fixture. He knew how to make that happen. How could she not offer him a bedroom when the transmission in his car would take three days to be repaired? Then, when the tree came down on her front porch, he had cleaned it up – she'd rented a chainsaw for him – and made the repairs needed to the trim on her porch. That meant taking Bruce down into David's workshop to retrieve needed tools. How could he help but be impressed with her husband's organization? He'd been captivated by the three workbenches, each built by David for specific jobs.

"I can't get over all this!" Bruce had kept exclaiming. "Your husband must have done some good work in his time. And look at all these implements and tools. There must be something here for every kind of task." He'd had his glasses in his hand and he used them to point out items in the workshop. "Look at the size of that lathe!"

"He used that to turn legs for a little stool upstairs. And to replace the bannisters on the stairwell."

"And all sorts of planes – every size you can imagine. He knew what he was doing, that's plain to see." A sure way into Esmerelda's good graces. She missed her husband and longed to talk about him. "What's that fan arrangement over there?" Bruce had put his glasses back on and smoothed his hair back. "It seems to be an exhaust system to the outside."

"David loved to finish furniture with a French polish. He'd do coat after coat until there was the highest gloss you could imagine. I'll show you a library table he refinished. It's in the conservatory."

"Was this his whole life?"

"Not at all. He also ran Grandma's Grahams, a huge enterprise. David was a study in opposites. He had an accountant's mind, the hands of an artisan and the heart of a poet. Somehow he managed to fit it all in. He loved to read too. We used to belong to two book clubs though that used to generate some real discussions between us. We often disagreed on what writers were trying to say. I'll show you the collection of his favorite authors upstairs, all in bookshelves he made himself." After turning off all the lights, including the halogen ones David used to spotlight certain projects, she had taken Bruce to show him the bookcases in the library that David had outfitted himself.

"Gosh! Did he do this all these? The wood is amazing. They're beautiful. The surrounds are gorgeous too, all carved with fancy flourishes."

Esmerelda had laughed. "Much like the passages he so enjoyed reading. David loved flowery writing, whereas I'm just the opposite."

"Truly awesome work, Esmerelda."

A little surprised that Bruce hadn't been interested in the books themselves, she'd replied, "He made shelves for me too, for ornaments in the dining room." Bruce had been duly impressed, had asked all the right questions, expressed amazement and respect.

"Your husband must have drawn the designs before he executed them. Do you still have his designs?" Three shallow drawers in the dining room buffet had been reserved for David's portfolio of designs that he'd drawn himself before doing any woodwork, relegating her fine lace tablecloths to the linen cupboard but she never minded. Even more so now, as these collections of David's drawings were far more valuable than Belgium lace. Showing all his work to Bruce had brought David to life, almost.

A man can make himself indispensable, especially to a widow who's all alone. Bruce started to shop for her groceries, drove her to appointments and the library and even washed her windows. She appreciated that and the admiring glances he garnered. To be escorted by an attractive and personable young man about town was a pleasure. She had few friends left, but getting a grin from the pharmacy cashier or a little bow from the girl in the flower shop perked her up as well as seeing Bruce's effect on women. To be with such a man made her feel alive again. Sometimes she wondered when he'd be moving on but, for some reason, she didn't ask. Perhaps she hadn't wanted to know. It was nice to have someone to talk to again. She'd felt it only right that she pay his expenses while he was doing so much for her. He anticipated her needs. As the autumn drew to a close with cold winds from the east Bruce suggested he caulk the windows to add some insulation.

"Not that you need to save money, Esmy. But why throw it away?"

"If you think it's necessary, Bruce." She'd begun to rely on the man, she realized. Then Jenny arrived, there on her doorstep midst the fallen leaves.

"Esmerelda, this is my girlfriend, Jenny," Bruce had drawn the girl close to him with his arm around her waist. The young woman's hand had moved up to brush Bruce's hair out of his eyes. "I didn't realize there was someone in your life, Bruce," Esmerelda had said.

The young woman had been a surprise, for some reason. Bruce was young and in his prime. What a foolish old woman she'd been.

"For about two years now."

"Bruce! It's been just a little over a year now," said Jenny. She had brought three pieces of luggage herself. "Can I take these through? Show me the way, Brucey."

Show me the way? Esmerelda had been taken aback as Bruce pointed down the hallway. The woman went ahead, but Bruce stood there with the heaviest suitcase in one hand. Esmerelda had gathered her courage, easier to do as she thought over events. Why had he never mentioned this girl throughout this past month? He'd talked about being alone, just like her. There's no fool like an old one. Finally she'd made herself inquire. "When...how long, Bruce, are you and Jenny planning to stay? What are your plans?" What an idiot she had been. Of course the young man would have someone somewhere. She hadn't given it a thought. How silly of her.

"Esmerelda! I'm sorry. I should have explained. I wanted Jenny to come on this trip with me but she couldn't get away until now. I thought I'd be down south by this time, but you know what a fine time we've been having! I should have moved on by now. Jenny's been wondering why I hadn't contacted her to have her join me. She's been waiting. You see, we'd like to settle down sometime and she thinks she should have a say as to where it will be." He laughed. "Of course, she's right. I can't make that decision alone."

"So you'll be moving on soon, I guess?"

"Esmerelda, you've been great and I really wanted you two to meet. Yes, I've got some feelers out and hope to hear pretty soon."

"Well, I've enjoyed your stay, Bruce, but I understand you have to get on with your life. If there's any way I can help, let me know." At least she'd have her home back to herself. It had been nice getting to know Susan's grandson, but that's as far as it went. Esmerelda was coming to her senses.

"Just keep your fingers crossed for us!" It didn't happen at once, of course. In the meantime the pair made the house their own. Jenny had a penchant for television quiz shows and never missed one. There was no television in their room so the den became Jenny's nesting place. What had once been Esmerelda's favorite room was no longer a place of solitude. It became littered with newspapers and magazines of the kind Esmy had never seen before, along with lots of food packages. The couple did a lot of their eating out of bags. When they moved the microwave into the den Esmerelda was too surprised to speak. The television was on morning and night too, with no peaceful moments. To get some solitude Esmerelda had eventually retired to her own wing of the house, and not just in the evenings.

With Jenny in the house Bruce was a changed man. She couldn't say he was no longer considerate. It was just that the emphasis was on them, rather than...Esmerelda. She chastised herself for being so selfish. Any young man would behave the same, of course. Whenever they happened to share a meal Bruce always wanted to talk about family, something Esmerelda felt uneasy about. He loved to tell how his grandmother Susan volunteered in the local library. He credited her with his love for books. Esmerelda suddenly remembered how she and her sister used to love playing librarians, even had a date stamp and marked all the books in the house. Of course, that was before electronic record- keeping. He answered her polite questions about her sister but, if she were being honest, Esmerelda really didn't listen much to his answers. Family should be important, she knew, but Susan had nipped that in the bud many years ago.

If anyone could use words as weapons, it had been Susan. "Father can't bear to talk about this, Esmy." Susan's words of decades ago were as fresh as if they were uttered yesterday. "What could you have been thinking?" Susan didn't wait for, or expected, any answers to her questions. "This is going to be the death of Father! Would you leave us orphans?" Esmerelda's mother had died giving life to Esmerelda, always an unspoken accusation from Susan. "What will people say? Esmy, you have absolutely no choice. We…Father has decided. You'll be going away for some months, until it's over. You can say you went to Europe or something."

If things had been different while David was alive, perhaps they would have patched up the wound. David was always on to her to forgive her sister. He put great stock in family, maybe because he had none. But now? Did it really matter? She could almost see David shaking his head and saying, "Esmy, the past is the past. This young man is the future. Get to know him."

So Bruce and Jenny had settled in and Esmerelda adapted. Talk of books had given her an idea. It would be a way of forgiving herself for the past. Or was it Bruce's idea at first? Either way it seemed a good one. Establishing a trust or some kind of financial arrangement to endow a library of her own would commemorate her husband and…. perhaps her sister too? That part was Bruce's contribution for sure, but it was one way to end the feud for once and for all in her mind. And wouldn't Bruce be the perfect one to handle all the arrangements, with his education and talents? Of course, that led to talk of her will and who would inherit.

"Don't want you to take this the wrong way, Esmerelda, but who will inherit after you're gone?" asked Bruce. At first she was affronted, but she had to realize he was family. Jenny sat reading one of her magazines and didn't seem interested in their words. Esmy had never even thought of Susan's side of the family being involved in her estate. Anonymity is very protective. Now she'd come to know Susan's progeny she couldn't pretend he didn't exist.

"There's no one left but me. And you." Thanks to Susan.

"No one else, Esmerelda?" Bruce's glasses were sitting propped on the end of his nose. With one finger he slid them back to the bridge as he looked at her intently.

"I have some charities I support. I've made arrangements for them to get some." The rustle of Jenny's skirt as she shifted position, closer to the arm of the couch and away from Bruce.

Bruce glanced at his girlfriend before saying, "That's good of you, Esmy. If you're serious about endowing a library though, that's going to take quite a bit."

"I'm not sure how to go about it. I'm a bit peckish. Would you like a drink, Bruce, and some biscuits? Jenny?"

"A drink?" asked Jenny.

"Hot chocolate, maybe? It helps me sleep."

"That will be fine," said Bruce quickly. Jenny shook her head and buried it in her magazine once again. Esmerelda went to the kitchen and prepared the night time snack for the three of them. When she got back Jenny had left the room.

"That looks good, Esmy. Jenny decided to call it an early night," Bruce said, taking the tray and putting it on the coffee table between them.

That meant no late night television, thought Esmy. She smiled at Bruce.

"I've been thinking," he said. "To make matters simple you could leave it to me, with the stipulation that I use the money to set up a library of the kind we've been speaking about. Here, I'll show you the kind of thing I mean." He had a legal pad ready and had already jotted down some figures. She'd have to include Bruce in her will and this idea of endowing a library was the way to do it and establish something permanent and it would take care of his part of the bequest, a library he could direct. Bruce couldn't complain about her motives, could he? With that they put their heads together and drafted a few statements outlining such a plan while Bruce took notes.

"This is great!" said Bruce. "Don't you think so?"

"Is it clear enough, do you think? Perhaps we should have my lawyer look over it when we're done."

"Sounds like a plan! Listen, why don't we add a bit about... Cripes!" Bruce jumped up. He'd spilled hot chocolate all over his hand and the pages they'd been writing on.

"Oh, gosh. I'm sorry Esmy. I've gone and ruined this whole draft."

"No, no, it's not ruined. I can read it – almost every word."

"I've gone and burned my hand too."

"Go and run cold water over it. Quick. Get some ice from the freezer."

"Can you..finish...?"

"I can write this up. Just take care of your hand. And better rinse the chocolate out of those chino pants too." Esmy rewrote the draft in final form while he tended to his wounds. She was pleased her money would be establishing something worthwhile, and a relative would be overseeing it, carrying out her wishes. Bruce would get his 'inheritance' on her terms. She signed the paper and drew a flourish under her signature.

On Bruce's return she said, "Remind me to have the lawyer take a look at this, won't you?"

"Tomorrow?"

"No rush, Bruce. Next month will be fine. I have an appointment then to deal with some things."

That's how Bruce Forrest got himself into her will. After Esmy retired for the night he took the paper and placed it safely in her important papers folder. It was crucial this codicil not get mislaid. Now for stage two of his plan.

CHAPTER SEVEN

The marks humans leave are too often scars.

John Green

"You see, Jenny? I told you! Just like taking candy from a baby. Esmy's the easiest target so far." They had just finished making love, quietly, not Bruce's usual style, but it was better than nothing. Bruce was feeling good. He wanted to impress his girlfriend even more.

Jenny was brushing her hair in front of the full length mirror on the outside of the bathroom door. They'd never been in a place this posh before. The bathroom had everything from body washes to a bidet. Bruce had to tell Jenny what it was for. She'd wrapped a velvety towel- there were several in different sizes but all in shades of pink- around her waist. With a hand towel she was patting her breasts dry. She knew Bruce was watching her like a hawk and she knew her breasts were her best feature. "But when you get the money you'll have to build a library, won't you? It wouldn't be your money." Bruce had come up with some good schemes, but this time might be different. She was having trouble seeing how he'd get any money from the woman if all they were going to do was open a library. Libraries had never been her favorite place. "What good would building a library do? Tell me that."

"I'd have to set up a library, yes. But it could just be some dinky little hole in the wall, or maybe even nothing at all." He tossed a pillow at her to make her turn around. Her breasts bounced as she tossed it back and he laughed. "Good catch, sweetie pie. Listen, everyone knows you can't leave people money with strict stipulations about what they do with it. I think it's called 'undue control from the grave'." At Jenny's puzzled expression he went on, "Undue control. You can't boss people around, especially from the grave." This time he threw his slipper at her. It successfully dislodged the knot in the towel, which fell to the floor. God, she had it all. "Come here, baby."

"Well, that makes sense. I mean how could someone boss you around when they're dead?" She picked up the towel and draped it over one shoulder, playing peek-a-boo. Teasing him, she moved the towel up and down over her torso. She saw the effect this had on Bruce and came closer to the bed, but just out of his grasp.

"Well, someone might stipulate...insist...that their son or daughter marry someone they'd named in the will." Bruce's hand grabbed the towel.

"People do that?" She fell beside him and they nestled into each other's arms.

"For sure, but they haven't got away with it. Or willed the money to them on the condition they take care of their cats for life."

"Well, I can sort of understand that, Brucey." She liked cats. When she was a little girl she'd had a little black kitten and named it Midnight. When her family moved, the fourth time in as many months, Midnight didn't choose to go with her. He leaped out of the car and her Daddy wouldn't go back to get it. He said it cost too much money to feed. She never understood that because all it ate was table scraps.

Bruce's chuckle interrupted her thoughts, saying, "If that happened to me, I'd make sure something happened to the cat."

Jenny drew away from him. "You wouldn't!" This was a side of Bruce she didn't like. He could be very cold-hearted, just like her Daddy. Her friend Sasha had told her women pick men just like their fathers. Maybe that was true.

"So, you see, Esmy can't tell me what to do after she's dead. We'll just have to do something in the spirit of her will, not use all of the money."

"So we'll get the whole shebang, Brucey?" Jenny kissed him behind his ear, the way he liked it. Her wet hair fell onto his shoulder

"Most of it. And you'll get that dream house you've always been wanting, with a spa and exercise room of your own, maybe even a stable for me and some horses!" Magic words. Later, when they were fully dressed, Jenny returned to the topic.

"I can't wait much longer, Brucey. Don't you have enough money by now, with all those jobs you did down south? Why do you keep wanting more? It could take years for her to die." She was sauntering around the room, opening drawers, sometimes tidying Bruce's belongings.

"Not if I have my way, Jenny." From a glass case he removed a pair of narrow wire glasses. He put them on, adjusting the frames around his ears carefully.

"What do you mean?" She may be greedy, but she sure wasn't willing to do anything too dangerous to get what she wanted. Jenny was a coward and was the first to admit it. Now she was at the wall-to-wall bookcase and touching the spines of books.

"Ask me no questions, I'll tell you no lies." He wondered what Grandmother Susan would think. Would she be pleased that he'd managed to get into Esmerelda's good graces and was going to take full advantage? "You know, Jenny, it's going to be so easy. I know my way around old broads."

Jenny raised her eyebrows but he didn't notice. And since when did he wear glasses? She'd come to a shelf holding china horses. Gingerly she took each one and held it in the palm of her hand. "Look, Brucey. Aren't these sweet? Little horses, perfect in every way. See this one's ears, all perked up?"

"Be careful, Jenny. Don't you go dropping one of them. Grandma always said Esmerelda could be led astray by a smooth talking man. It happened before when she came close to becoming the black sheep of the clan. Luckily, Grandma and her father dealt with things swiftly and it all turned out fine. No one knew what Esmerelda had done. You know, Esmerelda had some nerve! She hardly ever spoke to her father or Grandma Susan again after they saved her from a lifetime of shame! Can you believe it?" He took off his glasses and rubbed the bridge of his nose.

"How long did the....What do you call it when two parts of a family fight? I know! Feud! How long did the feud last?" asked Jenny. Pride at finding just the right word gave her courage to ask. "And why are you wearing those? Do you need glasses?" She put the last horse back in place and patted its rump. "You go back to the field now, with all your pals," she said in a little girl voice.

"I don't need glasses. I just bought these with plain glass in them. I thought they'd make me look more....endearing." Jenny raised her eyebrows again, keeping her thoughts to herself. "Good word, that, Jenny. Feud. That pretty well describes it. They rarely spoke. Years later, Grandma had to read about Esmerelda's wedding in the papers. Can you believe it?"

"In the newspaper?" Jenny was trying all the lamps in the room now. There were four. The night tables had swing lamps suspended from the wall that could swing into place as needed. Jenny tried all the positions, then the settings from low to bright. The mahogany desk had a hurricane lamp in brass and glass. The floor lamp by the armoire had crystal drops. Jenny lay on the chaise lounge and gathered her skirt about her. Bruce didn't like her to wear slacks. He said next to her breasts her legs were worth a million bucks.

"Yup. How Esmerelda managed to marry into money, Grandma could never understand. To get to marry someone like David Graham! What a coup! Boy, that made my grandmother even madder. And to not even be invited to the wedding!" Bruce had heard the stories many times over the years, especially near the end, when resentment seemed to strangle the dying woman. She was angry too about what seemed the final insult – that her sister would likely outlive her. Totally logical, of course, but Bruce had been raised on bitterness. "I'm going to make sure the woman shares her good fortune, for Grandma's sake." He took off the glasses again, this time to clean the lenses.

"It's not going to be that easy, Bruce. May I say something? If you keep fiddling with those specs she'll know you're not used to them." She lay back with her arms behind her head. The separation of her breasts distracted him.

"It certainly has been a long time. You are a sight for sore eyes."

"Maybe she'll decide not to, Bruce. You ever think of that? She seems to be a smart lady to me. Polite too. When I came barging in with my luggage she kept her thoughts to herself."

"Aw, it'll be easy – and I'll get used to these damn fool things." He took off the glasses and rubbed his eyes. "I know my way around old ladies. I should, after learning how to deal with Grandma Susan. If there's one thing I know, it's how to please, especially women. Wouldn't you agree?"

Jenny knew better than to disagree with Bruce. "You sure do, honey."

"And especially old women. Grandpa and I soon learned how to deal with Grandma. I was a lot better than Gramps, in fact, at looking like I was going along with Grandma's strictures, while not actually – if you get my meaning."

"I do, Brucey."

"I usually got my own way, in the long run. Of course, Grandma doted on me. I knew how to twist her around my little finger. I'd sit for hours listening to her go on and on, usually about how Esmerelda had ruined their family. I could take it. Grandpa would just get up and leave the room. He didn't want to hear any more of it. My sitting there nodding and speaking at the right times put me into Grandma's good books. I'm good at sitting and listening."

Jenny swallowed her laugh.

He noticed. "Well, not really listening. I guess it's about knowing when to interject just the right word at the right time. That's what old people like." He was peering at her over the rims of his glasses. Jenny thought he looked domineering, not endearing. Those were words she'd learned from Bruce. His Grandma had been domineering.

"Why was your Grandma Susan so filled with thoughts about Esmerelda? Didn't it get her down? Life goes on. Why did she keep harking back to the past."

"I used to wonder about that too. I think because Esmerelda went on to make such a success of her life. Grandma Susan thought she should have borne her guilt like an albatross and been forever grateful her sister and father had saved her. Grandma said Esmerelda never was the least bit appreciative. When Esmerelda married well, and for love, it fired up Grandma's resentment even more."

"But that had to have happened years ago!"

"Yeah, but incidents kept cropping up, igniting Grandma's anger all over again. News about how well the Graham shares were doing on the open market. Or a picture on the TV of Esmerelda endowing a wing of the local hospital. Even the coverage of David Graham's funeral fired up Grandma's ire. I remember how she peered at the picture and finally said how poorly her sister was looking. It wasn't true, of course, but I kept my opinion to myself. I just agreed with her as I usually did. Even in the fuzzy picture in the newspaper Esmerelda looked striking, especially compared to Grandma Susan whose health was rapidly deteriorating. Grandma's pride was sure prickly.

Bruce was the first to admit he wasn't a patient man, despite his relationship with his grandmother, or maybe because of it? He was sure he'd be able to arrange the financial side of things with Esmerelda, but he didn't want to have to wait years. The widow's health was just too good. Like Jenny, Bruce wasn't big on bravery either, so he gave lots of thought to the best way to achieve his plan. He wanted it to work the first time because, frankly, he didn't know if he'd have the courage to try again. He didn't see him and Jenny sitting around twiddling their thumbs waiting for the woman to die naturally. It could take years and he didn't have that long a wait in mind. The answer came after one of Esmy's visits to the doctor.

"Bruce, will you get a gallon of milk with the groceries? Dr. Emery says I need more calcium. Apparently my bones are getting brittle. I'll need some capsules too. Here's the name." She passed over a slip of paper.

"Brittle bones?" Bruce peered at the note through his glasses. He still wasn't used to them and he had a little blister on the side of his nose. But Bruce was a stubborn man.

"Oh, it happens to women. I've been taking a supplement but it hasn't done the trick. He says I haven't been doing enough walking either. Says I should get out more. He gave me a clean bill of health otherwise. Said I should live for years and years so I must make sure my bones can carry me through. His words scare me a bit, I have to admit. What if I took a fall? What if I break something? He says I haven't enough flesh on my bones, either." She hadn't told the doctor she didn't like Jenny's food. Too spicy. She didn't like dining as late as they did either so just nibbled at dinnertime. She was eating a lot less than usual.

Bruce was mulling over her words. Live for years and years? Again, not what he had in mind but the doctor had given a clue as to how to make sure that didn't happen. What if she took a fall? Old people break hips and often never recover. Their health wanes, their muscle tone goes, they get pneumonia. That's usually the end. He didn't voice his thoughts. "Esmy, you should stay right here, where you're safe and sound, not go gadding about." He encouraged Esmerelda in this plan of action and gradually Bruce and Jenny took over the running of the house, which made things easier for Esmerelda. They did all the errands, often bringing things into the house she'd never asked for. Decisions were taken out of her hands one at a time – like mealtimes. The two of them preferred their big meal in the evening whereas she'd rather have her dinner in the early afternoon with a light snack for supper. She didn't think it right to make an issue of this so she acquiesced. No wonder she ate even less. With the television on all day, she changed her own routine, staying pretty well to her own room. They did the shopping and started paying the bills and were in and out of the house all day. Because she didn't want to slow them down she left them to it, relinquishing much of her independence. It wasn't a good decision.

CHAPTER EIGHT

Anyone who says they're not afraid at the time of a hurricane is either a fool or a liar, or a little bit of both.

Anderson Cooper

"Just a sip this time," Harry said. "Thanks." The liquor felt good and, besides, he was curious. "Tell me about Huntz and Misty."

"He's a roofer who's come down for the work. Contractors are crying for labor these days." Gus pulled out a stool from the corner and perched on it. He picked up a couple of pencils from the counter and started tapping out a complicated but compelling rhythm. Harry's foot started tapping all on its own.

"Yeah, I can imagine. I never saw so many roofs off." Harry decided to sit down before he broke out into a dance. He was feeling much better and took a seat next to the old lady, being careful not to wake her. Her dog opened one eye and glanced at him. Then he deigned to give Harry a smell, stopped and stared again and then went back to sleep. Harry had passed inspection. A dog would be good company at the gallery. Make a good watchdog too, he thought.

"Huntz is from Canada. Don't know where he picked up Misty. He came in one day, checked in, and a few days later she appears. The fellow's been working since he arrived. Every contractor gives him a housing allowance. He lives here and pockets the other half of what they give him. He's raking it in. Says he has plans for the money." Doesn't everyone, thought Harry.

"Huntz deserves it," said Annie, awake again. "Hard worker, Huntz." She picked up the mutt and gave him a cuddle. As Gus' pencils got busy on a rumba she swayed the pup back and forth. The old woman had a good sense of rhythm too.

"You're right, Annie," said Gus. "He's good at what he does too. Works hard on every job he gets. Never wastes a moment. In between jobs he goes fishing, usually on the boss' boat, lucky sod. They all like him."

"Brought me a kettle one time."

"You cooking in your room, Annie?" Gus winked at Harry.

"What? Cooking? Me? No way. Just a cup of hot tea now and then." She put the pup down beside her between the two of them. "Sure could do with one right now." With that, Gus put down his pencils, got off his stool, turned around and plugged in the kettle. He had all the makings under his counter. He brought out three mugs, three tea bags and a spoon. A saint. Harry was feeling a lot better now. A hot drink would go down well. Without Gus' percussive accompaniment, the night sounds penetrated the little lobby. The ocean was slapping the shore and every so often a plaintive cry could be heard, one hardly human.

"What's making those sounds out there," he asked Gus.

Annie answered. "Feral cats, mister. If I let Little Bertie here loose, he'd take care of them."

"Now don't you go doing that, Annie. That pup's not street smart. They'd eat him alive," said Gus. He glanced at Harry. "They're wild cats making that noise. They get dumped here by their owners, at the side of the road. Nature being what it is, the felines mate and their offspring are even wilder. You can see them at night searching up and down this strip for food. Spend half their time under cover of dark looking for food and the other half procreating. That's what they're doing right now – calling to each other, checking out who's interested." It must have worked because, after a string of escalating cries, all Harry could hear was the rush of the waves.

"You wrote that letter for me, Gus?" Annie asked. The mutt uncurled himself and inched over to Harry's lap, took a sniff, then settled down.

"Letter...?" Gus frowned.

"To get me money from Jeb Bush. Jeb Bush is going to give me money, mister. It said on the TV." Annie smiled at him. The pup's approval was enough for her. She straightened out her housecoat and stretched her spindly legs. He could hear bones cracking or maybe it was his imagination.

Jeb Bush? Harry raised his eyebrows this time. Gus laughed and explained.

"Some counties are getting special funds to help low income folks, disabled people too, after the hurricanes."

"Four hurricanes we had, mister! I remember their names." She started counting them off on her fingertips. Tiny little hands with a simple wedding band on her third finger, left hand. That surprised Harry. "There was Charley...Frances...and..."

"And Jeanne," helped Gus.

"I can get them, Gus! Let me see......Darn, it! Gus! Which one did I forget?"

"The Russian one, Annie. Starts with an I. Ends with a vee-hicle. There's a clue. 'I' and a VEE-icle." Again with the elongated veee-hicle with the first syllable accented..

"I-? Vee? V? I know! Ivan! That's right. That name's funny. I-Van. Sounds like a car ad. The Russian one. I didn't like that hurricane, for sure."

"Governor Bush says they just have to write a letter, be over 60 years old and prove they have special circumstances. They have to need a helping hand 'cause of hurricane damage."

"My walker flew right away. Who knows where it landed! That's why I gave up looking. Could be in a tree somewhere."

"Or in someone's swimming pool. Should have brought it into your room, Annie."

"I can't remember everything, Gus. Those winds sure scared me. You going to write that letter tomorrow, Gus? I want one with wheels this time." Absentmindedly, her right hand was patting the pup, still asleep on Harry's lap.

"Yup, Annie, I'll write it. Don't you worry your head about it." She'd started patting his hand now, but Harry didn't mind. It was soothing.

"Maybe I could get one of them new-fangled ones with a basket? For when I go shopping?"

Harry couldn't help but add, "That would sure be handy for this little guy. You could put a little pillow in the bottom. He'd be nice and comfortable, wouldn't he?" Annie nodded.

"Shopping, Annie? So's you don't drop your bottle?"

She ignored his jibe. "With a little seat even? Mrs. Ewley has that kind. Thinks she's special, that one, with her wheelabout." She directed that comment to Harry, who nodded. He didn't know why. He felt as if he'd been sitting here for months with two old friends.

Gus seemed to know his way around official stuff. Harry decided to ask. "So, your inheritance? How long did the whole process take? Any hitches? Hold-ups? The law can be an ass sometimes."

"Not long. I was Rod's only living relative." Esmeralda's relative, Bruce Forrest, was out to get Harry but he knew something Forrest didn't. Esmeralda had given him a job to do and Harry wasn't going to let her down, even if Bruce was her only living relative, or so he thought.

"I have no living relatives," murmured Annie. Then she started to sob, quietly. More like little hiccups. Harry began to pat her hand this time. Little Bertie snuggled into her to help out too. Rod made her a tea, putting in two teaspoons of sugar. Harry put the pup right in the middle of her lap. She needed him right now.

Gus asked, "You hungry, Annie? Want some pizza? I've got a couple of pieces right here." The old lady stopped sobbing long enough to shake her head. Looking at Harry, Gus whispered, "This old dame keeps skimping on food. I try to get her to eat more and drink less." Then, in a louder voice, "I'll wrap it up and you can eat it tomorrow, Annie?" Gus took a pizza box and a plastic bag from behind his counter and dealt with the leftovers.

"I'll just get her to bed, if it's okay, Harry?" Harry nodded and watched as Gus let her put both hands on his arm to pull herself up. She nodded and continued holding onto him as he held her tea and the bag of pizza in his free hand. The little dog leaped to the floor and followed a step or two behind, knowing not to get tangled in the old woman's feet. Harry opened the door for them and stood watching as they inched across the forecourt. Gus opened the door to number 11 and guided Annie inside.

Harry reached down into his carryall and pulled out a copy of the letter from the lawyer. Reading it made his blood rage all over again. He'd been on a slow boil ever since the lawyer had contacted him. Esmerelda knew what she was doing. It was her idea in the first place. She wouldn't even listen to Harry saying it wasn't necessary. She'd set up his annuity for a reason. No way was she not in her right mind when she did that. Harry hoped she was in good health now. She had to be, but her last phone call couldn't be ignored. She hadn't fooled him. Something was wrong. He gulped down the sweet tea, shoved the letter back into his bag and sat down again on Annie's settee. Maybe he should just leave it to the legal guys. That was the advice of his own lawyer. The fellow kept telling him if he went barging in it would just make things worse. How much worse could they be? Plus Harry had something the others didn't know anything about. It was Esmeralda's secret, and his, for the time being.

CHAPTER NINE

You know that saying, bad things don't happen to good people? That's a lie.

Tori Amos

"Sorry about that," said Gus as he came back into the motel office. "You ready for forty winks?" Harry nodded. His knees were buckling. From fatigue, or the upcoming mission? He was a man who hated confrontation. From what he knew of this grand-nephew Bruce he didn't think they'd be friends. The couple of times they talked on the phone confirmed his opinion. Not until he knew Esmeralda had control of her life again did Harry take off south. He was pretty sure she could handle Bruce. Frankly Harry believed she'd seen the last of him. He hoped so. Esmy understood. She'd even sent him off with a nest egg, the annuity. Besides, there was someone new on the scene who had real blood ties with Esmy, not like Harry who was just a good friend.

With her computer and Harry's instructions she'd found her son. Bruce had no idea. For some reason Esmerelda felt it safer that way. She said she couldn't even explain it to herself, never mind to Harry. It was just a gut feeling she had to follow. She was in regular e-mail communication with her son now, though the man didn't know his mother's wealth. His adoptive parents had done a great job with the fellow. He welcomed Esmy's having found him, but wasn't clamoring for more. He was a mature man himself, with a family almost grown. He certainly had no idea his birth mother was the matriarch and almost the last remaining survivor of one of the wealthiest families in the northeast. That would be the icing to top the cake, Esmy said, after she passed on. Esmy insisted Harry had done enough and encouraged him to get on with his own life once she was mobile again. She'd got back her confidence, put some meat on her bones and the exercises he'd taught her had sharpened her mind while her painting had sharpened her spirit. She had got back in touch with reality – gone well beyond that, in fact. She was using her initiative and ingenuity. It was easy to imagine the young woman she'd been.

Harry knew she was pleased in her quiet way to have discovered his 'talent'. She took great delight in being the one to set him up on his own. She couldn't wait until he'd carried out her plans. Neither could Harry, truth be told. Who wouldn't be excited? A studio of his own, even a modest one, was going to be the beginning of the best of his life, he told her. Her annuity called his bluff, she said. It was now or never. She almost pushed him out of her house, literally, to get going on the plans they'd made together for him.

"Now you will have no excuse, Harry. Aren't you tired of saying 'if only I had the time'? Now you will have the time, and the place." She'd told him to pick anywhere. Did she secretly hope he'd stay in her neck of the country? But she wasn't really surprised when he picked Florida.

"I'm partial to sunsets," he quipped. Her scheme was a nice daydream, but it wasn't going to happen. "Maybe I'll go to Florida. Does this hurt?" He was massaging her ankle, rotating it through a full circle.

"No, it feels good, in fact. It's so much more mobile that it was. As if the arthritis had disappeared! Why Florida?"

"It seems a natural place to go." Harry motioned for her to lie on her side. "Why not have at least three seasons when you can get outside and paint the landscape?" He was being flippant. Harry just couldn't take this offer to heart. It was too far-fetched that he could be this lucky. He checked the symmetry of how her legs lay at rest, then did some manual adjustments along her spine.

"Sounds like heaven, Harry. And feels like it too."

Harry was just playing along with her because he truly couldn't believe she was serious. To be honest it was a game he enjoyed but when she kept harping on it he realized she wasn't fooling around. "This is ridiculous. I can't, Esmy. It's just not right taking money from you. We're talking...thousands!"

"I'm not giving it away. I'm investing in you. I'll be a shareholder. After five years I will get a return on my money, say, twenty per cent on your gross? Until then, I'll be a silent partner. How's that?"

Five years? How could a woman her age wait that long for a return on her money? He was too much of a gentleman to ask. They argued like this every day for weeks until she got fed up and took matters in her own hands.

"That's it, Harry. I'm tired of arguing with you. My agent has drawn up the papers for an annuity. All I need now is the name of your bank, a contact number." From the way she leaned both hands on her cane and clenched her knees – something he'd told her she shouldn't do because it wreaked havoc with her back – he knew she was finished with their game. She was playing for real this time.

Harry acquiesced. "You're serious, aren't you?" Maybe he could add a condition of his own. "My own back problems might right themselves if I lived where it was warmer most of the year, Esmy. It would do you good too. Why don't you come with me? Check out the real estate? Help me set up that art school." She laughed at that.

"And make everyone think you were my toy boy? I don't think so. I still have some dignity, even if my body doesn't stand up straight anymore. How about I'll aim for a return on your money before the five years is up?" The twinkle in her eyes registered the fact that she knew she had won. "I have to get on with the rest of my life too, Harry. I can't be lying around here all day having massages. I've got to get ready to meet my son." Her plans had evolved. She hoped to have a meeting with her son as soon as both were ready and that time was getting closer.

That was how things stood when Harry left two weeks later to go south, secure in the knowledge she would do okay. That was four months ago. But had she? This recent phone call had been a little alarming. He couldn't forget it. It niggled at him until it came to the point that he was here, staying at The Pelican Motel, still not quite sure he should be heading north, but compelled to. Would she see it as interference? Esmy's confidence had been a fragile thing once. Was it still?

"Here's an extra pillow." Gus took it out of a cupboard behind him, not from under the counter, thank goodness. It was nice and plump.

"That'll be great. Thanks again, for everything. The drink, the tea..."

"Maybe in the morning you'd like to see Uncle Rod's boat?" He checked his watch. "Just a minute. Almost news time. I'll see what the weather's going to be." He turned on the radio.

The idea was appealing. Maybe he should rethink things. Take a day and mull things over. "Might be nice." They were interrupted by the somber tones of a newscaster.

"In four days more than $534 million of state money has been spent on hurricane victims. The Florida Legislature's special session finished with more money being promised to help rebuild schools, restore beach dunes, pay people's insurance deductibles and cut property taxes on ruined homes."

"Wow. That's a lot of money," Harry said.

Gus shook his head. "That's not all. Along with all the federal money it comes to about $1 billion that's been given to communities down here.

"That should certainly help people."

"There have been other problems, as you might have heard. They've had to step in and stop insurers' practice of charging separate deductibles to policyholders hit by more than one hurricane."

"Yeah. I'd heard that. It's a complicated thing, though, isn't it?"

"Some people have received only a fraction from their insurers, not even a tenth, of what damages they suffered. People have been crying foul up and down the coast." Gus appeared to know a lot about this.

The radio announcer went on, adding more details. "Not addressed by the special session were insurance rate controls, tough deadlines for people to make claims, changes to the Hurricane Catastrophic Insurance Fund and coverage for windblown water damage to businesses and private dwellings." But there was no weather forecast.

"Damn. Guess we'll just have to hope it'll be nice in the morning. So maybe you'll come along with me?"

"I'll have a look at the map and see what's what."

"Sounds like a plan. There'll be a pot of coffee on in here, in any case. For when you wake up." The guy was clicking his fingers in a nice easy rhythm now. Picking up a pencil he sent it somersaulting from the index finger right down to his pinkie, and back again. He'd never seen a guy do that before. Then, with the tip of the pencil he flicked one of the keys off the board and handed it to Harry. "Number two, right next door. Nice and quiet."

"Thanks, Gus."

"Sleep well, now, you hear?"

Harry picked up his bag and went next door. The rush of the waves seemed to have gone to bed for the night. There was a hush about the place. Inside, the room was nondescript, like all motel accommodation. Nothing slick or modern, but there was no broken glass in the shower and no musty smell in the room. He went to pull out the letter again, but changed his mind and instead opened the thriller he was reading. After a sit on the john- glad to see the toilet flushed with no trouble- he showered in water more hot than tepid and dried himself on a threadbare towel. Back in the bedroom he threw two flat pillows down onto the floor, then positioned the third, the fat one, in the small of his back. He arranged his body for a good read. The light was good and he focused on the words where he'd left off. '*Should he enter the vault? Hadn't there been footsteps as he turned the corner? If so, he was a sitting duck. No way to go but forward.*' Sleep took him captive.

Though Harry hadn't completed the renovations of his new studio, they were all finished in his dream that night. The walls were filled with his own watercolors and with Esmy's art collection too, mostly French impressionism, her favorite. To be fair, she loved pen and ink sketches as well as lithographs. All in all, an interesting collection. She'd even framed some of her own efforts, but had hung those pictures in her home, in her bedroom rather than in the library or in the wide hallways. Viewing the scene in his dream Harry was surprised to see his work looked perfectly appropriate up on display with Cezanne and Manet. Then a peacock spread its plumes wide. That image seemed to be the button that lurched the dream into fast forward. The paintings suddenly turned to the wall. Then the gallery door flew open and Harry saw a New England winter, not the Florida sand and shore. When he went to shut the door a figure suddenly loomed in front of him, blocking his passage. A big brute. That's when the floor fell out from under him and he found himself in a locked vault. There was nothing left for him to do but count money.

CHAPTER TEN

If people sat outside and looked at the stars each night, I'll bet they'd live a lot differently.

Bill Watterson

Night time is the best time for some things, like stargazing. The skies were brilliant that night over the Pelican Motel, with millions of points of light piercing the blackness. Twice, falling stars shot across the heavens, but no one saw. A pair of young lovers frolicked in the surf but no one saw them either and they were glad. Sometimes people never want the day to end, and it shouldn't, especially in the lotus land that is Florida. It had been a week of warm temperatures and clear skies, too good to last. Most people up and down the coastal highway were asleep. Some of them were dreaming dreams they'd never remember. Some would wake in fright from reveries they'd rather forget. The odd driver only saw the bare road in front as mind fought with fatigue.

While Harry slept the sleep of the just Gus stayed awake the rest of the night. It was his favorite time. He'd always been a bit of a loner, but of late he realized he was starting to crave company, conversation, a sense of fellowship. He couldn't explain it. Even so, he liked the silence night offered. It wasn't always peaceful, of course. Sometimes the winds blew in off the ocean with an eerie howl, causing dry palm fronds to come crashing down to dot the forecourt of the hotel. He didn't mind, because they burned with a rush of flame, perfect for building a fire. A fire pit out back took care of most of his garbage. Other nights the quiet would be broken by the scream of sirens or someone's stereo, but tonight it was still, with a full moon. "The nuts will be out tonight," Gus muttered, scratching at his arm again. On his last job he'd hidden himself in some insulation and a nasty rash had resulted. It was clearing up, but taking its own sweet time. From his line of work Gus had quickly come to the conclusion that full moons were a force unto themselves. It was as if common sense flew out the window with some people and insanity took over. A man robs the corner store he shops at and thinks no one will recognize him because of the mask he has on, even though he's also wearing his favorite baseball cap and making a getaway on his own bike. Women batter their husbands and don't admit to themselves they'll be at the top of the list of suspects. During full moons, kids who had never stolen in their lives go on shoplifting sprees, model citizens run red lights and residents break out of convalescent homes. It was true. A guy last week had packed all his belongings into a bag he slung on the back of his wheelchair and rolled his way right out the front door. No one saw him because it was supposed to be nap time. Probably he pocketed his medication so he'd be awake enough to make a break for it. When the police caught up to him all he could say was, "Where's the state line? Just drop me on the other side." He'd even tried to bribe the cops with a bottle of peach brandy.

Every so often Gus turned on the radio to hear the weather, still hoping to go fishing in the morning, but night broadcasts don't give much weather, just more bad news. "Nearly one in five Floridians hasn't reached a settlement with their insurance company yet. The

Office of Insurance Regulation says 170,000 claims are still pending. Any policyholders reached by this station were too frustrated to put their feelings on record." Gus could imagine. Luckily, he wasn't one of them. He'd received a check for $30,000 just last month. The piece of roof that came off the back of the building was manna from heaven. With Huntz's help he'd fixed it up a few days ago and it was as dry as toast inside. "Homeowners, still dealing with destruction, are also being forced out of their homes by mold. With no money in hand from their claims, residents are finding it impossible to even start repairs. To date, only 58% of claims have reached settlement, months after the disasters." He turned off the radio and returned to his work. Better deal with Annie's letter too.

He didn't mind taking care of that for the old woman. She couldn't have done it herself. When he told her Governor Bush just might help her out with a little cash she was over the moon. She'd seen him on television and could put the name to the face. Ever since, she'd been talking about Jeb Bush as if he were a personal friend. It wasn't likely Jeb Bush had ever met someone like Annie. Gus had made sure he didn't tell Annie that the Governor's brother was the President of the United States. She wouldn't believe it. As a matter of fact, Gus couldn't either. That dynasty had sure taken hold of America. It was like a Monopoly game with one player cornering all the best cards. Still, if writing a letter to Jeb Bush got Annie some cash he'd do it. It was paperwork, not his favorite part of any job, but always necessary. Everything he did had to be backed up with proof- invoices, signed interviews, phone bills, bills of delivery, contracts – real or forged. Photos too, but computer technology had made that part of documentation much easier for him.

He'd enjoyed talking to that guy, Harry, telling him a bit about himself, but not the important parts. Harry even seemed interested. He wouldn't mind taking him fishing. Do some more talking about life. Gus was a little surprised at his dawning outlook on life. Maybe this place was getting to him. He'd have to get all his thoughts in order and out in the open about this motel. Maybe talking things over with the stranger would help. Get things straight. Hearing thoughts out loud sometimes makes them clearer. Spoken aloud, nonsense sounds like nonsense, and you know where you stand. You can fool yourself with bad logic otherwise. Writing ideas down on paper helps too, but that was paperwork again. He was a hands-on kind of guy. It's why he was good at his job, one of the best, because he wasn't afraid to get into the trenches and find out things for himself.

Normally, Gus wasn't one to share much with anyone. In his line of work it was best to listen. Surprising what people will tell you. You just have to appear a little curious, ask the right question and then pause. It's the pause that counts. Most folk can't stand empty air, especially down here in the south. They'll say anything, right or wrong, to be sociable. The stuff people spew out, accurate or not. You had to separate the wheat from the chaff, remembering there was always a kernel of truth in whatever anyone said. Sometimes it divulged a home truth about the talker himself, at the very least. Gus was smart enough to not take anything at face value. You had to put what info you got from a person into perspective. Don't jump to conclusions too early. Important to triple check the facts. Up north, people are a lot more reticent about divulging private information. They'll clam up soon as talk gets away from the weather. But one thing for sure, if people don't like talking about themselves – and that was very rare – they always like to talk about other people and their business. True the world over. Given half a chance, they'd discuss it, dissect it, judge it and then take great delight in predicting how things will end up, usually badly. I told you so – everyone's favorite mantra.

Talking to Harry like that, buddy to buddy, had done him good. Cemented something in his mind. He did like this place. He'd been hunkering down for quite awhile now and coming to see it was a great base of operations. Quiet. Nondescript. No one would ever suspect he was anything more than a bit of low life who'd staked out his corner of Paradise. Uncle Rod had been right. When he was alive he was always trying to get Gus to sell up and come stay with him. He should have listened. It was a nice bit of Nirvana down here. He could keep his own hours. Work when he wanted, and heaven knew there was lots of work down here. Always would be. If it weren't the regular citizens looking for an easy piece of the action there were always the transients attracted to the coast for their chance at luxury and fine living. Florida was a honeypot. Rich widows. Fly-by-night businesses. Tourist traps. Trade of all kinds. Like the tides, fortunes went up and down. Like his.

This time last year he'd been in New York where competition was fierce for private investigators like him. He had the knowledge to work in the electronic espionage sector, but couldn't hack it. Gus chuckled at that. Plain and simple, his stamina failed. Bored to death, he couldn't keep his nose to the grindstone. He much preferred working with people, even if their crimes were petty. The tomfoolery of some people entertained him. Men and women alike, all thinking they'll never get caught. Sometimes their false bravado inspired his respect. For sure, he was no nine-to-five guy himself and had to admire others who tried to avoid that kind of life. Of course, doing it illegally was never smart. Private investigation was the kind of work he liked, stuff that involved people though once in awhile he'd get pretty fed up with the stupidity. Some people were just too dumb to live life on the dark side. They'd always get caught. He got frustrated too in tying up all the ends. Sometimes he came to a brick wall, had to find another way to prove what's what. But always he enjoyed the interplay and liked reacting to the good and the bad of a job. It sure beat staring at a computer screen all day. Man against man – definitely more interesting than man against software. He needed to feel the beat of another's heart, the fear, even the triumph when someone escaped the net he was drawing closer. He liked trying to understand the workings of another's mind, figuring out the scheming and the strategies – the hustle of private investigation.

When Uncle Rod died Gus had a lot of regrets. His mother's brother had always been a little eccentric so Gus hadn't taken any of Rod's entreaties to come on south seriously. He'd been named the executor on his uncle's death and had no choice. He came south to close out the old man's estate and sell off his boat and belongings. That should have been it, easy for someone with Gus's know-how, but he found he couldn't tear himself away. At first, it was the boat that stole his heart. Then the life agreed with him during the two weeks he'd put aside for the task. Here on the coastal highway, the wash of the waves pulled on him like the moon on the ocean, sure and strong and steady. And real. It was a refreshing change from the life he'd been living. He had to admit it, he was hooked. He couldn't tear himself away. Uncle Rod seemed to be calling to him too, from the grave, telling him to take care of business. Like having Annie camped out in one of the rooms, a problem he hadn't foreseen. It didn't take long to get to realize she was one of life's simple souls, in need of protection. Funny, that was what made him pause in the first place. He couldn't just kick her out. It wouldn't have been simple. In all good conscience he would have had to contact some social service, get funds from somewhere and maybe contact medical people. Likely Uncle Rod knew that. Some might have seen the motel as a noose, with Annie as a stranglehold on him, but it had the opposite effect. He felt needed, by Annie and this motel, both sad reminders of past decades. This place was in a time warp, and Gus was finding it suited him.

CHAPTER ELEVEN

Humility is not thinking less of yourself, it's thinking of yourself less.

C. S. Lewis

Bruce should have been more patient. His first plan had serious flaws. It was a good job it didn't succeed and knock off Esmerelda. Finding a woman dead at the bottom of some stairs – with a bruise in the middle of her back – would have raised anyone's eyebrows. Perhaps that's why there were few repercussions. Someone intent on murder would surely have devised a better scheme. Jenny was not impressed.

"What's your plan now, bright boy?" asked Jenny. Bruce's first attempt at grabbing the brass ring – by pushing an old lady down the stairs – proved that bedding, and a consideration for others, can save a person's life. Esmy had been bringing a change of linen for Jenny and Bruce, a complete set with everything from satin sheets to a thick eiderdown. It made for a perfect landing platform, as well as cushioning Esmerelda's bumps on every other step and is why she only bruised her knee cap. Jenny felt terrible about that. Esmy was a really nice lady. She had literally let them take over the house. Jenny knew she wouldn't have been that generous and had tried to reciprocate by making some nice Mexican dishes for her, but Esmy didn't seem to take to them. Jenny hoped Bruce had no other ideas. Then she could get out of here. He was pursuing a path she didn't want to follow. It was definitely time to weigh her options. "I sure hope you're going to forget about hurting the lady."

"Be quiet. I'm thinking." Bruce had a headache. Could it be the glasses? He hated wearing the things. When Esmerelda's fall had not produced the right result he was befuddled. Switching from scheming murderer hoping to inherit to acting like a loving relative who couldn't do enough wasn't easy for a man whose emotional inventory was rooted in selfishness. Who would have thought the old woman to have such stamina in her? Of course, the blankets she'd been carrying had helped cushion her fall. Worse than that, subsequent events had really botched up the works with the arrival of that physiotherapist, Harry Somer, sent in by Esmerelda's doctor. Amazing what money can buy. Fate was working against him. When Harry had appeared on the doorstep, suitcase and exercise table in hand, Jenny said it was time to retreat and rethink their position for things had gone from bad to worse. Bruce agreed with her in part. Why had Esmerelda let the black guy in? It turned out that, under Somer's care, the woman became rejuvenated, holding a whole new lease on life. No one could be more surprised, or disappointed, than Bruce.

"Don't worry," Jenny advised. "After all, you're still named in her will. Everyone thinks the fall was an accident. I honestly don't know how you get away with these things."

"Guess I'm just lucky, I guess." But Bruce wasn't feeling lucky.

"Okay, okay. The woman's alive, but she's elderly. Things could still work in your favor. Just back off, Bruce," she advised. It was the closest she'd ever come to bossing him around. Jenny was surprised at her own tears when she saw Esmy crumpled at the foot of the stairs. The woman didn't even cry out. Instead, she hoisted herself to a sitting position and called out Jenny's name. Then she'd patted Jenny's hand and kept saying she was fine, before she asked her to ring the doctor, please. Jenny had never been this close to any of Bruce's victims, though she didn't believe he'd actually tried to knock someone off. Either way she decided she'd better get out as soon as possible.

Bruce couldn't be told a thing. He pretended to agree with Jenny. He knew how to deal with women. When he suggested they leave Esmerelda in the care of a physical therapist the doctor sent, Jenny was pleased. Maybe he had a streak of conscience, after all. The pair took off, leaving Esmerelda in Somer's care. Bruce resumed his previous activities with much success, and the funds he accumulated seemed to be keeping him satisfied, Jenny hoped, but secretly Bruce was planning to return when Esmerelda was on her own again. Sometimes retreat is a wise strategy. Best not to appear too eager.

That's why, two months later, after Esmerelda's recovery, Bruce was able to talk Jenny into returning and, to their surprise, they found not just a patient on the mend, but a vital, energetic woman. Jenny was thrilled and greeted Esmy with real affection. Bruce was less happy at the change in the woman. Esmy had not only recuperated, she'd been busy giving away some of Bruce's inheritance.

"It's mine, Jenny, isn't it?" Bruce moaned. "No one else's. I'm Esmerelda's only living relative, even if I'm only her grand-nephew." Worse than that the woman was fueled with enthusiasm and a zest for life. "I have to act like I'm interested and listen to her exciting description of how she's started painting and look at all her silly pictures. It's beyond me!"

Esmerelda didn't notice the effect her words were having on Bruce. "Harry was just wonderful. I really have to attribute my recovery to him. He's so much more than a physical therapist. He has a real talent for painting." And for conning a rich woman, thought Bruce. He should know —he was a master himself. The irony didn't make him laugh. Someone had moved in and taken over, using techniques Bruce thought he'd cornered the market on. Bruce was sure he was right about Somer. Bruce Forrest operated on a plane rooted in dishonesty – finding the fastest way to a buck. Even a hard woman like Grandma Susan could be wrapped around his little finger when he put his mind to it. Somer had probably used all the right tools – smooth talk, a personable demeanor and boyish charm. He really found it hard to believe that all this Harry fellow had ever wanted was to paint. Yeah, sure. Likely story, one he'd never thought of himself. Fostering sympathy was the approach he'd found most successful. Instead he nodded and smiled at her effusive admiration of Harry Somer. Behind his smiles he was entertaining other ways of doing away with her. An article in a newspaper gave him the idea. *EMOTIONAL STRESS LINKED TO HEART FAILURE, by Susan Jackson: Sudden emotional stress – from grief, anger, anger or shock – can cause heart failure in a little known and poorly understood syndrome that seems to affect women primarily, researchers reported Thursday.* Could he make her mad enough to croak? Maybe if he told her what he'd been doing with some of her husband's sketches – trying to sell them. *The victims are generally healthy, with no history of heart disease.* There'd be no murder weapon or fingerprints to worry about. It was an intriguing piece. *A death in the family, an armed robbery, a car accident, a biopsy and a surprise party were among the events that sent 18 women and one man to coronary care units in Baltimore with chest pains and weakening of the heart, according to an article in the New England Journal of Medicine.* Well, it's sure as shooting that a death in the family wouldn't work. Esmy had hardly seemed aggrieved at all at Grandma Susan's death. Armed robbery? Maybe he could pretend to be a burglar. No, he best not be involved at all, or at least to appear not to be. He'd have to attest he saw the robbery, describe what was stolen, all that, which would put him center stage. A car accident? Esmy didn't drive anymore because of macular degeneration. Biopsy- too complicated. Maybe Jenny and he could throw a surprise party? Nope, Esmy didn't have many people to invite. *Most were older: their median age was 62. But one was 27, another 32. Some had such poor heart functioning that they would have died without aggressive treatment to keep their blood circulating, the researchers said.* Well, Esmy was the right age – 72 – for a good scare to put an end to her days. *But all recovered.* Damn. *The new research on the condition, nicknamed broken heart syndrome by the doctors, suggests there may be some truth to the old idea that people can be scared to death or die from sorrow like characters in a romantic novel or a country song. "It's important for people to know that this is something that emotional stress truly can do," said Dr. Maurice Jones, a cardiologist at Johns Hopkins University School of Medicine and the article's lead author.* A good scare would be best, thought Bruce.

"Bruce, are you listening? I have to tell you something. I'm going to make Harry's dream possible. I'm helping him set up on his own, as an artist." Esmerelda had decided she best get her plans out in the open.

Talk about a good scare! Bruce was aghast. "What do you mean – set up on his own?"

"He's going to have his own gallery, Bruce. He'll never have to worry about giving deep massages to any more patients. His artistic talent shouldn't be wasted."

Bruce recalled the closing of the article in the paper. *How exactly it occurs is not clear, but the patients had unusually high levels of stress-related brain chemicals and hormones like adrenaline, which may have temporarily impaired their heart function.* He could believe it. He felt his heart pumping blood into his ears. His heart was racing. *Why nearly all the victims were female is also unknown.* Bruce could give them a clue.

Maybe that was the only way to dispose of these crotchety females who hung on too long. Share the wealth was his motto.

Bruce was appalled that Esmerelda Graham had given a hand-out to a mulatto of all people. He was boiling, but kept quiet. Later, with Jenny, he exploded.

"She should stick to her own kind! Why give money to a black guy?"

Jenny didn't know what that had to do with anything, but she wasn't going to press the point with Bruce, not in the mood he was in. "She has enough to go around, I guess."

Bruce got even angrier at Jenny's words. He was on a rant. "After a couple of questions I discovered she's set up an annuity for the man! She wouldn't tell me how much Somer will get every bloody year, but I can imagine!" Bruce's imagination had run wild trying to figure it out. "I made inquiries. One phone call to an insurance agent told me that even a modest annual income meant an investment of at least a million dollars initially! A million of *my* money!"

Murder was out of the question now, even death by scare, at least until he proved Esmerelda incompetent. "I have to get that annuity cancelled. I'm not about to share my money with anyone." I have to make sure her sanity comes under scrutiny. That'll make all her actions suspicious." If anyone could drive someone crazy, it was Bruce, thought Jenny.

He set about doing it and found it fun. The trick was to always act solicitous and not make a big deal out of any one thing. If they did Esmerelda might get suspicious and put two and two together and smell trickery. Esmy was a woman with a habit – everything with a place and everything in its place. So the smallest change made her uneasy. Why was she finding things where they shouldn't be? The address book on the piano stool? The silverware in a jumble instead of in their little flannel bags? This was the fun part, disrupting the peace of her organizational mind. He'd take her toothpaste out of the medicine cabinet and put it in a drawer. He'd move a plant out of the sunshine and out of alignment with the doily. Tricks in the kitchen were amusing too, switching the cutlery around, or mixing up the tea and coffee. The freezer and the fridge provided some interesting opportunities for confusion too. Dangerous items had to be dealt with more carefully and took more thought. How to get her to almost burn herself but not actually? Just something that would make her nervous but not take her to the doctor? That time when she slipped on the puddle of water that Jenny had left in the middle of the kitchen nearly put paid to their plans. He told Jenny she had to run any ideas by him first. His girlfriend got a little miffed at that, he noticed. He didn't care, as long as she knew she better stick to his plan and not come up with additions of her own. Little did he know that Jenny had not done it on purpose. She was appalled that he thought she could plan to hurt the little old lady and got busy planning her own escape from his clutches.

He didn't want Esmy needing medical help too soon. There would be the proper time for Esmerelda to see the doctor – when she was sure she was losing her marbles. Bruce wanted Esmerelda to be the author of her own misfortune, and Harry's too. If she were incompetent, that would make any annuity she set up for Harry null and void, wouldn't it? Welcome back, million bucks!

CHAPTER TWELVE

You can't have everything. Where would you put it?

Steven Wright

Harry wasn't the only one dreaming that night at the Pelican Motel. Annie snored some of the night away, finally getting a little peace. She was having visions of the love of her life, Big Bert. In her dream he was meeting Little Bertie for the first time. They were all walking down the promenade in their glad rags. Even Little Bertie had a bow tie around his ruff. He had a bounce in his step and Bert was holding her hand. They were planning where they'd go to get some dinner. Fish 'n chips or Chinese? They skipped for a bit, the pup bouncing along between them. Then Bert stopped and looked up into the sky. A brown pelican was breezing through the air, a fish sticking out of its mouth. "Some good fishers, those pelicans. You can't go wrong with a pelican for a pet." Annie wasn't sure whether Big Bert was joking or not. She laughed anyway.

She woke up chuckling. The sound startled her. She hadn't laughed in a long time. She forgot how good it felt. Big Bert loved to laugh. His laugh made her feel safe. Every morning they used to sit and watch the early morning cartoons on TV before they went to work at the Goodwill. Sometimes the shows made her sad because of the loud noises. She didn't know why. Bert would turn the sound down when she jumped and then he'd pat her hand. Why did sudden bangs make her want to leap out of her skin? Bert said not to try to figure it out. It was better that way. So she didn't. Then he'd laugh at something on the screen and she'd feel safe again.

Big Bert would like her new pet, and she was sure he'd really like that she called the puppy Little Bertie. It sure was nice of Gus to bring the little mutt home to her. A warm body next to her at night. The pup liked to sit beside her every waking moment too. Maybe he knew things about her. Maybe he loved her. He might. Too bad dogs can't talk. Turning onto her back, she felt Little Bertie shift his weight and then curl up in a new position next to her feet. Who needed words, anyway? Some hot water bottle, this little guy. I love him too, she realized. She'd never had that thought about another living thing, other than Big Bert.

Annie turned again in bed and looked across the room to the little table Huntz had got for her. The secret drawer wasn't hidden. It was there for everyone to see. What was secret was how it opened. You had to put your hand up under it and push it from behind. Last week Gus had teased her about keeping some secret money. Maybe he was just testing her. No money there, for sure. Every penny was where it should be, in envelopes in Gus' office. Gus said it was better that way. She wouldn't have to worry about thieves coming into her room, something she was always going on about. Gus had been right. Since Gus started keeping her money she didn't worry about it. It was always there when she needed it. He was a good friend. Big Bert had thought so too. She knew she'd gone on to Gus for a long time about how she didn't like living alone. How people might break in and steal everything she had. Finally, Gus had sat her down and put down on paper what she spent her money on. Then Gus had taken little brown envelopes and written numbers on them, a different amount on each brown packet. Annie liked the way the bills fit just so in the packets. Gus had to tell her to stop putting the money in and out and to listen. So she did. She liked Gus. She didn't mind doing what he told her.

She wasn't the same with most other people, especially that mean guy at The Goodwill. He'd yelled at her. "Get your hands off those books. You know you can't read!" Her friend Stacey told him to shut his mouth, he couldn't read either. Gus wasn't like that at all. He was teaching her to read. He was better than any teacher she'd ever had. Gus was nice, like Rod, who was almost as good a man as her Big Bert. Why did everyone she like drop dead like that, in their sleep? Maybe it's why she didn't sleep too well herself. What if she woke up one morning and found out she was dead?

After Gus and she had sorted out her paycheck and the government money it was all put into her brown envelopes – Gus called it her budget – and the packets were now in Gus' desk drawer for when she needed them. She'd learned to read and write some new words because he made her copy the letters under his, so she'd know which packet to take out when she needed something. PERSONAL- Gus said that one was for things like toothpaste. Silly man. She had to tell him she never used the stuff now she had false teeth. She had to buy round tablets to soak with her teeth at night. Said her teeth had more company than she had. That had made Gus laugh aloud, just like Big Bertie used to. TRANSPORTATION- she never knew she could spell such a big word. That was for her bus fare. She'd started walking more since the envelope system started, because Gus said any money left over at the end of the month was dis...dis...dis-something. She couldn't remember the word, but it meant she could spend it any way she liked. She tried to save some too from the FOOD envelope- that one she already knew how to spell. She'd taken to buying packets that could be mixed with hot water. Soup, hot cereal, even some desserts could be made that way. If Gus asked, she'd tell him that wasn't really cooking even though she could now have breakfast and lunch now in her room. She only had to worry about paying for one meal a day. Not always, because two times a week she got a meal free from the Good Samaritans and from the church down on Brody Street. She was saving a bit of money that way and it bought nice food for Little Bertie. He couldn't go hungry. She could spell RENT too, which she gave to Gus on the first of the month. He'd bought her a calendar with puppy pictures on it. It was hanging above the little table with the secret drawer right now. Gus had given her a bright red pen and on the first of the month she checked her calendar for days she should remember. Not that she had many appointments, but the chart had made her life easier. Her memory wasn't what it used to be and she hated trying to think of when she was supposed to show up somewhere. Now she knew when the library was open or when she had to go to the clinic for her vitamins and those big white pills she could hardly swallow. She liked to drop in on Stacey when it was her turn to be at the Goodwill. Those days were starred. She didn't love Stacey, of course. But Stacey had known Big Bert and she could talk to her about him. Sometimes Stacey brought her freshly baked cookies from home. Some days were better than others, but without Big Bert she knew she had to take care of herself now. Gus was showing her how.

Her secret drawer was where she put things she found on her walks. The walks started as a way to save bus fare. Then, when she got the pup it gave Little Bertie some exercise. Gus had insisted she get some good shoes from the Goodwill and she really enjoyed going everywhere now by foot. She saw things. Heard things too. Most times she didn't understand what she was seeing and hearing, and it was the things she picked up that made her walks special. Lying in bed, she could picture the contents of the deep drawer. A shiny key. Maybe she'd find the door for it. A jeweled ring, green, with gold. She'd like to put that on Little Bertie's collar. An envelope with a stamp, not even used. She hadn't read the letter inside. That wasn't her business and she suspected it might be even against the law. Besides, she doubted she could read what it said. It was the stamp that was special. All silver and blue with fancy red edges. She had a shell that looked like a baby's ear. So sweet. Annie wished she'd had a baby to cuddle and coo at. She shivered suddenly and felt like she was going to throw up. Little Bertie stretched under the covers, then licked her foot. Who needed a baby? Little Bertie was her baby. He needed her. She felt better.

She decided to remake the bed. Sometimes that helped her get back to sleep. When she stood up, Little Bertie jumped to the floor and sauntered over to the door, then looked back at her. Who needs words? Annie let Little Bertie outside, and left the door open while she watched him wander the courtyard, sniffing into dark corners. The night was lit by a full moon and she didn't rush Little Bertie. She could just see the outline of Gus' head on the couch in the office. Looked like he was reading something. Had he taken care of her letter to Jeb Bush? She sure hoped so. Would Jeb send her some money from his own wallet? She could tell Stacey Jeb Bush gave her some of his own money. Maybe Gus would help her write a thank you letter, like Mrs. Adamson used to make them write in the home whenever someone dropped off bags of old stuff – clothes that smelled funny, books with missing pages. Sometimes there'd be something nice, like a pretty blouse or warm mittens. A sudden breeze chilled her. It fluttered an American flag Gus had put at half mast in the center of the court- yard. He said it was because some guy he knew had been killed in the war. Guess that was worse than waking up dead. The flag flapped a bit, then died down. She went to dig out a cigarette but decided against it, inhaling the night air. Little Bertie, realizing he was getting some extra time outside, started to check out the doorways and their smells. When he got to Huntz's room Annie called him back.

"Don't you go nosing around other people's property, Little Bertie." She was afraid he'd leave something nasty on the walkway. "Wouldn't mind if that Misty stepped into it, but no way does Huntz deserve to have a mess there." Little Bertie whined so she knelt down to apologize for speaking rough to him. They went inside Room 11. Annie put down a treat for Little Bertie while she stripped the bed, then remade it. She liked smooth sheets and a cold pillow. Before she pulled the blanket taut she checked her secret drawer. She'd found something of Misty's last week and had been thinking about it for days. Did the woman even know it was missing? Annie didn't know what she was going to do with it, whether to give it to Huntz or to ask Gus to do it. One thing for sure, she wasn't going to give it back to that woman. It must be important though, because it was all covered with plastic, like those cards you have to keep for ID. She'd found it underneath the clothesline out back, where Misty hung her wash. Gus didn't have but one washer and dryer, industrial strength he called it, and Huntz's woman didn't want her fine things to be ruined, or so she said. Annie thought it was just to tease the guys having her undies flapping in the wind, get them thinking about her in that way. She was sure that was why Misty did her hand washing once a week and hung it out back. Silk blouses and panties and bras even. That's where Annie had found the card with Misty's picture on it – under the wash line. But it didn't have the right name. Even Annie was smart enough to know Misty starts with an M, like Mother. Not S. Her name and Misty's both sounded the same size too and the name beneath her picture on the card only had three letters. S-U-E. Who was the woman anyway? And what was she doing calling herself Misty? That's what Annie would like to know.

CHAPTER THIRTEEN

You can't blame gravity for falling in love.

Albert Einstein

"Too bad, Huntz," said Misty. She was disappointed their little holiday had been cancelled, but she was more concerned about Huntz, who needed a rest. He'd been working real hard these past weeks.

"Makes me want to throw away that cellphone. Had my mind all set to go fishing."

"You should have said no." She took his cellphone and pretended to throw it out the car window. "Want to see time fly?"

"And maybe not get any work for another ten days? I can't afford that. I wish you could go ahead and get rid of that thing. I hate carrying it with me, but it's how the bosses can contact me, so I'm stuck with it."

"You shouldn't be so generous with me, Huntz. Not if you're stint. Can't you afford to turn down work?" She put the phone into the glove compartment, which was neat as a pin. Huntz was certainly a good housekeeper. She was trying to do things his way and be tidier in the motel room. It was pretty easy because she hadn't brought much with her – just what she could carry, in fact, but Huntz was spoiling her, buying her whatever she needed. She'd learned to watch what she said because he'd just go out and get whatever she asked for. She didn't feel right about that.

"The reason I don't turn down work is because I want a good reputation, not because I need the money. Everybody knows I'll be there if they call. Bosses know they can depend on me. Besides, I got plans for the cash." Huntz didn't share those plans with Misty. It was way too early in their relationship. They'd only been together a couple of months. Things were great but Huntz knew from experience that was no guarantee. He was hoping this one took. Misty was a great gal. He swung the truck into the forecourt of The Pelican Motel.

"Look at that. Gus has got himself a customer. See that blue Chrysler there?" Misty grabbed their overnight bags and a parcel of food. Their plans might have changed but she wasn't going hungry. She had made Huntz stop at an all night grocery on their way back and pick up some snacks. It may be the middle of the night, but she had her mouth all set for a cheese sandwich on rye.

Knowing Gus' sleep patterns – or lack of them – they went into the office for a chat and explain their unexpected return, a job over on Palmetto Bay Road. Gus had the radio on again to see if it would be good fishing weather in the morning, but all he heard was yet another news bulletin. He went to turn it off but Huntz held up a hand to stop him. The word "Charged!" had caught his attention. The three stood listening.

"Police have laid charges against 13 roofing companies for operating without licenses. Homeowners are advised to call their local Chamber of Commerce before signing on with a roofer."

"Still going on," Gus said.

"Yup. I make sure I see the paperwork before I do any labor for these companies. We've sure seen the fly-by-nights around here, haven't we? I learned about that early."

Gus knew the man was speaking the truth. He'd first met Huntz in the line of investigation he was on right now, checking out the legitimacy of all these contracting companies who were going up and down the coast to take on the work of repairing the hurricane damage. Who knew how long the job would last? Likely the whole year. Coincidences sometimes happen and when Huntz checked into the motel Gus knew immediately he had a good source. He'd given Huntz a good background check and the guy was legit, a real roofer, down here to cash in on the scarcity of labor. He could trust Huntz, so told him about his own line of work. Huntz had seen some tricky dealings and didn't mind giving Gus inside information to get rid of the bad eggs. "I got three more contracting companies on my list for next week. New businesses just started up, out of nowhere. Can you believe it?" Gus asked.

"Couldn't they just be people trying to make a living?" asked Misty.

"Misty, the guy I started with tried to cut corners from the get-go," said Huntz. "He was cheating people all the way. I stayed there a week and got the hell out. Heard he's sitting in a jail cell right now, waiting for a court date. What goes around comes around, as they say."

"Glad you didn't get taken in, Huntz." she said. As the saying goes, Huntz was as honest as the day is long. How would she ever explain things to him? Come clean about her past?

"Makes you feel for the homeowners, though," said Gus. That's what kept him going, knowing he was helping out the innocent. Sounded corny, maybe, but Gus fancied himself a bit of a Robin Hood. Perhaps the man was in a time warp, born in the wrong century.

"Somehow these characters get the owners to pay up front. They say they need it to get in there first for materials, that it helps being able to pay up front," said Huntz, shaking his head. "You can imagine the rush for tiles and shingles and everything else, so it's a good line. Some people are too stupid to doubt and pay at least half of it before the trucks even arrive. Sometimes they cough up the whole cost!"

"And it's still going on," said Gus. He slammed a fat folder onto the desk. "Look at what I've got so far."

"That's why the police have to get involved," said Huntz. "It's fraud, front and center. The resident has trouble right away with the shoddy workmanship. What else can they do but get the law onto it? Those companies have to know they won't get away with anything. I wish they'd publicize the rotten eggs more. Give people a warning and let the con artists take a second think before they hone in on another poor fool. The penalties should be stiffer too."

"Eventually that might happen."

"Yeah, eventually." Huntz didn't appear to have faith. "You know, some of these people never even appear again after they've got the money. I don't want any part of that kind of tomfoolery," said Huntz. Gus wasn't surprised at his tenant's words. Huntz did a bit of hunting and gathering, like those sticks of furniture he got for Annie, but everyone had to admit to doing that after the storms. Huntz was a straight shooter at heart.

Gus had spent the night making a list of fencing and screen enclosure companies, getting ready to check out all of them in a radius of 60 miles. There were plenty. How many actually knew anything about construction? It was his job to find out. The hurricanes had been kind, giving work to all and sundry from odd job repair guys to private investigators like Gus. It was the run of the mill jobs like this assignment that brought in the cash, a sure and steady income for him. Sometimes he'd strike it rich once in awhile with a big case, one that got his blood going, giving him the excitement of the chase. Those kinds of jobs were the toughest too. He'd had one ongoing for three years now, a real corker. Some guy was swindling elderly widows by telling them he needed a liver transplant. Gus couldn't wait for the moment he finally proved the guy was a shyster, but the fellow had gone underground several months back. Gus couldn't find a trace of him. As gripping as these cases could be he didn't go looking for them anymore, being satisfied with regular work, no matter how routine it might be. It was a guaranteed source of income because, like it or not, people were always trying to rip off others. Right now he felt he was doing useful work making sure these companies got their comeuppance.

Gus felt like talking. "I got handed this interesting job last week. Something totally different. Some guy escaped from the Brown Creek Correctional Institute by clinging to the underbelly of a truck."

"You're kidding! Must have been some youngster."

"No, he's in his thirties."

"Must have wanted out pretty badly," laughed Misty.

"Turns out he had a toothache and went to a dentist when he made his escape."

"I think that would be the last place I'd go after flying the coop," said Huntz.

"Yeah, he had some work done, then set the office on fire that night."

"What? Why?" asked Misty.

"Had to destroy the records."

"What did he do then?"

"You won't believe this. He hid in an electronics store – for months, eating baby food he'd stolen. He routed water from the next door Toys "R" Us and took a mini-basketball set and Spider-Man DVDs to pass the time. You guys want a drink?"

A glance from Misty made Huntz turn down the offer. "No, early start in the morning and it's real late, Gus."

"Want a wake-up call?" asked Gus.

"No way," Huntz laughed. "I got my wake up call right here beside me." Misty grinned. The pair went out the door. Gus watched them grab each other's hand and Huntz brought hers to his lips to kiss her fingers. With her free hand Misty pulled his ear to make his mouth meet hers. They were like a statue there in the middle of the walkway. Like a photo. *Entwined in the Evening*, a good caption for a painting. A sudden breeze swept the woman's hair into her eyes and a strand or two must have got tangled in the man's watch strap because suddenly the two were giggling as one of Huntz's hands struggled to get free. Between the two they got Huntz's hand loose. He shook his arm, rubbing it, while she stared at the ground, as if searching for something as she tugged at her ear lobe. Then the man was pulling her toward the motel room and she gave in with little reluctance. Watching the scene, Gus couldn't help but be a little jealous. Huntz had found himself a woman who seemed to really care for him. She was a wonder, beautiful and quiet. But Huntz was too nice a guy to envy. Beside he'd been a big help to Gus.

Things were going pretty well, right now, Gus realized. No hitches. Everything was running smoothly. No back log. His Uncle Rod would be proud of him. The Pelican Motel was the best base he'd had for investigating cases. He liked the place and liked meeting the occasional traveler too, like that Harry. Fellow seemed bothered by something. Maybe he should offer to help? Like he said, no matter who it was, everybody has his problems. But no, Gus was way too busy right now.

He turned up the volume on the radio again. "A special session of the Florida legislature has tried to deal with urgent issues and has succeeded in providing additional funds to help rebuild schools, restore beach dunes, pay people's insurance deductibles and cut property taxes on ruined homes." Gus was glad to hear some good news. One fellow he talked to last week couldn't stop ranting. His home near the Indian River had $45,000 in damages done to it by two of the hurricanes. His insurance settlement came to a little over $1700. He was having to hit his retirement funds to come up with the rest, or let the damage get worse. Roofs had to be replaced, electrical circuitry protected, water removed....the list went on and on. "Not just government is trying to get something done. The National Football League has awarded $1 million to the United Way in Florida for hurricane relief."

CHAPTER FOURTEEN

Don't waste time on jealousy. Sometimes you're ahead,
sometimes you're behind.

Mary Schmich

Misty wasn't three steps inside the motel door before she was eating her bagel with ham and cheese. At the same time she started opening two boxes, shoes Huntz had bought for her on their short trip. She was a sucker for shoes, ones with high, slim heels. They made her legs look pretty special. She put on her favorite of the two pair – black suede with tiny silver buckles on the ankle straps. Huntz was sure good to her. She paraded up and down the length of the room, swaying her hips with each stride. They sure were more comfortable than they looked. When she heard the water stop running in the shower she quickly put the one pair of shoes back in the box, then placed it on the top shelf in the closet. Neat as a pin. But how messy could a pin be? She returned to the plastic tray on which she'd placed the makings for their sandwiches. When he came out of the shower she handed him a plate.

"Thanks, sweetie. Didn't realize how hungry I was." He took one bite and chewed with gusto. "This is great! You going to have your shower now? The water's nice and hot." He watched her nibbling a piece of cheese as she examined her feet in the shoes. She'd point one shoe, toe tapping the floor, then turn her body round so she could see the back. Pretty fetching. Hungry as he was, he put his own sandwich down on the paper plate, then reached out for her with his arms. She glanced up to see him grinning at her and her heart melted. She didn't even bother to take off her shoes as she came close to him. His hands encircled her waist, then dropped down to cup her hips. Such big hands, she thought. The high heels put her right where she should be in his arms. For a few seconds they slow danced, right there, in the middle of the room, as he hummed their favorite song deep into her ear. Their torsos took each other's shape as his sultry voice took her to another place. She couldn't move away. Didn't want to move away. His hair was still dripping with warm water and traces of it trickled down her cleavage. Giggling, she suddenly grabbed the towel from around his waist, making him hoot in surprise, and she started to towel dry his hair. She was singing now, the same song.

Annie heard the sounds and woke again. She lay still and listened.

Misty was gently scrunching the towel, massaging Huntz's scalp at the same time. Her words had dwindled to a hum. His hands roamed over her body. Every once in awhile she'd stoop to kiss the back of his neck. The man had her mesmerized. She couldn't believe what she'd done to be with him. She couldn't tear herself away. She'd lost control, was completely in his spell.

"Hey, honey," Huntz whispered, "I think I'm ready for bed. Are you?" He stood up straight, a fine figure of a man, and she stared at every inch of him. Her mind wasn't on food, or wet hair or the fact she hadn't had her own shower yet. She quickly slipped off her heels – Annie heard them hit the floor – and Huntz had her under the covers before she could even undress. Between them they managed that side of things with a little laughter and a lot of good-natured wrestling.

Huntz knew his way around a woman and the things he did made her squeal in delight. He never entered her until she was truly ready. Huntz said he never wanted to go where man wasn't welcome, so she made sure to welcome him with open hands and whatever else she had on offer. Huntz had staying power too, the kind that lit you up all night, if need be. Late as it was, the pair engaged in a mutual love fest, perhaps not as long as usual, but just as satisfying. Finally they slept in the nooks of each other's bodies, like oysters in their shells.

Annie listened to it all. Misty, you slut. Just you wait until I find out who you really are, Miss S-U-E. Annie got up and went to her little table, pushed her hand up inside and pushed. Out slid the secret drawer. She handled each item with loving care, and ended with the laminated identity card. She read 'S-U-E', certainly a first name. Shorter than Misty. She just might ask Gus what it said. But then he'd see Misty's picture and ask Annie where she got it and probably a whole bunch of other questions. Annie didn't know if she could handle that. She had to think, but she was tired. Somehow she had to let Huntz know he was hooked up with a phony.

She went back to bed to think about it. The sounds next door annoyed her and she yelled out a couple of times but the couple were too involved with each other to take notice of Annie's complaints. Truth be told, she didn't yell all that loud because she liked Huntz. When it quietened down next door Annie thought of Big Bert and their lovemaking. She hadn't liked that part of marriage all that much. It made her feel like an animal when they did it. Cuddling was nice, and holding hands and talking in whispers in the middle of the night. But the best part of their marriage was the wedding. Annie never thought she'd be a bride and when it happened it was like a fairy tale come true. Stacey came with her to pick out her wedding dress. It was rented and had been worn by a movie star once in a movie. She couldn't remember the name of the movie or the star. But Annie bet the star looked just as good in it as she did. Bert said she looked real famous. He wore his one suit, the one they gave him when he graduated from Normal School. That was what he called it. Normal School. She didn't get to go to that school. When Bert came to pick her up that morning they walked to the office downtown, hand in hand, all dressed up. People along the street looked at them and pointed. Annie felt proud for the first time in her life. When they got to the place where the man would marry them Stacey was already there. She put a veil on Annie and handed her flowers. Real flowers that made her remember. She didn't like real flowers. They reminded her of her father's funeral. She didn't like seeing him lying there in a box. She said nothing to Stacey because she knew Stacey thought they looked pretty. Rod, Gus's uncle, put one flower in Big Bert's buttonhole. If she had to have real flowers she would have liked just one, like Bert had. It took the man only about fifteen minutes to make them man and wife. Annie was surprised at how easy it was. She was sure there would be a test or something, but all they had to do was answer simple questions. Stacey had told her even if she didn't understand the man's words she was to just say 'I do' whenever he looked at her. Then the four had a big Chinese dinner that Rod paid for. He let them have the best room in the Pelican Motel for their honeymoon and then went fishing to give them privacy. Rod was a honey, for sure. Bert and she weren't quite sure how to do it, but Bert had asked Rod before so they just did what Rod suggested. That first time wasn't pleasant at all. It took the two of them a few weeks before they tried again and that time things went better. Annie finally fell asleep dreaming of organza and flowers and plastic identity cards.

CHAPTER FIFTEEN

Nothing will work unless you do.

Maya Angelou

Huntz never needed a wake up call. It was like he had an alarm clock in his brain. Clear conscience, likely. By six-thirty the next morning he'd slipped out of bed leaving Misty all tucked up into the pillows. He knew she felt the cold, so he added an extra blanket. Gus kept extras in the bottom drawers of the dressers in the motel rooms. Huntz's late night hadn't affected his performance or his commitment to being on the job on time. As far as he was concerned, if a job needed doing, it should be done right. That applied to everything in his life. He shaved and washed quietly so as not to disturb Misty, then cleaned the sink and towel dried it. Women hated finding bits of hair sticking to the sides of the bowl when they went to wash. Misty said that was real sweet of him. She liked that he always remembered to put down the toilet seat too. He had clean work clothes ready to go in one of the drawers. After he shoved the clothes he wore yesterday into a duffle bag he kept just for that purpose – when it was full he knew it was time for the weekly wash. Misty thought that was a good idea and was doing the same with her stuff, except for her fine things like silken underwear and nighties. She always hand-washed those. He liked to watch her as she stood over the sink with her arms in the water rubbing and rinsing. Her hips moved in time with the rhythm of her scrubbing. It was some sight. Sometimes she'd stop and remove her bra and panties and do them in the sink too. She wasn't ashamed of her body and didn't mind him feasting on her with his eyes.

After he'd tidied up he pulled on his jacket and patted the pockets and found his keys and a little package – plush slippers he'd picked up for Annie when Misty was busy trying on shoes. The old woman needed a new pair and she sure couldn't buy them for herself. He went outside and along the walkway to Annie's room and hung the bag on her doorknob. She'd find them. Back in his own room he left the keys to the truck on the night table in case Misty needed wheels today, grabbed the sandwich he hadn't bothered to finish last night and went to meet his ride on the corner of Heron Drive and Mayfair.

Dan was late as usual. Huntz sat on the curb and ate the sandwich, remembering last night. That girl could sure take his mind off things. He didn't mind waiting this morning. It gave him time to think. In the truck all the fellows would be joking around and sharing stuff they'd heard. Or made up. Huntz never knew whether to believe some of their tales. The truck would be full of noise. You couldn't get a word, or a thought, in edgewise. He didn't talk much when he was on the job either. He'd known fellows break their backs from being distracted while they were roofing. Not smart to be talking up a storm or looking round at the next fella. Because of his concentration, Huntz was one of the best workers and was why he could pick and choose his jobs. He never turned up hung over either, or out of sorts. Another bonus when you hired Huntz. No moods, no tantrums, no fights. Sitting on the curb he thought of Misty. She and he were really hitting it off. She never talked much but when she did say something it was worth listening to. Once she disagreed with him when he said everyone should take care of their mother, no matter what. Mothers should be respected and honored. Misty wasn't having any of that.

"Maybe your mother, Huntz. But not everyone may have had as great a time as you, you know. Ever consider that? My mother was..... well, there's no word for it... except ignorant. A drop-out."

Huntz was taken aback. "What about your father, Misty?"

"Huntz, I don't even know my Daddy."

"Did he leave your Mama?" Huntz asked.

"Leave? He was never there to stay."

"What do you mean?"

"I mean he was just one of her one night stands. I don't even know who my Daddy is." Another hard thing for Huntz to hear. Was he treating Misty like her Daddy did to her Mama? But it seemed to be a mutual attraction between the two of them, him and Misty. They'd met a couple of months ago and after a real fun night they'd come down to Florida. Well, he came first, wondering if she'd be as good as her word. She was, following him three days later. Said she had to stay behind to clear up some things. Neither of them had talked about next year, next month or even next week. They were playing it a day at a time. All he knew was she said she had some vacation time coming and she'd come along on his trek to Florida. It might be fun, she said. He was glad of the company. Misty. He liked the name. It reminded him of the song he'd always loved. It was playing the first time they danced together and she'd laughed at his singing the song the whole way through. He knew all the lyrics. She said at the end of the dance, when they introduced themselves, that they were meant to be! It was real weird, she said. Her name was Misty, just like the song. He couldn't believe it. He liked her company. He'd been so set on his plan of late that he'd become a bit of a loner, depriving himself of company.

Huntz had to get a sizable amount of money. Acquaintances often wondered why he was so frugal, but not with others, as Misty had found out. Annie too. He had a soft spot in his heart for women. Women of all ages. Though Huntz was generous, he saved most of what he made. He had to. He couldn't even make plans for the rest of his life until he'd accomplished his goal, getting rid of the debt hanging over his head. He was whittling it away, but sometimes he wondered if it would go on forever. His father had left him with a millstone the size of a two story house. Well, actually, it was really a bungalow. Mom would not lose her home. That's what he told the creditors in just those words. Mom will not lose her home. So they'd all agreed, and he had the law behind him on this. They had to accept regular monthly payments, no matter the size. Something was better than nothing and bankruptcy wasn't his way of doing things. He had his pride. A friend who knew legal stuff had managed to have the interest rate lowered so he wouldn't be paying an arm and a leg extra. The way things were going lately though, Huntz saw the load would soon be off his back. He just might accomplish what he'd set out to do three years ago. He thought it would take at least ten. This hurricane season in Florida had been heaven sent. He never turned down a job, and he was never idle, not since the first day he drove into the sunshine state. His payments to the creditors had doubled and some weeks tripled.

"Hey! Huntz! Wake up!" Dan's van was idling at the curb. Huntz climbed into the back seat and another fellow was there, curled into a corner – Simon, the fattest guy on the crew, but strong as a horse. The man could whip the packages of shingles around as if they were cartons of tissue paper. He never spoke, but had a smile that would light up Jacksonville. Simon opened one eye, winked at Huntz, and then closed it again. Huntz grinned and leaned over the front seat for a second.

"Thanks, Dan. Glad you didn't just go on right by me."

"Hey, why would I go and do that? You're my lucky charm." Dan flicked the turn indicator with two fingers and took the turn without slowing down. Simon fell over onto Huntz, who nudged the big man back into his corner.

"What do you mean, lucky charm?" asked Huntz.

"Why, I ain't been out of work since you came to town. Don't know why that is, but I been working steadily since February."

"Might be because there's so bloody many roofs to be replaced. Ever thought of that?" said Neville, the youngest in the crew, sitting in the front seat beside Dan. He was roofing to get money to go to college. He was a surly youth who realized this was no way to earn a living. He'd come to that decision fast, at the end of the first week, when his shoulders wouldn't stop pulsing with pain. He'd had to soak in a hot tub every night since. He turned on the radio and started fiddling with it. Loud rock suddenly shook the van. Shouts from the others and a horn honk from Dan made him switch it off fast. The three men in the back bench seat applauded and laughed. Simon opened one eye again and looked around, confused.

"Lots of work, for sure," said Dan. "We could say it's raining work!"

"Lots of work for the insurance companies too!" spat one of the men.

"If they ever get their act together," added another.

"I heard there's a government committee investigating why they're so slow at settling all these claims," said Huntz. "It's been months and months for some. Some people who can't do repairs because they don't have the money now have an extra problem – mold because of the dampness."

Simon spoke. Rare for him, so everyone listened. "It's a senate committee doing the investigating. And you know what I heard? This guy, one of the head haunchos of insurance companies, invited all the members of that committee up to his dream home for a party."

"You don't say!" yelled Dan.

"His way of saying thank you to the people on the committee."

"Christ!....."

"Yeah....."

"Geez!!".

"Likely not the first time he's held a little party."

"Nope. He's a major contributor to political parties so when....." Simon stopped. "Ah, it just makes me despair about this world." He was quiet again. So was everyone else. Neville was busy figuring out how many more weeks he'd have to do this to have enough for his tuition. Maybe if he asked his Dad for a loan? Nope, Dad had decided one degree was enough. If he wanted to do something else in his life than be an accountant he'd better pay for it himself. Was a journalism degree worth all this shit? Simon was asleep dreaming of having dinner at Mama Linguini's, the best Italian restaurant this side of Tampa, with the best looking woman running the kitchen. Rosa always gave him an extra big helping and then would say, "Bon appetito!" and wink at him. One day he just might get up the courage to....or maybe not. Dan was wondering what that noise was under the engine. This truck had better make it to the end of the month when he made his last payment. It would be the first truck he'd ever owned outright. Huntz had his eyes closed, picturing Misty waking up in their bed.

They had to make two more stops before they had everyone Dan was supposed to collect for today's job, a condominium complex over on the ocean side. Everyone seemed quiet today, maybe because their weekend had been cut short. This job would last at least two weeks. The boss needed all the parking spaces for suppliers and dumpsters, so workers were brought to the site in vans like Dan's. At the end of the working day each was delivered back to his pick up spot. Sometimes they stayed long after dinnertime, depending on the weather. Bonuses would be paid out for jobs that finished quicker than the allotted time. Food wagons made the rounds of sites, selling snacks and quick meals to crews that worked long hours. Everyone was making money from the hurricane damage.

CHAPTER SIXTEEN

The great advantage about telling the truth is that nobody ever believes it.

Dorothy L. Sayers

Misty woke shivering. Huntz had gone already. She hated when that happened. She liked to waken in his arms. She'd never felt safer. The room was cold from the air conditioning because Huntz said it was healthier for sleeping. She looked around the room trying to locate her big bulky sweater, the one that hung to her knees. Huntz liked her to sleep nude – okay as long as he was in bed with her, but alone she was chilled to the bone. She stood up and ran over to the thermostat and adjusted the temperature. She looked at herself in the full length mirror beside the air conditioner stuck into the wall. She still looked good, even at her age, the wrong side of thirty. Her breasts were full and didn't hang too far to the sides, but faced front, proudly. Her nipples stiffened in the chilly room. Huntz said he didn't know if he liked her breasts best or her hips. She wasn't crazy about her buttocks. She turned to look at them over her shoulder. Too big to fit into tapered pants. On a whim she ran to the closet and took out the second pair of shoes, the ones she hadn't tried on. They were red,

with acrylic heels and had the tiniest little bows just where the straps
touched her ankles. She pranced in front of the mirror – even did a
couple of kicks and surprised herself by how high she could raise her
leg. She had to giggle. She'd have to demonstrate for Huntz tonight.
He'd get a kick out of it. She laughed aloud at that. "I get a kick
out of you!" she sang to the mirror. Her skin was all in goosebumps.
Hurriedly she located her clothes under the bedclothes where she'd
stripped them off in a hurry last night. Huntz had that effect on her.
Just thinking about him made her weak in the knees and gave her a
funny feeling down deep. She pulled the wool sweater over her head
and scurried into the bathroom, barely touching the floor. She must
buy some slippers today. She started the shower to get it warm and sat
on the toilet until steam filled the little room.

Misty showered for a long time in hot water, remembering the night.
Leaving Huntz would be hard. Coming here to Florida to meet up with
him had been a big gamble. She'd almost been afraid to take the plunge.
Had she been too headstrong? She should have thought about it more,
but the way things had gone with Huntz, she'd felt it was the right thing
to do. The only thing she could do. Fellows like Huntz don't turn up
every day, that was for sure. Is that what had come over her?

She shouldn't have taken Marjorie's money. She knew that. She'd
never done anything like that before. One thing for sure, she couldn't
ever go back. She didn't want to, she realized. Could she stay here
with Huntz? Follow him to wherever? Would he want her to? Had
she thrown everything away just for a chance at the brass ring? She
was discovering the man had an honest streak a mile long. He would
never understand her actions. What a predicament. She stopped the
water and sat on the edge of the tub to dry herself, remembering the
beauty parlor. The smell of shampoo and soap must have triggered
her memory. She was right back in Marjorie's salon, sitting at her
station during a lull in business, listening to her boss.

"The cash float's there in the cupboard. At the end of the day you'll do your ledger work, separate the money you've taken in and put it into the zippered bag on top of the float." She'd been getting instructions for operating the cash register at the salon where she worked. Marjorie, the owner, who wanted to take a day off here and there, was going to give her more responsibility.

"Okay, I guess. I hope I can handle it." But really Misty was unsure. She didn't think she had a head for math. That's what all her teachers had thought too.

"Well, the clients like you. You have a nice way with them." That was true. Misty loved to talk and she was a good listener too. Those two traits didn't always come in the same person. "Time to have some more responsibility, I think. Then you make out a deposit slip and take it to the bank with the money." Marjorie had some samples and had Misty copy what she did. "See, you're catching on. It's easy."

"I like doing hair, Marjorie. Listening to the women too. Makes my own life seem simple to hear some of the problems they have! But I'm not so sure about handling money, though. Are you sure you need me to do this?" She was scared about carrying money to the bank. What if she were robbed?

"Yes, Sue. This way you can open up and close at the end of the day. You have a steady clientele. It won't mean you putting in any more hours. You're almost fully booked every day. I'm sure you can handle the money, Sue. Once you do it a few times it'll be easy as pie."

Sue. That was her name. She had no idea why she told Huntz it was Misty. If she had to explain it, she'd say he hypnotized her. With that first dance, she knew she was hooked. He sang that song into her ear, stroking her hair at the same time and she was putty in his hands. Something just made her say those words. "This is meant to be, Huntz. You singing that song! My name's Misty. Imagine that!"

It seemed important to connect with him. So she followed him to Florida when he suggested it.

Marjorie would be hopping mad. How could she have done that to such a nice lady? Marjorie had trusted her. What would she do? Especially when she discovered the cash float was gone and her piggy bank too, the one that held all the tips? Sue also took the cash the owner kept in her extra purse that was stashed in the back cupboard – another reason she had to stick to her new name. Maybe the robbery would be announced on the radio, or be in the papers, though she didn't think anyone would come chasing her to Florida. After all, it wasn't all that much money for them to think of sending cops out of state. Not that much money to them but it sure was to her. To think she'd been afraid of carrying money to the bank! When she headed to Florida she had more money on her than she'd ever had in her life at one time. Still, any report naming Sue Robinson would give her away to Huntz and she didn't want that to happen. So Sue Robinson became Misty Brody. Brody was her brother's name, the one who used to stick up for her at home. He protected her from the time she could walk. Protected her at home from her stepfather, at school in the playground and even when boys started to hang around. When Brody joined the army she thought her heart would break. It didn't, not then, not until later when his tank exploded and her mother got the news. Her new name made her feel her brother was guiding her, telling her to go for it. Maybe so. Suddenly she felt nauseous and dropped her head between her knees.

Every time she worried about this she got a headache. She stood up slowly, holding the sink with one hand and opened the medicine cabinet with the other. Not much there, of course. Huntz's condoms and anti-perspirant, his shaving stuff, all neat and in a row, from smallest to tallest. She took his deodorant and took off the lid and inhaled. Her knees shook as she smelled Huntz's signature aroma. On the second shelf was her make-up and her soaps and lotions for massages. Her clients at Marjorie's Beauty Emporium had come to like booking a massage just before they had their hair done. It had started slowly but caught on, for sure. She was good at that too. Huntz loved a good rub down after work. He said it was the secret to not having any aching muscles after a day of running up and down ladders. He couldn't believe the difference it made to his body. But the massage had to be done after they made love, not before, because once she got her hands on him she couldn't concentrate until he'd satisfied her. Her desire would bubble up like shampoo in hot water. No man had ever had such an effect on her.

She really couldn't believe her actions of the last couple of months. She looked at her line up of pills. Birth control, stress vitamins, headache. She took a couple of the last and ran the cold water tap to get a nice cold glass of water. Maybe if she ate something too? She wasn't sure what she should do to kill time while Huntz was on the job. Each day it was getting harder to just stay around the motel. Huntz said this job would last another couple of months, at least. Perhaps she should think of getting a job. Huntz was entirely too generous and she had a hard time saying no to him. She wanted to be paying her own way, but she was really hesitant to dip into the money she'd taken from Marjorie. A job would be best. She'd love to get back to doing hair. Could she, with no references? If she were honest, she'd even be the dogs body and wash hair, just to get started. Would Huntz get bored with her if she hung around too long?

CHAPTER SEVENTEEN

A woman's heart is a deep ocean of secrets.

Gloria Stuart

Annie stirred under her covers. She had a bad taste in her mouth. Darn teeth. She'd forgotten to take them out last night. She shivered. Like always the room was chilly this morning. Even so she managed to drag herself out from under the covers. At least she had her flannelette nightie on, the one with little doggies all over it. Stacey had saved it for her from the donations that came into the Goodwill. Annie only had to pay one dollar for it, Stacey said. That made things legal, whatever that meant. Annie loved it because it had a little dog on it just like Little Bertie. More than one, in fact. Seventeen. She'd counted them the first time she took it out of the dryer at the laundromat. She put on her housecoat, doing the buttons up from the bottom like she'd been taught in the home, then shuffled over to the thermostat and squinted at it. Grimacing, she pushed the lever up a bit, then went into the bathroom to fill her kettle. She could hear that darn Misty next door peeing. Annie pounded on the wall, though it wasn't really a pound. With Annie's strength it was more like a tap. Misty never heard her because she was stepping into the shower but

Annie didn't know that. She filled her kettle. It took a little time as she had to fill a cup with water, then pour it into the spout of the kettle. The thing was too big to fit under the tap. Annie's bare feet curled under her as she tried not to make contact with the cold floor. Finally water poured out of the spout showing it was full.

Shuffling back into the bedroom Annie took the kettle over to the night table. Then she went over to the little table Huntz had found for her. Along with the secret drawer, it had two shelves where Annie kept her food. To make things easy for herself she had decided to keep the top shelf for breakfast and the bottom one for lunch. That one was empty as she'd finished her jar of peanut butter and her bread was all gone except for a hard crust. She would give that to the birds today. She was pleased to see lots of stuff on the top shelf: three bagels from the day old section of the bakery, packets of jam and honey from her favorite restaurant and cereal that came in envelopes. Imagine that. At the home they used to make huge pans of cereal every morning, and eggs too. It all tasted funny. She always stuck to the cold cereal and toast. She didn't like breakfasts then. Stacey had taught her about these packets. At first, Annie didn't want anything to do with hot cereal but Stacey convinced her it would be good, but made Annie promise she'd be careful with the hot water. All she had to do was stir some boiling water into a bowl with what was inside the packets and she had oatmeal that tasted of brown sugar and maple syrup. Yummy. At the home all they had was thin milk and a bit of white sugar and the hot cereal there always tasted like wallpaper paste. She knew because she used to eat that in school.

Of course, she could have the leftover pizza Gus had given her last night. She stood looking at it all, then finally decided. She pulled out a package of oatmeal because she wanted something warm. She plugged in the kettle to start her breakfast and went back to bed to cuddle Little Bertie while the kettle came to a boil. The pup stirred under the covers when he heard her return and came out from under to lick her face. For some reason she felt happier today. Little Bertie curled up into the small of her back. When the kettle turned itself off she had almost fallen asleep again, but Little Bertie jumped out of bed and ran to the door. She knew he needed out, fast. She got back up and shuffled to the door and opened it.

Little Bertie sauntered until he found just the right spot. Annie was pleased to see a bright, sunny morning outside. A nice day for walking, she thought. She might get down to the Goodwill. Was it Stacey's day to work? She'd have to remember to look at her calendar. She stretched out her arms and felt the sun. It was like having a bath in sunshine. So warm. For several moments she sat there with her eyes closed, feeling her body unwind from the night's tossings and turnings while Little Bertie nosed around the courtyard. She could trust him to stay near. He wasn't a dog that would wander. Some days it was just nice to wake up. Today was one of those days, she realized as her eyes snapped open and she grinned. She felt good. Something glinting in the sun caught her attention, something there among the shells Gus scattered around the pathways. She stood up and shuffled over to the bed of shells, then stooped down. With her fingers she separated the shells. Maybe she'd found today's treasure! She tried to find something every day, but never had it happened first thing in the morning. Sometimes it took all day and if she hadn't discovered anything by evening she often would pick up any old thing because, for some reason, she just had to find something every day. It was like having a daily good luck charm and she couldn't admit she'd had no good luck. Every day would start the same – she'd start looking again for something special. This just might be her lucky day, finding her good luck charm right off, first thing in the day. Shiny things were her favorite. She pulled the object out of the bed and laid it in her hand. She stared at it. It looked familiar. In her palm was a gold earring. She knew it was gold because the yellow was soft, not bright like the foil they put around some chocolates. Why did she think she'd seen it before? And where?

Annie knew it took her time to remember things, so she decided to sit outside for a bit and let her brain rest. She was pleased with her find, even if she didn't know why she thought she'd seen it before. It was no good. Her mind didn't have any answers. She carefully placed it in the bottom of her left hand pocket and stood. Left for lucky. She could remember that. Left for lucky. She turned to open the door to her room. A bag was hanging there. Another surprise!? Annie thought her heart would burst. Two surprises in one day? She couldn't get it off the knob fast enough. Staying outside, she shut the door, then took her time moving to the iron lawn chair outside her room. She had so few real surprises she liked to stretch them out. And imagine, a double day! What could it be? A picture frame? For the picture of her and Big Bert? The only one she had. Nope, too soft. A new pillow? She'd sure like a fluffy new pillow. Nope, too small. A package of cookies? With the white centers? Nope, no crinkly sound when she smushed it. Little Bertie had come back and jumped into her lap, landing on the package.

"Hey, Little Bertie! You be careful. I got me a nice surprise here and I don't want you breaking it, you hear?" The dog looked at her, then licked her chin. "Aw, it's okay. I'm not mad at you. It didn't break. I didn't hear any smashing sounds. Did you? Nope. Let's see." She opened the bag and took out another package, one in sturdy plastic. It even had a little button closing. She could see through it – something pretty and pink. Taking her time she undid the button and pulled out first one slipper, then the next. Soft. She had to undo the slippers themselves too, for the toes were nesting in the heels. That was fun, releasing the toes, then putting them back, then releasing them again. Finally she put the slippers on her bare feet. Warm and snuggly. She wriggled her toes. Wonderful. Where had they come from? Then she examined the empty plastic pouch.

"You know, Little Bertie? This would make a really nice purse." With that she fished into her left housecoat pocket and pulled out the earring. Giving her brain a rest must have worked because she remembered where she'd seen it before. On Misty's ear. That's when she knew what she had to do. She'd put that card with Misty's picture on it into her new purse, along with the earring. Then she'd show the purse to Misty. She knew just what she'd say.

"Misty, do you like my new purse?

CHAPTER EIGHTEEN

Insomnia is my greatest inspiration.

Jon Stewart

Gus awoke from another of his cat naps. He rarely slept a full night. Never had. A couple of hours solid sleep suited him best. This worked out well for his work too, as he was out and about at all hours, depending on the job. The odd time he'd go to bed at ten and sleep right through to the following day. That would set him up for another two weeks. Maybe it came from all those years on the road as a drummer, or perhaps it was his metabolism. His mother said he'd been like that as a baby. Awake half the night. Not complaining, just walking around seeing what's what. When he pushed a chair up to the front door to try to open it she'd gone to the clinic at once, frantic with worry and lack of sleep. She'd been in the habit of waking every time she heard him climb out of his crib. After putting him back to bed and gently rubbing his back she'd return to her own bed, only to be awakened twenty minutes later to go through the whole routine again. She'd finally taken to sleeping outside his room. The doctor told her she had to lock him in for his own good, and for hers. She couldn't sit on a chair outside his room and catnap just so she'd be there if he got up and started wandering. Who knew what trouble a two-year old could get into? It was probably why Gus hated being closed in now. He didn't blame his mother because he didn't know what he would have done in the same circumstances, but Gus grew up not liking locked doors and small rooms. That proved to be a handicap in his job sometimes, when he had to secrete himself in cupboards or under stairs or inside the trunks of cars. It didn't happen that often, but often enough for someone with claustrophobia. Some jobs meant hiding in a cupboard or behind a bank of filing cabinets until he could catch someone doing what he shouldn't. It was surprising the culprits never heard his deep breathing to keep himself calm, or smelled the sweat that poured from him in tight situations. He was too old for those kinds of shenanigans. Maybe that's why he was enjoying the routine jobs more and more.

Gus set about tidying up the foyer, ready for a new day. He never did hear a weather report, but going by the sun out there he just might make it to Rod's boat. He took a brush out from behind the counter and swept off the divan, then folded the afghan after giving it a shake outside. He should be tossing it in the wash soon. When he placed it on the arm of the old couch he grimaced at a couple of new tears in the plastic. Little Bertie's claws. He should take the pup to the vet and have his needles and nails done. Looking around the foyer he had a thought. Maybe he should redecorate? But why? For the odd client or two like Harry? Shrugging, he took the dirty cups and glasses and put them into a dishpan under the counter. He'd wash them later in his room at the back. His living space was not much bigger than one of the motel rooms but it was divided into two. In one room he had a counter that ran the length of one wall and had a little fridge and microwave. A table and two chairs completed his kitchen. His bedroom had a big desk with all his files. The business end of the room overwhelmed the room. He'd taken the

bed out and put in a recliner chair. That was enough for his sleeping needs. Gathering up the newspapers his eyes noticed a headline:
SETTLEMENT DEADLINES MAY NOT BE BEST SOLUTION.
Apparently the major insurance companies had been given a hand
slap, because the deadlines to settle claims – November 22 for hurricanes Charley and Frances and December 8 for Ivan and Jeanne
– hadn't been met by many insurers. Polled businesses were reporting
the percentage of claims closed and they varied from 59% to 90%.
No one had completed all claims by the target dates, but there was no
Florida law in place to back up such a scheme, even during ordinary
times. Senator Tom Lee had some strong opinions on the subject,
Gus read. He smiled at the man's words. "I have no illusions about
the behavior of big corporations when they see an opportunity to
frustrate the public with the way they conduct their business operations. There's no doubt that the more difficult you make it for people
to collect their money, the more likely it is they will go away." That's
telling them, thought Gus. He read a Vero Beach Republican thought
Lee was being a bit hard, saying it's not fair to change the rules in the
middle of the game, as he put it.

Gus knew, working from the inside as he did, that the insurance
companies weren't dragging their heels on purpose in some cases.
There just weren't enough insurance adjusters to go around, or investigators. That's why he was getting so much – too much – work. He
knew of nine companies who were overwhelmed by claims. It was
also pretty difficult to close claims due to most clients contesting the
settlements because of the four prongs of the multi hurricane attack.
All in all, a confusing situation for everyone. He sighed and folded
the paper until his attention was caught by a photo. He sat down and
read the headline, then the whole article, finally staring at the picture
off to the side. He recognized that face.

"Gus?" He jumped as Misty came into the room.

"Misty! Hi. I was reading something. Something important. Want a coffee, Misty?"

She nodded.

"About a job I'm on."

"Oh." She poured herself a cup of coffee, half full. Never a woman to ask questions. Gus liked that about Misty. He didn't know if Huntz had filled her in on what he did for a living. Probably not. Those two did little talking, he was sure of that. "Gus, can I take a look at some of that paper?"

"Which section?"

"Classified. I'm thinking maybe I should be getting a job down here. Just to tide me over."

"What kind of a job, Misty?" He envisioned Misty modeling lingerie or serving drinks at an upscale bar.

"Nothing to do with money." She shouldn't have said that, she realized. "I mean, I don't like making change, working a cash register. I'm not against money, you understand." She was babbling, for some reason. "I wouldn't mind working where I can get tips, you know?

"Like a restaurant?" Gus was skeptical. His mind was wandering. He could picture her escorting the rich and famous around town or appearing at boat shows, draped over the deck of the biggest and best yacht.

"No, too hectic. I'm a hair stylist, Gus." She said it as if he should have known. Hadn't he noticed her hair? She was mighty proud of her hair.

"Yours always looks pretty, Misty." That made her smile.

"I do manicures too, body art, everything. I'm quite artistic."

"I believe that, Misty." Gus' imagination took off. "You do all that other stuff too? Even massages?" He wasn't sure he really wanted to hear the answer.

"Yup. No one's ever complained after one of my full body treatments." Huntz had really lucked out, Gus thought. He managed to hide a groan of envy.

"I could do you one right now. You look like you slept in that there chair of yours." She'd been in the back once, with Huntz. Gus had to pick up his recorder to tape something Huntz wanted to tell him. She'd been surprised at how basic the man's living quarters were. He didn't even have a tablecloth. His dishes were piled up, clean, in one corner of the counter, ready for the next microwaved meal. How long had he been living like this? "That chair can't be good for your back, Gus."

That made him pause. He almost succumbed. "Better not." He was afraid to have her touch him. He might melt on the spot. "Hairdresser, eh? Would you believe it? There's a beauty place up there." Gus pointed to the ceiling.

"A salon? Up there?"

"Yeah, a salon. That's right. On the second floor."

"Second floor? You kidding me, Gus?"

"No, really. A woman used to run it back in my Uncle Rod's time. It's not too big. It has two sinks and chairs and all that stuff."

"It has two stations?" asked Misty.

"Guess so. Is that what you call them? The place was locked up when I got here. I took a look once but, to be honest, I'd forgotten all about it."

"Where'd that woman go to?"

"Apparently one day she just packed her suitcase and took off with a trucker. Who knows where she is now? She used to give haircuts to men and did a few women's hairdos around here. At least that's what Annie says. It was way before my time. The woman used to do Annie's hair in exchange for cleaning duties."

"Would you let me have a look at it?"

"You thinking you might hang around here a bit? Would you seriously open up a beauty parlor?"

"Tell you the truth, I don't know what I'm doing. Maybe. A lot depends on Huntz, of course. It would give me something to do if I could book a few appointments. Brush up my skills." She giggled at that. "Brush up! That's funny, eh, Gus?"

Gus' mind was still on massages. "Truckers would sure appreciate a nice rub down. Ordinary drivers too, like that Harry. The way he was standing I think he was in some pain."

"Gus, can I see it? Now?"

Gus had never seen Misty so animated. He wondered what Huntz would think of this. Maybe he shouldn't have said anything to the girl. Gus had to admit he wouldn't mind having her working up there. It would add a little more substance to the motel somehow, give him more reason to spruce up the place, make it a going concern. He'd clean up the foyer and put in new carpeting. A mahogany counter top would be nice. He'd buy a new lounge suite, a small one with a love-seat and matching chair, something that would fit in the corner, with a nice Tiffany lamp hanging from the ceiling. That would save on floor space, but would be a nice welcoming touch. "I'm not sure where the key is. Let me think for a moment." He rummaged under the counter, pretending to look for the key while he made up his mind. The screen door squeaked. Gus looked up and was relieved to see his guest. "Hi, Harry? You been up long?"

CHAPTER NINETEEN

One word frees us of all the weight and pain of life: that word is love.

Sophocles

Dear mother,

How are you? You haven't told me much about your state of health. I am interested. I hope you're fine. We're all great here. I told young Carrie that she has – in fact – three grandmothers, not two. I asked Mom first before I did that, of course. I wouldn't want to do anything that would upset her but she agreed it was something I should do. Carrie wasn't as shocked or confused as I thought she would be. She was quite intrigued, really. She thinks you should come out here and meet us. She's quite excited and hopes you will.

Esmerelda knew it might seem strange if she didn't go. Finding the son you gave up for adoption long ago would have inspired anyone to action, especially when that son had agreed to meet, but Esmerelda felt it was just too late to forge a relationship. She'd given it a lot of thought and fought with her fervent desire to meet the man. After due consideration she felt it best to ignore the impulse, a selfish one for sure. What could she offer the man, other than her money? And she didn't want that to be the prime factor.

At her age, the lost years would be too apparent. Esmerelda didn't know if she could deal with the enormous sadness of it all. She also wanted her son to know her as she once was, not as a weathered old woman. She had some pride still. Harry knew where everything was kept and she'd given him instructions. Let Teddy, her son, look at home movies and photo albums and see the woman she had been, not the decrepit, senile being she'd become, now getting more broken-down as each day passed. What had hastened her decline?

Was it a self-fulfilled prophesy? Had she really turned the last corner, gone right round the bend? How could any person, even a son – especially a long lost son given away years ago – forgive – much less love – someone who was so dysfunctional? Simply put, she was ashamed to have Teddy meet her. Maybe she'd do or say something embarrassing. Should the son's first knowledge of his birth mother be so distressful? He'd likely feel he had to help her somehow. Why saddle him with such responsibility? Judging by the man's emails he had a conscience and would likely not hesitate to take over the care of his birth mother, even if he had no personal relationship with her to speak of. He seemed to be that kind of man. Esmy was thankful to see that side of his character. He'd grown up well, with a sense of compassion. She could tell that already. Perhaps he even had taken after Esmy a bit. Thankfully he seemed to harbor no bitterness like Susan's.

When Harry left for Florida she'd promised him she'd be arranging a meeting soon with Teddy but she didn't know then what she knew now. Was she balmy? This time for real? Of course, to be honest, she had another reason too. Esmerelda didn't want Teddy anywhere near Bruce. When she died, Esmerelda was leaving all she had to her firstborn, her only born, with just a token amount to Bruce to keep it legal. She'd given the papers to her lawyer and was counting on Harry to carry out her wishes – to add the personal touch. If Teddy's only contacts after her death were a lawyer and then Bruce he'd have a very poor opinion of his mother. She needed an advocate, to explain her side of things. She also wanted to be fleshed out in her son's eyes. Harry would do it, kindly. He was the only one she could trust with the job.

> *I told Mom it is your decision and I wasn't going to talk you into anything. I guess you won't be surprised to know she seemed relieved, though Mom knows she can never be replaced. She's my mom, always will be. You're my mother. I care about you too, very much, but not in the same way. Mom understands, though I don't know if Dad would have if he were alive.*

> *Anyway, Carrie insisted on writing you a letter. She wanted to take her time over it and wants to mail it to you. But I really think she doesn't want me to know anything she's writing, truth be told. So, I didn't argue with her. The only problem, mother, is I don't have your address. Carrie thought it 'was weird that I hadn't asked you for it'.*

> *So I am now.*

> *With love,*

> *Your son,*

> *Teddy*

Your son. With love. That was a first. Those four little words brought her to tears. For a few minutes she had trouble catching her breath.

She should have shared it with Harry, told him about the breakthrough in her son's letters. He had accepted her. He was letting her into his life, letting his daughter contact Esmerelda. This was so much more than she had expected. But if she'd told Harry all this, he'd certainly have wondered why she hadn't arranged a meeting as soon as possible. How could she tell him she was going nuts? Imagining things? Losing touch with reality – just as it was getting interesting? How could she meet her son for the first time now? No man should get a scare like that. Best to keep her distance.

What should she do? The solution, of course – get a Post Office Box. Esmy was pleased. she still had some faculties. When her mind functioned this way she almost thought she hadn't lost her marbles.

CHAPTER TWENTY

Numbing the pain for a while will make it worse when you finally feel it.

J.K. Rowling, *Harry Potter and the Goblet of Fire*

Why had Esmerelda never tried to find her child before Harry came along? With her money she could have hired any number of private investigators. An easy answer would be to say that she'd never wanted to, but then how would she explain the dreams, once a month at least, all through her life? They were always followed by a sadness too sore to speak of. Perhaps a therapist would have been able to get her to express it, but she'd adopted the party line the family had taken. That episode was a part of her life that was dead and buried. And forgotten? Not by her, no matter how good a face she put on for her family. The dreams started coming about three years after she'd given up the child. Perhaps they were what finally allowed her to start thinking about her little baby and where he might be, and try to imagine his life. She kept the dreams and these thoughts to herself. By that time she was seventeen, about to graduate from high school, being reassured by her family – her father and sister – that they had forgiven her indiscretion. Her indiscretion – that's how it was referred to whenever it was mentioned, which wasn't often. Indiscretion, a triviality, not worth the time of day. Truth be told, it was never talked about, just referred to obliquely. To control her? Everyone's allowed only one indiscretion, Esmy, so think twice before you make another. That always preceded anything she was considering from the most trivial to the serious. Discretion is the better part of valor. Buy that dress, it's discreet. Go to that school, you'll meet your own kind. Eat this. Go there. Date that boy. That boy. The first time they'd said those two words their intonation revealed their disdain. "That boy's the father? That boy!? How could you even think of it, Esmerelda?"

Esmerelda never knew which they were most upset about, her pregnancy or the fact that 'that boy' had been the father. Jackie had been a nice lad, a sweet and insecure soul, like her. Is that why they'd gravitated to each other, even though it was definitely not the thing to do? Rich and poor don't mix. Neither do the races, but they had loved each other with an innocent, uncompromising kind of love, totally accepting of each other. She, overshadowed by her domineering sister, and he, who lost his father before his eighth birthday, were both struggling to find an identity. To each other, they provided comfort in uncomfortable times. Being spirited off to the next town to the home for unwed mothers finished that. She never saw him again. Did he even know why? Likely not. Fathers had no rights back then.

In another time and place she would have tried to find her baby. Truly shamed by Esmerelda's predicament her family did the usual – buried it under the carpet. She'd forfeited her rights and become even more docile as she carried out their wishes. When she finally came home she followed their lead. By then she'd learned well how to keep her feelings to herself, stuffed down deep. It took several years for them to fight their way free like a drowning body struggling to break the surface to gasp for air with pounding lungs.

She always remembered the one time she'd held her baby. For one afternoon she was allowed to see her infant son and to talk to him, cuddle him, soothe him. With her eyes and hands she'd examined every inch of the miracle and found that, yes, people do count fingers and toes. The baby was truly beautiful, with black curly swirls of hair from his forehead to the nape of his neck. His fingers were long and so were his limbs, like his father. He had Esmy's nose, tilted ever so slightly at the end. But it was his big eyes that seemed to stare into her soul that moved Esmerelda to hug the child with a love that surprised her. She'd recalled the science lesson about magnetism. She too was drawn, like iron filings to a magnet, gripped by a feeling of oneness with the infant. The nurse said that the baby couldn't see her, for babies took days to even be able to focus, but Esmy hadn't believed her. The baby had looked right into her face and somehow she knew he liked what he saw. That's not a smile – it's gas, said the nurse, patting Esmerelda. She was the kind nurse, the one who'd smuggled the infant in to visit with his birth mother. Esmerelda realized years later how much courage that had taken. She'd never really thanked the woman properly so eager was she to see her infant son. It was against the rules for girls like her – girls who'd been shipped to the hospital to deliver illegitimate children – to be allowed to see their babies. It was felt at that time that this would make it easier to give up the babies, all part of the indoctrination of the home where the girls stayed until it was time to deliver.

She'd cried for three days after giving birth. The delivery itself hadn't hurt half as much as Esmerelda had thought it would. Much like a really bad period for many hours, but not as much as the three or four days of agony Esmy often experienced when it was her time of month. After the baby was born her periods became much more comfortable. She'd cried because she'd never experienced such a yearning, a separation, an emptiness. She had also missed the baby moving inside her. For the few months after movement started Esmy used to love to lie still and delight in the flutterings inside her. Later her baby's somersaults often had surprised her into laughter. After giving birth, she had almost felt bereft, as if something had died instead of the opposite. Of course, it had for her. She couldn't have her baby, now out in the world. Try as she might, she hadn't been able to stop sobbing. Maybe that's why the nurse let her hold the little baby boy.

After the nurse had taken her baby away, never to be held again, something happened to Esmerelda. She froze. She went home, carried through her daily routine, going to school, studying, music lessons, all with little joy or involvement. Time heals all wounds, they say, and it did in Esmerelda's case. She wouldn't use the word heal, it was more like a freezing over inside her heart and when, years later, the thaw occurred it came with a price, a meltdown of trust. From the beginning Esmerelda had adopted her family's party line and gone on with her life. She never tried to find the child because she thought that, as everyone said at the time, it wasn't a good thing to do. Perhaps the race card intimidated her. Had the boy been adopted into a black family? Would her arrival on the scene make things worse for her son? It certainly had to be considered.

Later, when she was truly an adult she could have pursued the matter. Maybe she should have hired someone to help find her son, but habits die hard. The cloud of shame she'd lived under for so many years, both in her own mind and in Susan's, was hard to shed. Simply put, she just couldn't talk to anyone about it. Intellectually she knew she should cast off such a dated attitude, but emotionally she couldn't muster together the courage.

Had Esmerelda ever forgiven herself? She felt she managed to forgive her sister and her father to some degree, but forgiving herself was impossible. It was meeting David that became the impetus to truly live her life. Her husband had told her it was all right with him if she decided to find her boy, but by that time Esmerelda knew her son was likely an adult herself. It was too late. The sadness was always there, underlining her activities, but the melancholy no longer ruled her life. David and she had a love that allowed Esmerelda to blossom and give much to the world.

And it gave it back to her. David Graham's business – Granny's Grahams – flourished and the two lived a life of luxury. No children were born from their union. Six years into the marriage, when Esmerelda was in her early thirties, she learned she could not have children due to fibroid tumors that were crowding her uterus. A hysterectomy removed the problem, and her chance to have a family of her own. Again, David was her guide to sanity. Why had they never adopted? Esmerelda had a knee-jerk reaction to that. If she voiced her thoughts she'd have to say she didn't deserve to adopt a child, not after what she'd done. People can forgive and forget, but do they ever really recover?

CHAPTER TWENTY-ONE

I say luck is when an opportunity comes along and you're prepared for it.

Denzel Washington

Esmerelda couldn't believe it. Dr. Emery had agreed to morning walks as long as she bundled up! At first she and her nurse Eileen went only a few houses and then back again, a matter of fifteen minutes or so – not much time on the clock, but it was a major change in what had become a reclusive lifestyle. Gradually they extended their walks to over an hour. Spring was rushing to arrive in swollen streams, banked with rapidly melting snowy mounds. Children were skipping home from school, ready to enjoy the last rays of the day's sun. Once a little girl stopped and asked her how old she was. The child wasn't being rude. She was merely curious. Esmerelda answered her honestly. That provoked a long conversation about the child's Grandma who visited her every other Sunday and always brought treats for the freezer. When she looked expectantly at Esmy, the old woman had to laugh aloud. The little girl joined in before skipping off. Cats skulked under bushes, waiting expectantly. Birds were chasing each other in and out of trees before swooping into puddles for a refreshing splash. All of it lifted Esmerelda's spirits. Sometimes she and Eileen stopped to talk to her neighbors when they were out shoveling the last little bit of snow or were warming up their cars. They always greeted her with surprised pleasure. Sometimes she and Eileen were invited in for tea. That put paid to her lethargy and she started to feel her old self again. Soon they were walking around blocks, a different route each day. The two women talked on these walks and Esmerelda discovered the nurse was simply an efficient type, and not the uncaring soul as she'd thought. Things were going swimmingly until the slip on some ice and a broken leg.

But it wasn't Esmerelda who fell. It was Eileen. There she was, splayed out on the sidewalk, in agony. The poor woman couldn't move but an inch to take the pressure off her broken femur. It happened on a stretch where there were no houses. It was left to Esmerelda to make her way home. It had taken her some time but she'd managed to do it with no mishap and phoned Dr. Emery's service who arranged for medical help for their nurse.

Esmy was delighted. It made her feel competent again. What a relief. Two days later she was still assuring Dr. Emery she was going to be all right on her own.

"Are you sure, Esmy? I have no one on my list right now, but I'll contact some other services and see who they have available."

"Doctor, I'm fine. Look who fell! Not me! And I was able to do everything necessary. I was able to get home and make the phone call to you. I didn't even get lost!" she said, a trace of smugness in her voice. "In these two days I haven't set the house on fire or swallowed any bleach." She laughed at his reaction, and he had to chuckle. She convinced him she was feeling much better. It's amazing how functioning in an emergency can create a sense of confidence, she said to Dr. Emery, who didn't need more reassurance. Eileen had been there for a reason, to protect Esmy, and not from herself. Dr. Mark Emery didn't like Bruce. He'd had suspicions that guy was up to no good. He didn't really believe the man would actually harm the old woman, but he knew that Bruce's presence upset his aunt. Dr. Emery liked his patients to be as happy as possible. Perhaps he should have just come right out and told Esmy to send Bruce packing. However, the man was a relative and he, as a doctor, had no right to suggest such a thing.

Esmy was enjoying having her house to herself. She got up early and sat in her housecoat in the empty study, staring out the window at the rapidly melting ice in the trees. All through her marriage she'd always liked a quiet time before David, who was an early riser himself, got up. For many years this was when she meditated and now she got into the routine again. She spent time going into herself, as she described it. Sometimes she closed her eyes, but most often she would look at one thing outside, as she used to years ago when it might be a bird on the birdbath or a leaf just ready to fall in the autumn. Sometimes it was a beautiful piece of bark on the Japanese cherry or merely a bloom in the garden. She'd lose herself in it, letting her mind come to rest. Sometimes she chanted softly. After quietening her mind in this way she'd always found she could face the day and whatever challenges it had to offer. Back then it might be fund-raising for her charities, organizing a dinner for twelve for her husband's business obligations, volunteer work at the hospital, or chairing meetings and luncheons. These days it was to get back her integrity, as she put it to herself, become herself again, a woman with courage, fortitude and, hopefully, a regained sense of peace.

She admitted her life had certainly deteriorated. When had that all happened? After David's death she'd kept up some of her obligations, but gradually she'd become somewhat reclusive, but still at peace with the world and herself. When Bruce and Jenny moved in her world changed from a quiet, contemplative place to one of noise. The TV went on first thing in the morning. Their life was accompanied by either the television or the radio or the stereo. Esmerelda realized her walls weren't soundproof. She could hardly escape the frenzy of sound. To give them credit, whenever she asked for quiet, the couple always turned things off, then walked around whispering, making Esmy feel badly. So she soon stopped asking. After all, they were kin. With Bruce and Jenny in the house Esmerelda had gradually retreated to one wing of the house, staying in her bedroom or her sitting room and only coming out to eat. It was easier that way. Maybe she made it too easy for Bruce to start taking over the running of the house, especially when she gave him carte blanche in using her credit cards to pay bills. Before she knew it, new things appeared in the house. Exercise bikes. Big screen television. Gourmet cooking utensils, which they said she shouldn't use as they required special care. Why did they need fancy cookware, she thought, when she was served warmed up soup for lunch? Why did they need these things if they were moving on? How had things turned out this way? She didn't have the stamina to start a discussion, though.

Esmy continued to recall the chain of events. Things improved when Harry moved in to take care of her after her bad fall. That accident was odd. She was going down the stairs from the upper landing carrying a pile of clean bedding for the guest quarters on the main floor where Bruce and Jenny were staying. Suddenly she was pitching forward. The doctor said if it hadn't been for the bedding she would have broken something and not just hurt her knee. Of course, her body was covered with bruises and when Dr. Emery examined her he kept shaking his head. She'd never seen him like that before. He wouldn't stop muttering to himself as he poked and probed her. She was relieved when she finally heard his verdict. "Amazing you're as well as you are." But her relief was short-lived when he added, "Esmy, you need someone in that house."

"Bruce and Jenny are there."

That didn't seem to satisfy the doctor. "I mean, someone with medical knowledge. You're going to need some physiotherapy as your body heals. Muscle tone will go without some massages and exercises. Who are those two anyway? Do they have nursing experience?"

"A bit. Bruce is my sister's grandson. He took care of her at the end." The doctor's expression was hard to read. She explained. "They're businesspeople, I think. He comes and goes on trips. Sometimes she accompanies him, sometimes not."

"Well, I know someone who'll be perfect and will be there all the time for you. A fellow named Harry Somer. He's a physiotherapist, one of the best. I think he should move in and give you round the clock care."

"Surely I don't need that!"

"Yes, you do. I don't want any arguments. Let's have a trial period of six weeks of care. See how you do, then we'll evaluate. He'll take care of your recuperation and he's not averse to running households either. Damn good cook, too, from what I hear. You need some flesh putting on you, I can see." Another person in the house, she thought. Would her life never return to normal? "Do you have enough room?"

CHAPTER TWENTY-TWO

No matter what sort of difficulties, how painful experience is,
if we lose our hope, that's our real disaster.

Dalai Lama XIV

"Oh, yes. There's another spare room." Esmerelda remembered suppressing a tone of resignation at the medic's suggestion. It was more than a suggestion, she realized. She had so wanted to bite back the words. Why hadn't she just said, "No, there's no more room at the inn, Doctor. I'm tired of having people in my house. I don't need one more person in my home, Doctor. Please, no. I don't need any more help." But the doctor was determined and she knew it, so she didn't argue. At that time she couldn't understand why Dr. Emery had been so insistent. She'd resented his plan. A hired physical therapist? Was that really necessary, she asked her doctor, but he was brooking no argument from her. Having Bruce and Jenny in the house was bad enough. Now there'd be someone else changing her life and bossing her around. How could she cope? She was too old for this, but she had been too tired to argue.

"It's settled then," said Doctor Emery. By the end of the next day Harry Somer had moved in and she was surprised to be instantly charmed by the man's ready smile. He wasn't a big talker, either. He spent a lot of time examining her collection of art, staying out of the way when she explained things to Bruce and Jenny. That had turned out much better than she expected.

"Doctor Emery said I need someone trained. My knee and ankles are in bad shape." Bruce hadn't liked it. "Esmy, I wish you'd checked with me. Maybe I could have done the exercises with you. I could have learned." Esmerelda found the idea repulsive. Maybe the doctor had been right to insist she have the physical therapist.

"You have your own life. Your business......you should be seeing to it." She was glad she hadn't had the courage to tell them before Somer arrived. Secretly, she was pleased at the couple's reaction. Jenny stood behind Bruce, nodding her head in agreement with everything the man said.

"You know you like to have your house to yourself," said Bruce. Why then hadn't they moved on, if they understood that? "Maybe we should leave this fellow to it." Did they really understand she felt overwhelmed by having a houseful of people? The pair suddenly remembered some business they had to see to in the next state. A bonus! For that alone, she was grateful to Harry. From that moment things turned brighter. She almost phoned Doctor Emery to thank him.

Dr. Emery's plan turned out to be a godsend. Her life changed in ways she could never have imagined. The house became quiet again and she could breathe easily. Six weeks turned into sixteen until she'd recovered from her injuries and walk with confidence and without sticks. More than recovered – she'd found a friend for life and much, much more. Not only was she better physically, Harry had got her painting and she was secretly thrilled with the results. Hours would pass when she took up her brushes. Every week they visited a different art gallery and argued about their favorites. Then he got her onto the computer and that became a daily part of her regime too. How wonderful it would be if he stayed forever, but she knew that was impossible. Her health had recovered. Even Dr. Emery was amazed at the change in her. Reluctantly and against her own selfish desires, she made Harry go off to live his own life, even though she knew she'd miss him terribly. Before he left, he had one thing left to do, he said. He asked her for 24 hours more – and no questions – and locked himself in his room. Twice that day he left and came back with boxes under each arm. Then it was time.

"Esmy! Can you come and see my room now?"

He must have done a good job of cleaning it, she thought. What a nice man. She was wrong. "Oh!" she exclaimed. And again, "Oh, Harry! Oh, my!" The room was clean, she had to admit, but he'd done so much more. An easel stood beside the sparkling picture window. Beside it was a little stand with paint pots and a palette. In front of the easel was a stool.

"It's adjustable, Esmy. If you feel like standing you can move it up like this," he said as he demonstrated. "Or sit, like this, with just a push on this lever."

"It's amazing!" Her eyes darted around the room. She saw picture frames stacked in a box tidily, all ready on a workbench.

"Those are for you to frame your favorite efforts! And see, here are some little nails and a hammer. I think you should start hanging your work. Don't you?"

"Oh, Harry...and you have pads too."

"*You* have painting pads, you mean. All shapes and sizes. And pencils and tapes and brushes." Everything was stored in a container to suit. It was a beautiful sight – a studio of her own. Who needed a third guest room?

"I love it, Harry. I wish you could stay and use it...."

"When I'm in Florida I can picture you in here, working away. It's as much for you as me."

"You've been a wonderful teacher, Harry."

"Well, you've given me confidence to go and do it on my own. I loved teaching you. Now I know I'm suited to it. You've given me more than confidence, as you know."

"And you must teach! And produce your own work. Open that gallery! I'm going to want to hear all about it."

Her plans for Harry came to fruition. He did leave and for a time life was as before, shortly after David had passed away. She was lonely, but she coped. With her new computer skills and the little art studio, she was happily busy. A peace settled around her. Finally. Yes, Harry had given her a new lease on life.

Until Bruce came back. He said he had to tie up a few loose ends. And, of course, to help Esmy if needed. How desperately she wanted to say no. When he mentioned it would only be a short time before heading on, she was reassured, but the prison gate closed again. Days stretched into weeks. Bruce got to her, just as he had before. She couldn't fight back, for some reason. Can some people cast evil spells? During that time she declined again, even faster, losing much more than physical mobility this time. This time it was different, much worse. In fact, she was sure she was losing her mind.

Doctor Emery scoffed at that. She wished she never mentioned anything to the man. As usual, he interfered, insisting again on her having live-in help and, seeing Somer had left the state, contacted Eileen, the nurse. All these people. Why hadn't she kept her thoughts to herself, just gone quietly mad? Esmy was frustrated. Would her life never be her own? Nurse Eileen was a real go-getter too. First thing every morning, she fussed around to make sure Esmy ate. Then she had to have her bath before choosing the clothes of the day. Why did so much have to be done so early, Esmy wondered.

Bruce suddenly had a business emergency and he and Jenny left. Again. There was beginning to be a pattern, Esmy realized. Maybe she was destined to always have someone in the house. If she had to do that just to keep Bruce at bay, it might be a good idea, a relief in one way, at least. So much had happened in the last year. Such confusion, no wonder she couldn't think straight. Falling down the stairs like that. People moving in and people moving out. Then her mind deteriorating.

But now, thanks to Eileen's own fall she was finally alone. Like the early days, and she was enjoying every minute of it. Going by the last year she had no idea how long the peace would last and she would relish every second. Her phone rang, interrupting her musing.

"Mrs. Graham?"

"Hello?"

"It's Danny. My truck's broken down. I won't be able to come and plow your driveway today or tomorrow. Apparently there's one last snowfall due, a big one. Shall I arrange for someone else to do it? I don't want you stuck inside if you have places to go."

"Oh! Danny, thank you, but it's fine. I'm staying in and I think it's too cold for walks right now. Don't worry about it."

"Okay. Thanks, Mrs. Graham. I'll get there as soon as I can. Maybe by Tuesday?"

"That's fine. Bye." She had enough groceries. There was no need to go out. The house was hers. She almost hugged herself. Poor Eileen. A nice person, really. Thanks to her, Esmy was feeling stronger. She must order an arrangement of flowers and let her know I'm thinking about her.

Eileen had been a great help. she knew. There'd been no more silly incidents after Eileen arrived. Curious, that. Things stayed in their normal places. She didn't hear any voices. She was handling bills and the mail with no problems. The nurse's vote of confidence had certainly helped. Eileen had said she was just fine and a nurse so full of common sense certainly should know. Mistakes can happen to anyone, Eileen said. As for moving furniture, she must have dreamt it, said Eileen. Nightmares can explain a lot of things. After all, ever since she came on the scene, Esmy had had no disturbing incidents, right? With that no nonsense approach how could Esmy argue? Esmy had to admit it. She had her confidence back. She wasn't going crazy after all.

Perhaps while she was nestled into this renewed winter wonderland, shut off from the outside world, she should plan the meeting that would take place between Teddy and herself. Maybe Teddy could come east, and bring Carrie. A grandchild. A son and a grandchild! The youngster sounded a lot like Esmy was at that age. Ready to take on the world. Asking a million questions. Three people might be a better number for their first conversation, so no one person felt the pressure of having to keep the ball rolling. Here? Or somewhere public? The phone rang again.

"Hello?" Esmy heard no response. "Hello? Is anyone there?" She hung up. Probably a wrong number. She went back to the sitting room window and stared out at the white playground. A hair rose on the back of her neck. Silly old woman, she told herself. Brace yourself.

CHAPTER TWENTY-THREE

Appreciation is a wonderful thing. It makes what is excellent in others belong to us as well.

Voltaire

When Teddy got the email with a post office box as a return address, he couldn't help but be a little miffed. His newfound mother was certainly making herself inaccessible. Why? Was she afraid of Teddy coming to see her? Was she ashamed of something? Likely that. Giving up a baby when you're a young girl doesn't bode well for the rest of your life. Should he be relieved she hadn't kept him and taken him along for the ride of his life? His own feelings were too mixed-up to decipher. He imagined his birth mother was even more confused. He certainly wasn't going to push things and embarrass the old woman. Teddy was 56 years old. His birth mother must have had him when she was in her teens. That meant she had to be in her seventies now. Too old to be hassled.

Teddy's life had been uneventful, progressing as it should. Growing up as an only child, he had two parents who thought he was the best thing ever, but in spite of being the center of their attention Teddy had a good head on his shoulders. He recalled kids in high school, the stuck up kind, but they weren't his friends. Their attitude toward him never counted for much. He spent his time volunteering in hospitals, something his father, the doctor, had insisted upon. It had kept him on an even keel. Life was precious – the most precious thing of all, far better than sports cars and European vacations, though he'd had them too. His schooling had centered around playing clarinet in the band and acting as stage hand in plays. That, and getting through exams, which seemed more a chore than a hardship. Good marks came easily to him. That's how he spent his teen years, not like his mother, and it must have been especially hard back then, giving birth out of wedlock, never mind having given birth to a bi-racial child. His father had access to all the records and knew what had happened to his birth mother and tried to understand it. In those days unwed pregnancy was shameful and girls were spirited off to the next town to languish in a house filled with other bad girls, as they were called. He'd done some reading about it.

He followed in his adoptive father's footsteps, became a doctor, and married another intern while he was still in school. Family followed the opening of their joint practice. He'd had a good life and he made sure he told his birth mother that. Dad had died just last year so Mom lived with him and Bess now, in one of the children's rooms. They'd had three sons, all of whom were now out on their own. A surprise fourth child, a girl finally, had arrived when he and his wife were in their early forties. She brought delight to the whole family with her sunny disposition. Their menopause baby – they should have known better. Carrie was fun to have around, a last spurt of youth for all the family.

Teddy had fulfilled his life's desires and one of them had never been to find his birth parents, even though he knew from the time he was seven that his parents had chosen him, not like the rest of the neighborhood who had to take what was delivered. He smiled at that phrase. He used to say it whenever he was asked about being adopted. Had his parents told him that? Or had a little boy simply dealt with the surprise in a practical manner? Teddy had always been that way, turning anything that came to his life into something positive.

Mothers. He had two of them. The rest of the family was relatively disinterested, maybe because finding a grandmother who was in her seventies, or even older, wasn't going to have much impact on them now. Practical Teddy should have felt the same but for some reason he didn't. This mother, who didn't think it necessary to meet, was a mystery he couldn't decipher. He had to admit he was more than a little curious.

But not as curious as Carrie, the free spirit of the family. His daughter had a million questions. Why has she contacted you now, Dad? When did she start searching? Has she been looking for years and years? Is she having help? I mean, an old lady, searching the web for the child she gave up sixty years ago! That's amazing! It could be a movie, for heaven's sakes! Then Carrie had started this business of wanting to write to her mystery Grandma, as she called her. She believed there was a lot more to the woman's reticence to meet than her father was even considering. Carrie always loved to untangle problems, often in unique ways. Wait until she got home and was told she could mail her letter after all, not to her Grandma's home, but to a post office box.

CHAPTER TWENTY-FOUR

I feel a very unusual sensation — if it is not indigestion, it must be gratitude.

Benjamin Disraeli

Harry woke with a start. It took him a moment to remember where he was. He stretched his arms out above his head and tentatively wriggled his spine. No twinges. Sleeping on the floor always worked. He moved the pillow out from under his back and hugged it. He closed his eyes and tried to plan the next few days.

He promised Esmerelda if she ever needed him he'd hightail it up there. He had that last task she'd assigned and would do it when the time came, but he hoped it wouldn't be for a long while yet. It was the only reason he could leave the lady and head down to Florida. She'd earned his respect and he'd come to admire her. He knew he couldn't hang around her place forever. He was a little afraid too to take advantage of the big chance she was giving him. What if her faith in him didn't materialize? He was a coward, she'd teased him more than once. Finally, he agreed, on the condition that he'd come running back at one flick of her finger. If she ever needed him he'd be there. He meant it. She'd made him a guardian of her wishes and he didn't want to betray her trust, not for a second. Only Esmy's lawyer and he knew about the safe deposit box and about Esmy's newfound relative. Bruce Forrest was in for a big surprise. It was Harry's job to bring it to Bruce's attention after Esmerelda was gone. She didn't want the lawyers to do it. The personal touch –that's what she wanted – for both 'wings' of the family. One wing, Bruce, a vulture, the other innocent as a dove. That was the bargain he had made with Esmy. He was to tell Bruce and make sure he took his leave and then he was to contact Teddy, her son given up for adoption at birth, and break the news to him that he was about to receive quite an inheritance. He would have done it for nothing but Esmy had insisted his services should be paid for, the same as an executor. Thus, the yearly stipend, the key she gave him for a whole new life.

Her annuity let him stop worrying about making a living. As luck would have it that's when his work started to sell. He could finally give up physiotherapy and give his back a rest. They say that's the way things happen sometimes. When you stop wanting something so much, it falls into your lap. Well, it had with him. He was even having fun teaching some art classes down in the Keys and was accepted as an artist. Esmerelda had no idea how much she had changed his life. It was like being born again. He kept trying to tell her, whenever they talked, but she was adamant about not receiving the credit she deserved. A couple of galleries were hounding him to produce more work. It all was new and he hadn't quite wrapped his mind around it. Life had changed and he owed it all to Esmeralda.

Both their lives had altered, all because of her fall. When he became her physical therapist his life changed for the better, certainly, far beyond any expectations he could have had. Truth to tell, it was just another job when he started but it turned his life around. Esmerelda's too. With his help she'd been able to find a relative she thought she'd lost forever. A relative Bruce Forrest didn't know about.

It would be a shock, for sure. Bruce had got himself into Esmy's will with high expectations, thinking he would be her sole survivor. Not so, because Esmy had found Teddy. No second cousin, or sister-in-law or grandnephew like Bruce. Teddy was no distant kin like Bruce, if that scoundrel actually was related to her. From the moment Harry met him he somehow doubted it. It was just a gut feeling, really. Was Bruce really related to her? It was always highly suspicious the way he turned up out of the blue like that, whenever she was most vulnerable. How different he was from Esmy. He sure didn't seem to have her best interests at heart. You knew that just to look at him.

No matter. Now Esmy had someone much better, an immediate relative. A son. Harry promised Esmy he'd follow her instructions. Her deepest wish was that Bruce and his family never had to know about the fellow, ever, but that was impossible if he was to get what was coming to him. Esmy and Harry had got all the information organized and put all the documentation- after getting her lawyer to do the legal stuff- birth certificate, adoption papers, medical tests- into a safe deposit box and Esmy had given Harry the key for when the time came. She wanted to make sure her son would come out on top, with Bruce left out on a limb with just enough to keep him quiet. She'd come a long way from the trust she once had in him. When did she start to suspect Bruce wasn't all he said he was?

Harry couldn't wait to see the expression on Bruce's face when he realized what a small part of the pie was going to be his, if any. Revenge is sweetest when served cold? Certainly for Esmy if her health had declined that much. Harry had to drag it all out of her because she was mightily ashamed. He'd made her life a misery in fact. When Bruce moved in and started running the house she appreciated it at first, but it wasn't long before resentment reigned, especially after his girlfriend Jenny showed up. Esmy couldn't abide it, but was too sweet to say anything. He was family, after all, and she couldn't cause another rift, not like the first that had left her childless. It wasn't long before she'd lost her will. Breaking down a person's self-confidence also breaks down their backbone. He treated her as if she was an imbecile instead of just an old lady so that by the time Harry came into the picture she was reticent and shy. He'd cut back on her creature comforts too, while he and his woman bought themselves all the toys and trappings of modern life.

Harry came into the picture after she fell. Or was she pushed? She would never answer that question, but finally appeared relieved to have some protection after at first balking. Harry was her physical therapist and got to see firsthand how they'd intruded on her living space. When the doctor suggested Harry move in with her for daily treatments it meant Bruce had to change his tactics. He did – he left the scene – and that said something, didn't it? The doctor had his own suspicions, Harry thought, and it was his strategy for fixing the situation without making blatant accusations. The man had to protect his professional reputation, Harry guessed, and couldn't go around making assertions that might be false. The nice thing was after Harry moved his things into Esmy's spacious home, she eventually got back her mobility and more. Their conversations about art meant she soon insisted on seeing some of his stuff and then wanted to try a hand at painting too. Turns out it was a fabulous form of therapy. Anyone who paints knows how damned difficult it can be but at the same time totally cathartic. Her pictures were primitive and satisfying. They gave her just the kickstart she needed, a sense of accomplishment, and Esmy took a decided turn for the better. Her doctor was pleased with how his scheme worked out.

Seeing Harry's laptop was the incentive for Esmy to get one of her own. He showed her how to play a few games and search the web for fun and that was when she blossomed, spending hours at her desk, doing searches. And it's how she finally got in contact with her long lost son, given up for adoption at birth.

She'd only been in her teens when she'd got pregnant and had no power over her own life. Much as she wanted the baby, Esmy's sister and father had arranged everything and the young girl had no recourse. The whole story blew Harry away. You never think rich families can have the very same problems as everyone else. The child's father had been the gardener's son. Esmerelda was forever grateful to Harry because he'd made it possible for her to revisit the biggest regret of her life and try to make it better. In her mind, it was appropriate to give Harry a new life too, just as she'd regained the one she'd given away decades ago. Esmerelda had that kind of sense of justice. An eye for an eye? No, one good turn deserves another. Esmerelda had a ledger sheet view of life. She wouldn't let Harry turn down her annuity, no matter how hard he insisted.

CHAPTER TWENTY-FIVE

One thing you can't hide — is when you're crippled inside.

John Lennon

"I'm getting tired of this, baby." Jenny was short on patience and long on whining. "I made a call..."

"I'm fed up with waiting, too," Bruce shouted, throwing his glasses down on the couch beside him. "Don't you know that? But things have been going just as I planned. She's sure she's batty. She's even been to the doctor. It's documented now, isn't it? Just what I wanted."

"So the doctor knows she nuts? Or thinks she is?"

"Yup. That'll get back the money she gave away on that annuity, for sure."

"You sure about that?" Jenny needed more than just Bruce's wishful thinking.

"Didn't the doctor get a nurse to keep an eye on her? Isn't that proof he knows she needs care?"

"Yeah, well, she's not there now."

"Who isn't? What do you mean? Has Esmy gone somewhere? How could she?"

"I'm telling you- if you'd only listen! I made a call. I got sick of hanging around here. I wanted to know how she was. I hoped she'd been admitted to some kind of sanatarium. She sure hasn't. Get this. Esmy's in the house – all by herself – again."

"Esmy's alone again?"

"Aren't you listening? Yes, she's alone."

"You stupid bitch. Did she know it was you calling?"

Jenny bit her tongue. If he thought he could talk to her like that...... "No way. I did one of those sales pitch things and asked to talk to the lady of the house. Esmy answered. You know she never answers the phone if there's hired help in the house."

"Are you sure she didn't recognize your voice? Are you sure she was alone?"

"Yes. I called again and pretended I was from the nursing service and she answered again and said her nurse was off sick. Listen to this! The nurse fell and broke her leg!"

"You're kidding! I can't believe it! If only it had been Esmy."

"Didn't I think that too? Everything would have slipped into place, like you'd planned – if it had been a bad fall, of course, and not just a broken leg."

"When did this happen, Jenny? Did she say?"

"Just a day ago. My timing was perfect, wasn't it?"

"Looks like we'll have to take fate into our own hands, won't we? Surely you can see everything's in the right place now for us to go ahead?"

"How do you mean?" Why couldn't he even acknowledge how smart she was to have made the call?

"Esmy's alone. The doctor knows she's nuts. Before he goes and gets someone else into that house we have to be there. We can't waste time. This is our golden opportunity to finish her off."

"You mean...?"

"Yes. I'll do it right his time." Like most criminals, Bruce didn't have much imagination. Another fall would do it. This time he'd push her down a longer flight of stairs and he'd make sure she wasn't carrying anything that would cushion the fall. That should work. Maybe an extra bang on the head might be needed. He thought he might be able to manage that. Just think of the money, he told himself, and his grandmother Susan and how she'd felt about Esmerelda Graham. "I mean, how many falls can an old lady take anyway?"

"Won't they suspect?" Jenny was wondering how soon she could pack her bags. She'd like to get the hell out of here.

"Suspect what? Who? Me? No way. They'll think I'm in another state! With you."

Jenny was relieved. Bruce didn't expect her to be an accessory. She was finished with this man. He scared her. "I don't need any more trouble, Bruce."

"More trouble? What do you mean? Your record's clean, isn't it?"

Jenny frowned. Well, almost clean with just some petty larceny, but she was planning a change. Those days were over. Best to turn over a new leaf. She didn't have the nerves for this anymore. Bruce didn't know all that much about her. Best to pretend innocence. "Of course. What about yours?"

"Me? I'm as clean as the driven snow." An artful liar at work. "And I'm her rightful heir."

"Won't that make them suspect you?"

Bruce didn't like it when Jenny talked sense. He liked women swallowing every word he spouted. His grandmother always did. He was able to talk her around to anything, especially after fueling her anger by having her recount the feud over and over. In doing so, he got more and more valuable information about the wealthy Graham family. The info had come in handy. "Not if I'm nowhere in sight," he stated.

Jenny was to do as he outlined: check into a motel, order room service for two and play movies throughout the stay, some of them only a man would order. He was totally confident she'd carry out his orders. Jenny took off. He was surprised how quickly she got all her stuff together. That was step one. Now step two. In only a matter of hours he was back in Esmy's neighborhood, letting himself in with his copy of her house key, the one he'd made months before.

Bruce was better at talking. His bravado in outlining the deed to Jenny wasn't so straightforward now he was here. What if she just got banged up again? What if she saw him and didn't die? What if someone came by? That was silly because everyone was snow-bound. He'd had real trouble getting down the driveway. Getting into the house was the easiest part as he had a key. By that time he was exhausted and had to catch his breath. It had been hard going. Luckily no one had seen him struggling through the snow, trying to get a foothold. He'd carried a big branch behind him to obliterate his footprints and that had slowed him down a lot. Where had the snowplow guy got to?

It didn't take him long to confirm that Jenny was right. Esmerelda was in the house alone. No stereo on, no TV either, not even the radio. From the living room he crept to the foot of the stairs and listened. He could hear the soft chanting of Esmerelda's meditations. Crazy woman. She really was. That made him feel better about what he was going to do. Sitting up there with crossed legs at her age and moaning to beat the band. He was right to drive her over the edge. People like that don't need to people the earth. Sitting cross-legged on a bundle of cash – the picture sprang to mind and he giggled. That money would be his soon. Incentive enough.

Bruce's hesitation to do the deed was borne out by his actions during the next three hours. He disconnected the furnace thermo-stat- maybe she would freeze to death and who would be the wiser?

He pulled the phone line out of its jack because it seemed a good idea. Then he made strange noises by tapping, scratching and fiddling with the radio to make static. He thought he could unnerve Esmy, but in reality he had no clear-cut plan other than to maneuver her into a position so that he could send her for a headlong fall into oblivion. When he heard her coming down the stairs from the second floor slowly and carefully, he decided to head back to the basement. The woman's mutterings revealed her intent. "So cold...wonder why...?" She was going to check the furnace to see why it was getting so cold. Disconnecting the thermostat had been a good idea, he thought. He scooted back down the cellar stairs.

CHAPTER TWENTY-SIX

Confusion now hath made his masterpiece.

William Shakespeare, Macbeth

Maybe Teddy would come east and bring her granddaughter Carrie. A son and a granddaughter! The youngster sounded a lot like Esmerelda at that age. Ready to take on the world. Asking a million questions. Having her along might make conversation easier between Esmy and her son, too. It certainly would be hard to get the ball rolling. Where should the get-together take place? Here? Or some place neutral like a restaurant? Esmy's mind imagined what would happen. Her son would stride into the place, holding his daughter's hand. He'd introduce her to Esmy. He'd say, "Carrie, this is your grandmother Esmy. She's been looking forward to meeting you." He'd look at Esmy and smile. He'd put one hand on her elbow as he shook her hand. Then, almost as an afterthought he'd circle her with both arms and give her a big hug. She could feel the warmth of his embrace. She'd whisper, "My son, my own sweet son," in his ear. Esmerelda shook her head just a little. "Now, you silly old woman, just you stop your daydreaming."

She picked up the phone in the hall to the kitchen. "Hello?" Esmy heard no response. "Hello? Is anyone there?" She hung up. Still out. She went back to the sitting room window and stared out at the winter white playground. A hair rose on the back of her neck and she shivered. Cold out there, and in here. Perhaps she'd invite Teddy here. It would be hard to explain in a public place. She needed privacy to tell him about his father. She wanted to give him time to ask questions, tell him her reasons for not fighting her family. The big question would be why? Why had she not fought back? Insisted she keep the baby – him? Describing the temperature of the times wouldn't be easy. Then Esmerelda had another thought. This was a grown man she'd be talking to. He'd likely know all that. Maybe he just wanted to meet her, plain and simple. Maybe he didn't expect any explanation. What's done is done. He might say, we're meeting now, and here's your grandchild. Isn't that enough?

Silly old woman, she thought again. Better try again to order that bouquet for Eileen. She went to the phone in the foyer and picked up the receiver. Still no dial tone. Okay, okay. Ice – of course! Ice must have knocked out the phone lines. They usually do. She shivered again. Instead of returning to the sitting room she went back to the hall closet and took down an extra warm sweater. She heard the furnace turn itself off. Why? It didn't seem that warm in here. She walked to the thermostat by the basement stairs. She'd set it at 74 degrees. Higher than usual, but she felt the cold more these days. It certainly wasn't 74 in here. She went back to the sunroom and looked at the indoor/outdoor thermometer attached to the window outside. Outside temperature – well below freezing. Inside temperature, 65. How could that be? She tapped it. It remained the same. Esmerelda stood wondering in the silent house.

Bruce figured she'd come down into the cellar to investigate the workings of the furnace. This would be the best place to do what he wanted. *The confidence man did it in the basement with the.....what?* Bruce used the last of the day's sunlight seeping into the dark space to search out a weapon. Should he hit her on the head? No, evidence of foul play. Smother her? That might work. He ambled around the shelving trying to find something. In a carryall he found some rags David Graham probably used for staining his carpentry. Three shammies rolled neatly together would be better. They might do just the job, and not hurt Esmy. Leave no bruises. Out of curiosity he opened some drawers that slid slowly and silently. It was obvious Esmerelda's husband had kept everything oiled and shipshape. Inside one drawer were Cuban cigar boxes. When Bruce opened one, he found an assortment of seals and two blocks of wax. In another he found shiny shavings of gold leaf. When Bruce touched one it clung to his finger like plastic wrap. He couldn't remove it. He closed the box and scraped his finger along it to get off most of the gold. Should he take the collection of gold leaf? Better not. He had to travel light when he finally made his way back down the driveway. Had it stopped snowing?

Bruce's search revealed nothing else that would help him in his scheme of financial freedom. Tools like hammers and wrenches were disregarded – too violent, and likely to leave marks. Concoctions such as paint thinner and methylated spirits might be potent enough, but impossible to administer. Even Bruce knew that. He was becoming slightly bored until he found the bag of golf clubs. He practiced his putting until he heard the door open to the cellar way.

Esmerelda knew nothing about furnaces. Maybe the pilot light had gone off. But where was that, she wondered. She did know that no ordinary person should try to light a gas pilot light. You were sup-posed to call in the gas company to do that, weren't you? Maybe the thermostat itself was broken. She could do nothing about that either. She did remember there was a space heater in the basement. Electric, it was, just the thing. Bring it up and put it in one room and close the door. Get the space nice and warm and stay there until the storm passed and the utilities were restored.

When Bruce heard her open the door to the cellar stairs he shrank into a corner under the risers. This was it. He'd better steel himself and do it right this time. In his hand was the putter.

Esmy opened the door and flicked on the light switch that flooded the stairs with light. She could see well enough but her bifocal glasses prevented her from seeing what was directly underfoot. A putter, stuck out at an odd angle between the risers. At the third step from the top she tripped and fell the whole way, landing on the cement floor with an appalling thud. A slow rivulet of red seeped across the floor. That should have been enough for Bruce but he had to place his finger on her carotid artery to ensure he'd done the job right this time. Not even a hint of a pulse. He removed his hand, place the golf club back in the bag, restored the shammies to their drawer before leaving the premises. Everything in its place.

Except for the sliver of gold leaf on Esmy's throat.

CHAPTER TWENTY-SEVEN

You aren't sure if you're making the right decision — about anything, ever.

Joan Didion

The day dawned early for Harry, though not everyone. Gus was having a siesta when Harry entered the office. Asleep on the divan, he was slouched into a corner like a bear finally beginning his hibernation. Had he stayed up the whole night? Coffee was there, hot and ready, just as promised. Harry poured himself a cup, then went outside to drink it. The sunrise was over, but streaks of blues and pinks jazzed up the sky in shades too commercial to be true, matching the garish colors of the motel's metal chairs. He sat down in one and took a deep gulp of coffee. A decent brew that did its job. Things looked better this morning and the view wasn't bad either. On the other side of the road the ocean's waves pounded the shore. Nice, steady and dependable. Maybe he should take some time to check his strategy, rethink things. Perhaps a day's stopover? He closed his eyes and breathed in the sea air. A slight breeze promised oblivion. His back was just fine this morning. In fact, he felt better than he had in days. Even his jaw had stopped aching. A car pulling a boat trailer drove into the circular driveway of the motel. The driver got out, nodded, then checked his hitch.

"Thought I heard a scraping sound. Wasn't sure what it was," he explained when he saw Harry watching, who nodded back and took another sip. A sign on the boat said, "For sail". The guy smiled at Harry, got back into his car and drove off. A couple of pelicans swooped overhead, crossing the road toward the surf. Breakfast time. Harry decided to walk over for a better look. The shore was alive with birds and boats, all facing life head-on, into the wind. Three pelicans were lined up in a trio, floating with the current, looking like jazz singers, ready to do a number. They were rocking in rhythm, a wing's width apart, heads cocked at the same angle, in feathered finery. Abruptly they rose as one and swooped off in unison. On uplift they separated and did a wild tango, their twisting tails high into the air. They were now only within sight of each other, giving needed space for their acrobatics. They stopped, hung there briefly in the atmosphere, upside down. Then, beaks down, they free fell into the ocean, beaks piercing the surface. Two got fish. The third tried again, repeating the airlift and dive, successful this time. Again, the three resumed their floating phase, side by side. Harry sat down on a piece of driftwood and watched for a bit, listening to the cacophony of bird cackles.

The sun's warmth felt good and it wasn't even near noon yet. Harry definitely needed to stop dithering. Picking up a stick he started to draw lines in the sand. Pros and cons. Should he interfere? Or not? He'd read somewhere that when people get to drawing up this kind of list, they've already made up their minds. They're just going through the motions, putting things down, appearing rational when, in fact, they're stacking one side, the side they want to win because their minds have already made a decision. Let's see what his mind had decided. He made two columns. 'Yes' for interfere and 'No' for not. He started on the second list first. One. She should have given this job to someone with power, some family member, but there was no one. Two. Bruce was family, after all. Three. With time on his side. Four. And the resources. At that point his mind went blank. On to the flip side.

One. Bruce didn't deserve a penny. Two. He didn't have all the facts. Three. Harry did. That was important. Four. Esmy wanted Harry to have the annuity, and for it he'd promised to help her. Five. How could he forget her disturbing phone calls? Six. She'd had the foresight to give him the job. Seven. Most importantly, he'd promised her he'd do it and he never went back on his word. That was the clinching argument and, seeing the second list was longer, interfere he must. Now what would be the most effective way to fulfill his promise? More importantly, would he be there in time?

CHAPTER TWENTY-EIGHT

Someone has to die in order that the rest of us should value life more.

Virginia Woolf

After packing his luggage Harry returned to the office and saw Gus had company. Her eyes took him in as she sipped her coffee. They were as brown as the caffeine, and just as steamy. As was the rest of her. Harry could tell even though she was enveloped in a bulky sweater, except for her skintight jeans.

"Misty, meet Harry. He's on his way north," Gus said, reaching out with the coffeepot. Harry held out his cup for a refill.

"Hi," she said. So this was the Misty of Annie's wrath. Pure jealousy, he'd say. There were no sharp edges sticking out of her, just smooth, rounded bits in all the right places. Half Annie's age, with a wit about her. Harry couldn't keep his eyes off the woman and she knew it.

"Hello," he answered. "Nice day. The sun's doing its thing out there." What an idiot.

"Yeah? Guess I'll do some tanning." Harry would have liked to stay around for that. The woman went back to reading the paper.

"Decided to leave?" asked Gus. This guy could read Harry's mind, he was sure of it. "Are you needed up north? Or can you hang around a bit?"

"Well, there's a bit of a problem up there. I've got someone handling it, but I just don't know if I should give him a free hand. It's pretty important."

"Need to use my phone, maybe?"

"Might be a good idea...." Misty was sitting down, circling something in the paper, using a red pen with silver glitter. Legs crossed at the knees, one shoe was dangling from toes dressed up in blood red nail polish as she swung her leg languidly. She was in no hurry. Maybe Harry shouldn't be either.

"Here, use my phone. Got a phone card?" Harry nodded and pulled it out of his wallet and showed it to him. "Misty and I'll take a stroll outside." With his words, the woman stood up, pulled down her sweater and straightened her leather belt – that was worth watching – and picked up one section of the paper and tucked it under her arm, dropping the other sections onto the counter. Harry pulled out his little notebook for the lawyer's number and moved to use the phone only to see Bruce Forrest's face smirking at him. What was his photo doing in the newspaper? Had something happened? Harry dropped the phone card and the notebook, grabbed the paper and started reading. When Gus came back in he was sitting on the divan, head down. Esmy had died. And the vultures were swooping.

"Sorry. I just need to get a key," interrupted Gus.

"I can't wait to see the salon!" gushed Misty. "Gosh, a place of my own? It might work!" The woman took in Gus' silence and stared at Harry. Then her hand reached out to pat his arm.

"Sure, but remember it hasn't been cleaned in a bit," said Gus, recovering. "Annie could do that for you. She'd love to, I think. It would remind her of the old days..." Gus saw Harry's crumpled state and he shut up too. He stood quietly. Then he untangled the paper from Harry's hand. Gus smoothed out the page on his counter top. "You okay? Anything I can do, Harry?"

Harry looked up. "Can't see how. Someone I know...knew...has just passed away. I was heading north to see her, in fact. I'm too late. I'm a shithead."

"Was she a relative?"

"No, but she felt like one. Like a favorite aunt. No. More than that – like a mother. You know what I mean?"

"Yeah, I do, Harry. Sorry for your loss." He shrugged. "I don't mean to sound so formal. No one really knows what to say when there's a death. You'd think we would. There's so much of it around. Just a minute, Harry." He turned to Misty. "Look, Misty. Go and talk to Annie. Get her to show you around the place. Okay?" He handed a key to Misty, who almost ran out of the room. Then he asked Harry, "You know this guy?"

He was pointing to the picture of Bruce that accompanied the article about the death of Esmeralda Graham, heiress to the company that had made a fortune providing baked goods to the whole country.

"Yeah. A scuzzball, for sure. I knew Esmy – Esmeralda Graham – the woman who died. She helped me out once after I did a good turn for her. I got that Bruce out of her house for her."

"Is he related to the woman?"

"Yup. Esmy came to hate the sight of him. The guy's just been waiting for her to die. In fact, I have my suspicions he once tried to hurry that along. I could be wrong, but if you met this guy..."

"It says here her nephew's devastated by her death," Gus said, reading the item.

"She was his grandmother's sister."

"Picture of him here at the cemetery, at her funeral. I got news for you, Harry. This nephew...or great-grandson..or whatever he calls himself is going to have the biggest surprise of his life," said Gus. He had a big grin.

"What do you mean?" Harry asked. Something in the man's attitude brought Harry to his feet. Gus was pacing like a birddog on the scent. He took a deep breath before answering the question.

"He's going to be put inside for extortion... fraud.... whatever you want to call it. I'll leave that to the legal guys."

"Bruce Forrest?"

"Not the name he's been using as far as I know. Guy Feviere is what he's been calling himself down here. A while back he was courting rich widows and taking them for the ride of their lives, leaving them a lot poorer and, sadly, wiser. Now I know where he is I can wrap it all up and hand the case over to the authorities. He's been in and out of the state over the last two years. Sometimes he'd disappear for months, then back he'd be again. He must have been up with your lady in the off times."

"Rich widows?"

"Yup. He has this scheme. I can't get over how well it worked. I guess everyone wants to feel needed. You see, it seems he was dying of liver cancer and was short of funds. See his face? You can see he's upset the cameraman caught a good shot of him. That wouldn't be good for any of his patsies to see he's actually someone else."

"Bruce? Dying of liver cancer?"

"That's what he tells them, that he needs money for a transplant or he'll die. So far, he's managed to squeeze over three million dollars from less than a half dozen women, as far as I can gather. I was hired...."

"You were hired?" Harry's mind was reeling.

CHAPTER TWENTY-NINE

Forget injuries, never forget kindnesses.

Confucius

Annie's favorite singer, Dolly Parton, was singing raptures about her traveling man. The old lady turned up the volume and danced in her pretty pink slippers. She was cradling Little Bertie in her arms, enjoying herself, when she heard a tap at the door. No one ever called on Annie. It frightened her for a moment. She stood still.

"Annie?" A high-pitched voice. Little Bertie whined.

"Sh!" whispered Annie.

"Annie, you in there? It's Misty."

Misty, indeed. Didn't she mean S-U-E? She'd soon see about that. "What do you want? My radio ain't on loud. Not as loud as yours."

"Annie, my radio isn't even on. It's broken."

"So?"

"Can you open the door? Gus wants you to do something."

That was different. She put Little Bertie onto the bed, then went back to the door and opened it a bit.

"What does Gus want?"

"He wants you to help me." Annie looked at her. "He said you'd be the only one who could," explained Misty. The old woman couldn't hide her surprise."Really, Annie. Listen, can I come in and explain?"

"I guess so." Annie turned and let the woman follow her into the room. She sat on the bed and motioned Misty to the one chair in the room.

"Sweet doggy. He certainly loves you. I've seen how he won't leave your side."

That made Annie smile, in spite of herself. "Gus gave him to me."

"Gus is a nice fellow, isn't he?" asked Misty.

"Sure is. You can trust Gus. He's who he says he is." Annie thought that was a good stab.

Misty frowned. "Who he says he is? I suppose so..."

"What does he want?"

"Want? Who? The dog?" asked Misty.

Misty's confusion made Annie feel smart. "What does *Gus* want?"she said slowly, then added, "Gus is honest. You can trust *him.*"

"Oh! Yeah. I'm sure you're right, Annie." Misty realized something was bothering Annie, but had no idea what it was. She took her time explaining. "Listen, you used to help out a woman who had a beauty parlor over there on the second floor?"

"Yeah. Sharon. How did you know?"

"Gus told me. He said you used to clean for her."

"Not for free. She used to do my hair once a week. And cut Big Bert's too."

"Who's Big Bert?" asked Misty.

"He was my husband. He's dead now."

"Annie! I had no idea. I'm so sorry. That must be really hard for you. Is that why you named your dog Little Bertie?"

"Yes. Didn't you know about my Bert?"

"No. Life must be so different without him. You're all alone? That must be hard."

"I have Little Bertie." Annie didn't want Misty's sympathy. "And Gus keeps an eye on me too." She couldn't help adding, "Sometimes he bullies me, trying to make me buy things and eat every day and stuff like that."

"But he's a good friend to you?"

"You could say that."

"Would you like me to do your hair, Annie?"

Annie was dumbstruck. This wasn't the way things were supposed to go.

"Could you?"

"Yeah, I'm a hairdresser."

"Could you...cut it? I hate the way it scrapes on my neck. I like short hair."

"Sure, any way you'd like. I think you would look good with bangs too. Have you ever worn bangs?"

"No." Annie wasn't sure if she had. What were bangs? "Why would you do that for me, anyway?"

"I need the practice. I wouldn't charge you, Annie. You'd be my model."

"A model!" That sounded pretty exciting.

"And there's a place where we could do it, isn't there, Annie? That's what Gus wants. He said to have you show me the place and tell me how Sharon organized it and all. See, he gave me the keys."

Annie couldn't remember what she wanted to ask Misty. She knew it was important but she was so excited she'd forgotten her animosity toward the young woman who understood how it felt to be alone. No one other than Gus and Stacey had ever made her feel as if someone understood.

"Now?"

"If you have the time?" Misty stood up. Little Bertie jumped out of bed and trotted over to sniff at Misty's new shoes. "Do you like my new heels, Annie? Huntz bought them for me. I see you're wearing the slippers he picked up for you. I told him you'd like pink better than purple. They match that little jacket you wear a lot."

One mystery solved. "That was real nice of Huntz. I wondered where they came from. I should have known. I love pink."

"I'll just sit outside in the sun until you're ready. Is that okay?"

"Yeah. I won't be long." Annie had that Christmas morning feeling. Three surprises in one day! When Annie was ready the two women walked across the forecourt of the Pelican Motel to a set of stairs beside the front lobby. Little Bertie bobbed along behind. Misty realized she'd seen Annie often sitting on the bottom of this flight of steps but she'd never wondered where they led. None of the second floor rooms were ever rented so of course there had never been anyone mounting these steps with luggage, or much else, it appeared. Debris and dust filled the corners of each tread and the two women watched where they stepped. Customers wouldn't like too many stairs, thought Misty, but there were only a few in the first flight, which turned a corner to about eight more risers. Misty gave Annie the key, which pleased her. She managed to give Misty a smile.

"I used to have this key every Sunday. I used to come in here and clean up for Sharon. She was a real neat person, though, so it was really just polishing things clean and putting away the garbage." She picked up her dog and plopped him into one of the chairs.

"Yes, it's important to keep your equipment clean when you're working with people. You have to watch health regulations." Misty was looking around. "It looks like she just took off, Annie! I can't believe what she left behind."

"Looks about the same as when I used to clean up in here. Here's her drawer with all the brushes, lined up just so. The shelves are pretty full too, with shampoos and stuff."

"They're so neat!"

"Line them up in size, from smallest to biggest. That's what I did, just like we had to do in school with the glue bottles."

"You kept things neat like this, Annie? You're worth your weight in gold!"

"What does that mean?" asked Annie, though she had the feeling it was something good.

"It means you're a treasure, Annie."

"Why are you really wanting to see this place? Just to do my hair?"

"Not really sure. I'm thinking it might be a nice place to do business. If I were staying around."

"Do business? You'd open this up? Do hair and everything? You'd need a cleaner. Would you want me to clean up for you?"

"Sure would! Housework's not one of my talents. I hate it, in fact." That didn't surprise Annie. "But, in the meantime, why don't we girls just have a manicure and a shampoo and set?"

"You mean it?"

"Looks like there's everything here we'll need." Misty had been opening cupboards and drawers. She turned on the two hair dryers and heat shot out. Gus hadn't cut off the electricity to this part of the building. "Do you know where the cleaning supplies are?"

Annie answered by opening a door to a tall storage closet in the corner of the room. "Right here."

"Well, let's get to work and see what we can clean up. You tell me what you want me to do, Annie. You'll be the boss in cleaning. I'll take care of the beauty side of things."

"Sharon used to do my hair nice. It lasted for days."

"For days?" asked Misty. The magic of hair spray.

"Yup. I looked real good back then."

"You look fine now, Annie. Nice and slim. I wish I could get my hips down to your size."

Annie had something that Misty wanted? Slim hips? "Well, you look just fine, Misty." She could afford to be generous. "Huntz certainly thinks so." She was amazed to see Misty blush.

"Huntz is the finest man I've ever met," said Misty.

"Yeah, I'd say he's pretty good. Just like Rod and his nephew Gus. Good men too," said Annie.

"Imagine, Annie. Here we are in a little corner of one of the nicest parts of the world and we have here some of the finest men we've ever met. Who would have thought it?" The two women laughed at that. "What was your husband like, Annie?"

"He was fine too." Annie didn't find it easy to talk about Bert. She missed him every day. "He was my best friend. Ever."

"Is that so? They say that's what makes a good marriage. I hear that all the time, on Oprah and Dr. Phil and all those talk shows. You have to be best friends first if you want a good marriage."

"Well, we was. When we came here to help out Gus's uncle, life got really good. Then Bert died. In his sleep."

"How awful for you, Annie! What did you do?"

"At first I thought he was just playing a joke on me. He wouldn't talk. That was a nice thing when we first woke up. We'd sit and talk about the day before. But he wouldn't answer. I got up and came around his side of the bed. I knew right away he wasn't right. I stood there for awhile. I hoped it was a dream. I didn't know what to do, Misty."

"I can imagine!"

"Finally I went and told Gus. He saw to things. But he couldn't make things right. They've never been right since."

"Really? Are you unhappy here?"

Annie gave it some thought. Since Gus gave her Little Bertie and showed her how to manage her money she felt better. Less lost. And now, Misty was going to do her hair, and was talking to her like a real person. "No, I guess not. Things are getting nice. Like right now! I'm really happy you're going to cut my hair. I don't really know how to take care of it. I just usually wash it with my bar of soap and let it dry. Sometimes I wake up in the morning and I look like something Little Bertie dragged in off the street."

Misty laughed. "Bed head!"

"Bed head? That's funny. Did you make it up?" giggled Annie.

"Oh, no," laughed Misty.

"That's like down....town!"

"Or no fuss Gus!" suggested Misty.

"No fuss Gus! Or......Little Bertie in the dirt!"

"Annie with no fanny!" The two women started to laugh uncontrollably. Annie, because she hadn't in a long time, and Misty because she was back doing hair and being herself. "Now, shall we go with the bangs, Annie?" she asked, scissors poised.

"I guess so!" Annie was surprised she was putting her trust in Misty. "Tell me again. What will they look like?"

"I'll cut them to about here, and with your natural curl they'll sit just above your eyebrows. Then you can pull the rest of your hair back under a hairband or just let it go loose. It's not so long now as it was, especially at the back. It's going to look real nice. Just wait until I dry it."

Annie sat down in the chair beside Little Bertie. Misty whipped a plastic cover around her shoulders and tied it with a neat bow. It was nice to be doing hair again. Changing Annie's look was a challenge she was up to.

"Okay. Cut away." Annie squeezed her eyes shut and kept them that way until Misty started the hair dryer, blowing sections of hair dry one at a time. "Oh, my gosh! My hair don't look so gray! What happened?"

"You have a nice pepper and salt color, all mixed in together."

"And your hair's a nice...ketchup color, Misty." Annie wanted to give her a compliment.

Misty laughed. "Ketchup? I'll have you know that's called strawberry blonde, my dear." But she laughed along with Annie who thought it was funny to describe hair with food names- salt and pepper and strawberries.

"Big Bert had chocolate hair."

"Dark brown?"

"Yup."

"And Huntz has Cola hair!" laughed Misty.

"Black?" She was getting the hang of this. Even though she was having a good time Annie couldn't forget the card with Misty's picture on it and the three letter word, S-U-E. Should she?

"You know those slippers Huntz gave me?"

"Yeah. The pink ones."

"Well....." Annie's curiosity overcame her. "Well, I'm using the little purse they came in."

"Little purse?" asked Misty.

"Yeah. Let me get it." She jumped out of the chair and ran to grab her purse from the counter by the front door. "See!" She held it up. "You can see everything inside. That way you know if you've remembered your keys and bus pass and things like that." She shoved the plastic bag into Misty's face. The ID card was plainly visible through the front window.

Misty gasped. "Where did you find that?" Her voice was barely a whisper.

Annie wasn't a good actress. Her eyes gave her away.

"Annie! You know exactly what I mean. Where did you find my ID?"

"Yours? S-U-E. Is that your name? Even I know Misty doesn't start with an S."

"Answer me, Annie." In a softer voice she added, "Please?"

"Outside, by the wash line."

"It must have fallen out of one of my blouses..." Misty was biting her lip. The dryer wasn't aimed at Annie's head now. It was just hanging from Misty's hand. Annie was regretting what she'd done. The look on Misty's face scared her a little. Misty was close to tears. So was Annie.

"My hair.....?" Annie directed the barrel of the dryer onto her bangs.

"Wha...? Oh, I'm sorry." Misty tried to concentrate on the last of the styling, though her mind was obviously elsewhere.

Annie was regretting having brought up the whole matter, no matter how curious she had been. They'd been having such fun. Why had she ruined it all? She no longer cared who Misty really was. This was the closest she'd come to having a new friend in a long time.

"Listen. Take it. I just found it." Was Misty crying? She threw the ID card on the counter. It landed midst the combs and brushes. "I really like my bangs."

"Annie.....you can't tell Huntz...."

"Tell Huntz? Why would I?"

"....I didn't tell him my real name. It's Sue. He thinks it's Misty. We were dancing, you see, and I knew I really liked this guy so I said...."

"You don't have to tell me, Misty. Ain't my business."

"....so I said my name was Misty. It's the name of his favorite song, you see. I thought it would make things click. You know?"

Annie didn't understand at all, but didn't admit it. "Sure. I understand. So what's wrong with that anyway? I'd like to be called Marilyn. After Marilyn Monroe. I loved her."

"Well, there's more than just giving him the wrong name." Misty wanted to tell all, she realized. The weight of carrying it had got her down. Maybe she'd try things out on Annie first.

"I did something very wrong, Annie." And she told about stealing from her previous employer. When all the details were out Annie didn't know what to say. Never before had someone confided in her. Though it was a good feeling to know someone's secret, at the same time she hoped Misty –Sue – wouldn't ask for advice. The problem seemed enormous to Annie.

"You just left? Like that? Do you think the police are after you?"

"Somehow I don't really think so, Annie. The money helped me out, for sure, but it wasn't a huge amount."

"How much?"

"A little less than five hundred bucks."

Two months' living. Annie gasped. It seemed like a lot of money to her.

"Do you have any of it left?"

"About half. I've decided not to spend the rest. I need to make some money of my own, until I decide what to do."

"What do you think you'll do?" asked Annie.

"Save up until I have enough and send it all back."

"That would be good!"

"Or send a little at a time until it's all paid off."

"Why don't you ask Huntz for it and then you can pay it back all at once?"

"I don't want Huntz to know! He'll hate me!"

Annie thought Huntz was a pretty understanding guy, actually.

"Maybe you want me to tell him for you? Would that help? Huntz treats me real nice. He won't get mad. I could tell him you're really sorry?"

"Annie, this has been just awful. I've felt so badly about it. I've been so afraid to look behind me. Afraid she's chasing me. I'll never do anything like that again, in my whole life. I just want to be back to my old self. To Sue, but without that name. But be here, in Florida, with Huntz. I've grown used to Misty, especially the way Huntz says it. But please, don't tell him. Not until I've decided what to do. All I know is the sooner I get this thing settled the better I'm going to feel."

"Okay. Your secret's safe with me. If you need some money I can help a bit. I have eight dollars in my 'extra' envelope."

"No, Annie, no! But you're so sweet to offer."

They'd each found a friend.

Misty finished Annie's hair styling and told her to look at herself. When she did there was silence. Then it was Annie's turn to cry. She gasped, then her hands flew up to her cheeks and her eyes started to water. Silent tears.

"Oh! Annie, I'm sorry. You don't like it!" Misty felt terrible to have upset the old lady like this. "I can try to change it. Just let me start again. I can't make it longer, of course, but maybe I could part it differently...."

"No! Don't change anything. I can't get over it! I.....I......I'm pretty!" Annie's hands were touching the wisps of hair around her eyes, then patting the bounce of curls at the nape of her neck. "It's so soft! How did you do that?"

"Though it doesn't look it, it's much shorter. I thinned it out too, quite a bit, Annie. And layered it. That makes it nice and soft and springy. With your curl all you'll need to do is towel dry it, then style it with your fingers."

"How do you mean?"

"Well, like this." Misty demonstrated by moving the tresses this way and that with her hands. "But you must use a conditioner after you shampoo. There must be one here I can give you. Yes, this one will do fine." She thrust a bottle from the shelves into Annie's hands who held it as if it were some award, with both hands. Her tears had stopped and a grin of happiness shone back at her.

"You are good at what you do. Just like Huntz." Annie could not have paid her a better compliment, thought Misty. At that moment she felt as if she hadn't a care in the world.

"Thank you, Annie." She patted the old lady's shoulder before whipping off the plastic apron. "Let's doll up Little Bertie too, shall we?"

"Oh! Really? Can you do that too, Misty?"

"Of course I can. Let's give him a shampoo first, shall we?" The women had fun placing the little dog into one of the sinks. Annie saw how gently Misty handled her little fellow and that sealed her gratitude forever. Misty sterilized some scissors, then snipped away at the little dog's facial hair first. His eyes popped out as the shaping took place.

"Gosh! Look at how handsome he is!" blurted Annie.

"Yes, he's adorable. I'll take a little off his body and his little legs. You'll be able to keep him cleaner this way, too." The dog liked all the attention he was getting. He took turns licking the hands of one woman and then those of the other. "Shall we put a little bow in his hair, Annie? About here?"

"Oh, yes!"

Misty checked through the drawers. The third one held a variety of bobby pins, and hair clips. "Here's one with a little plaid bow. Do you like that one, Annie?"

"Oh, yes. Isn't he sweet?" Little Bertie seemed to be looking at himself in the mirror, he was sitting so still. Misty had no trouble fastening the clip between his perky ears.

"Now, shall we go show Gus?" Misty took a few moments to take one last look at the place, then closed the door and locked it.

"Won't he be surprised!" Annie went down the stairs faster than she'd gone up them, so much so that Misty had trouble keeping up with her. Little Bertie seemed to have an extra dose of energy too.

Misty wasn't there to see Gus' first reaction but what she saw was enough. He was bowing from the waist and saying to Annie, "I'm not sure I know your name, ma'am. Do you come here often?"

Annie was laughing and exclaiming, "Gus, it's me! Annie! Misty did my hair. Do you like it?"

"I can't get over the change in you, Annie. You look....look different, for sure. What a change. Annie! You're beautiful!" The woman didn't take offense. She just kept smiling.

"Look at Little Bertie, Gus!"

"Little Bertie? Look at the little guy! Ain't he a handsome fellow?" At that point Huntz entered the motel office. He said a quick hello to Gus and nodded his head to Annie, then put his arm around Misty's waist saying, "Hi, love. Have you had a nice day?"

"Look, Annie! Huntz didn't recognize you either!" laughed Misty. "Or Little Bertie!"

Annie glowed. "Hi, Huntz."

Huntz was confused. He looked at Annie, then Misty, then did a double take. "Annie? Annie! You're looking darn pretty today."

"It's all because of Misty," said Annie, grabbing her new friend's hand.

"Misty? What do you mean?"

"Misty's going to open up a beauty parlor. I'm going to clean it for her. She's going to do my hair once a week. I'll always look like this!" Annie's words came spilling out.

"Misty's opening a beauty parlor?" asked Huntz.

"You liked the place, eh?" asked Gus, holding his hand out for the key.

"Maybe. I don't know," said Misty, not ready to relinquish the keychain.

"If you can work your magic like this, I'd say it's all yours," said Gus. Misty laughed and tossed him the circlet. He caught it with his index finger.

"I'm just thinking about it, I tell you," repeated Misty. "But, if what you're saying is true, if I decide to do this, it'll be all right with you Gus if I open it up?"

"Sure thing."

"I'd pay rent and utilities and stuff, of course."

"We can work all that out later. Listen, going by Huntz's expression I think it might be wise if you and he go and have a talk. You can explain things. There's no rush. That salon isn't going to walk away, is it?"

"No, you're right. I do need to talk to Huntz," said Misty. She and Annie exchanged glances. Annie winked. Misty smiled weakly. "I'm glad you like your hair, Annie." She leaned down to Little Bertie, who licked her hand. "You too, sweetie pie!"

CHAPTER THIRTY

Behind every beautiful thing, there's some kind of pain.

Bob Dylan

Now that someone knew her secret Misty felt better. She thought she'd be mortified if anyone knew what she had done. The last few weeks had been torture, she had to admit, in spite of being so wrapped up in this man. It was wonderful to have told someone and not have the earth open up and swallow her. Maybe she could tell Huntz? She knew she should. It certainly wasn't fair that Annie should know and not him. Besides, it was too big a secret for Annie to have to keep, if she could. She'd likely blurt it out to Gus or, even worse, Huntz. Misty knew she had decided to tell him. But how? When? What would he do? Say?

Back in their room Huntz was barely inside the door before he started speaking. "Honey, you did that to Annie? I bet she's in seventh heaven. What a change! I didn't know you could do hair. And what's all this about opening a beauty parlor? Where? Gus seemed to know all about it."

"One thing at a time, Huntz. I'm a beauty specialist. That was how I make my living. I thought I told you."

"I thought you were a masseur. I know you give damn good massages."

"I do all that, and style hair and do body art. I'm a trained artist."

"Misty, don't I know you're good at all kinds of things?" laughed Huntz.

"Get serious, please. You see, I worked in a beauty salon when I met you."

"Okay, I'm with you. I'm listening..."

"I was thinking I should get a job, earn some money to pay my way..."

"You don't need to worry about that..." interrupted Huntz, moving toward her, his arms out.

"Yes. Yes, I do. Let me finish, Huntz." Misty stepped back and managed to put the bed between them.

"Okay, okay, I'm listening." Huntz plopped on the bed and lay there, his arms behind his head. He gave her his full attention, eyes wide open.

"So I went into Gus's office and looked at the classifieds and Gus got to talking to me about what kind of a job I was interested in and I told him and it turns out there's a salon above the motel office. It's even got all the equipment."

"Really? You certainly sound all excited. Slow down, and tell me all about it."

"I am excited. Can you believe it? Turns out Annie used to do the cleaning. Gus gave me the key and got Annie to show me around. We decided to do her hair while we were up there. Did you really like it?"

"Honey, she looks.....glowing, Misty. I've never see her so happy, and that's magic, for sure. You did a damn fine job. You're good for sure! So, you're going to hang around here then." He sat up straighter and pushed a pillow behind his back. He patted the space beside him.

Misty sat down primly, her feet planted on the floor. She didn't want to be distracted.

"Well, Huntz, that's what we need to talk about. Is your job lasting much longer?"

"At least a couple of months. After that, there'll likely be another. I think it's a good idea, Misty. A beauty parlor for you. This is a good base for me. It'll give you something to do while I'm off working. If that's what you want to do."

"Well, I do, but....." Should she tell him why she really needed the job?

"There's more?"

"Yes." Now or never. "You're not going to be happy. You might not like this part, Huntz." He searched her face for a clue. With his full gaze on her she blurted, "I need the money."

"No, honey, I've got enough for the both of us." He tried to pull her closer.

Misty stood up. "Huntz, I need the money. I have to pay back a debt."

"You owe someone money? Much?" They were more alike than she knew, he thought. Both working to pay off a debt. How bad was that?

"Depends what you mean by much. And yes, I owe someone money. Money I took to get down here."

"Oh. A loan. Well, I can understand that. Why wouldn't I like that?" He leaned back and stretched his arms above his head again. His shoulders loosened.

"Not a loan, Huntz. I took the money." Misty couldn't look at him now. She stared at her feet.

"Took it?" She could hear the bed squeak as Huntz sat up.

"Stole it." The words were out. She glanced at him. His eyes registered nothing. "Stole the money, Huntz. From the lady who owned the beauty parlor. I just pocketed every cent she had on the premises and walked out."

He said nothing. His feet were on the floor now too.

Misty wished she could turn back the clock. "I knew it. You hate me. But believe this, if nothing else, I've never done a thing like this in my life before."

"How much?" Two words only.

"Four hundred and eighty-five dollars."

"Misty! You had me imagining thousands! Is that what you've been having nightmares about?"

"Yes. But it's theft, even if it's not thousands!"

"Oh, I know. But look at how much simpler the solution is. We can raise that. It's not that much to find."

"Well, I do have some left, Huntz."

"You do? How much?"

Misty went to her clutch purse and got out the remains of the money. She had to count it three times because it was all in low denominations, twos and fives and ones with a couple of tens, and she kept getting a different total. As she did it, Huntz was doing his own tallying. This was no hardened thief – if she was worrying about a matter of taking a few hundreds. Going by her sleeplessness she was having real trouble with her conscience.

"I have, if I've counted it right, one hundred and twelve dollars left. Now, I told Annie I'd like to send it back somehow...."

"Annie knows?"

"While I was doing her hair we got to talking. You know how it is." She was madly chewing the inside of her lip.

"Okay, okay, I was just a little surprised you told her, that's all." Huntz was leaning on the back of the one soft chair in the room.

"What's the best way to send it back? Not through the mail, surely?"

"No, that's no good. Do you know her bank and her account number? You could just have it deposited."

"That simple?"

"Yup. Here, I'm going to write you a check for the whole amount..." He moved over to the table on his side of the bed.

"No, Huntz! You can't!"

"Why not?"

She was a loss for words. "Because...."

"You can pay it back to me, when you get the salon going."

"I could? You're right, I could. You're okay with me doing that? You're sure?"

"Yup."

"Do you hate me for what I did? Huntz, I'm never going to do anything like that again, in my whole life. It's just been awful!"

"So, why did you in the first place?" He was sitting on his side of the bed now.

"I met you. And I wanted to come south with you. And I had no money. I guess. I think I just went mad for a bit."

"Mad to come to Florida?"

She stood there, afraid to smile. All she knew is she never felt so good. "For you, Huntz. I went mad for you. But I was incredibly stupid."

"As my mom used to say – everything happens for a reason."

"I think I should give Marjorie a call and confess, shouldn't I? Tell her I want to give the money back?"

"With interest. Tell her you're going to give her the current interest rate. You can work that out. She'll have no reason to complain then." He was lying down now, relaxed once more.

"Guess I better learn to handle cash better if I'm going to open my own place, eh?" Misty sat down, propping pillows behind her back and turned so she could see Huntz's face.

He was grinning. "Yeah, Misty. You'll have to watch who you hire." Misty looked askance at him but Huntz was teasing her, going by the way he threw the pillows onto the floor before stretching out full length beside her before wrapping his arms around her.

"Huntz....I will pay you every cent..."

"I know, sweetie....." He started to sing in her ear.

CHAPTER THIRTY-ONE

Silent gratitude isn't much to anyone.

Gertrude Stein

Fred Henderson had spent hours pouring over his notes, trying to find how he could carry through on his promise to help Harry Somer keep his annuity. The old woman had had a history of batty behavior. Not good. Granted, most of it was witnessed only by what they call 'an interested party'. How to discredit the words of that Bruce Forrest? Any gift given during a time of dementia had to be questioned. As a lawyer, he would query it himself. Coupled with the fact that the woman herself had thought she was going nuts, not once but twice. That was well documented. Her doctor stepped in to bring her back from the brink of senility, two times, it seemed. Granted, the physician said it was more her imagination than any actual deterioration of brain cells. That would help Harry's case, especially when the nurse Eileen Grover seconded the doctor's opinion. Asserting that no such incidents as Esmerelda Graham had first reported had ever happened when she was in the house, she maintained the old woman's poor state of mind could be attributed to, of all things, nervousness and a poor diet. Talk about practical nursing. In fact, she said the woman's thought processes were better than her own at times. Listening to the news and discussing current events were part of the old lady's daily routine. Her favorite game was chess, but the old woman had resigned herself to playing checkers with Grover each evening. She also used the computer daily. Amazing for someone in her seventies.

Still, her confusion was a matter of record. Bruce Forrest had lots of stories to recount. Esmerelda too had reported some of the same to her doctor. Her confusion. Her memory lapses. The minor accidents. Leading up to the last fatal one? That didn't bode well for Harry Somer's chances to keep his annuity. Granted, he liked having the money, but he also said Esmerelda Graham had wanted to know she'd changed someone's life for the better. She told Harry it had been a long time since she'd accomplished something noteworthy. Anyone would suspect Harry's motives, of course. The woman appeared to have had a real soft spot for the man. Henderson wondered why? Was there another motive? Imagine having a regular, guaranteed income for life! Fred would like that himself. However, after listening to his client he came to believe in the man. It was his job to ensure that Harry keep his gallery and continue painting, but was it possible?

Bruce Forrest was claiming undue influence, attacking Harry and his motives. As a lawyer, Henderson's job was to show Esmerelda Graham had insisted Harry take the money, proving the man hadn't wheedled it out of the matron. A sizable amount of money. To set up a yearly stipend of $30,000 required more than a million dollars. No wonder Forrest was questioning it. A bit of a chunk out of the Graham fortune. The lawyer pulled out a yellow legal pad and started to make notes. It was imperative to prove competency. Get others' opinions. Harry said there was an art group she used to participate in, even did some painting of her own. What would their opinion be of the lady? Had she made some wise purchases at that time, any sculptures or paintings? That would prove mental acuity. Contact the insurance agent who set up the annuity and ask him his opinion. That party could also help him with the time frame and the chain of events. According to Somer she'd got the paperwork going while he was still balking at the idea. Timing was important.

Also, did the woman set up the annuity simply because she liked the man and his artwork? That would be a bit tricky, may even provide Forrest with proof that Harry had sweet-talked her into it. If they could prove it was in payment for a service, Somer would stand in a better position. An exchange, one service for another perhaps? It would show the woman had a reason for her generosity. Henderson realized at the same time that it would have to be something pretty important for a million dollar bestowment. Just cause would eliminate undue influence. What service could the artist have provided an old lady? He'd better have another talk with his client.

He'd need the dates of the physiotherapy when Harry had lived in the mansion giving her treatment and did Harry have any document from the woman explaining her motives? He sensed Harry was holding something back. But what? And now things were going to be much more tricky to prove. The woman was dead and she couldn't even speak on Somer's behalf. Terrible thing, that. Broken neck from a fall down the stairs. They didn't find her body until the handyman arrived three days later to get his payment for clearing the snow from the driveway. He couldn't understand why no one answered, knowing she couldn't get out on her own.

Since her death Forrest was pushing things, wanting everything settled as fast as possible. Did he have a personal vendetta against Somer, wanting to settle some score? To be fair, Forrest was the closest relative, though it was a tenuous connection, and Harry wasn't even related, for God's sake. What hope had he?

CHAPTER THIRTY-TWO

Turn your wounds into wisdom.

Oprah Winfrey

"Yeah, I was hired. You know I'm an investigator," Gus was explaining his business to Harry. "I do insurance jobs and government cases when they need someone local who they can trust. But I also work for private individuals. The daughter of one of the widows hired me. She was livid at what her mother had done – signed over an insurance policy to this guy so he could borrow on it."

"My friend, Esmy – that's Esmeralda Graham – fell for his line too. This Bruce insinuated himself into her life. Sounds like he has a real way with words, or something. I don't think he faked illness or anything like that. This was a different kind of scam. He's actually related to her and that certainly helped, I guess, but it didn't take long before she'd regretted it. She knew something wasn't right about that guy. She hated Bruce's guts, I'm pretty sure. She made sure he was in her will, but just enough to prevent his contesting it when she died. From what you say he got tired of waiting to inherit from her and started his own retirement investment program, hauling in other women's money. He seems to like to concentrate on widows." Harry couldn't talk fast enough. "Listen, can I hire you to do something for me? For Esmy? Contact my lawyer? Tell him what you know about Bruce? It's just what we need to stop the man in his tracks. The guy's trying to inherit all of Esmy's money, even what she set aside for me. He's been claiming undue influence on my part. Can you believe it? Esmy would hate that, I know."

"Well, it looks like the table's turning on him. It's likely he's the one who used all sorts of influence, plus a lot of lies, to get himself into her will."

"Bruce milked the family relationship for all it was worth. A couple of incidents even made me start worrying he wouldn't balk at hurrying his inheritance along. I believe her doctor felt so too. Bruce Forrest must be his real name. He'd have to make sure the will was legal. But I know something he doesn't. It may just mean he won't get a cent."

"What do you mean?" asked Gus.

"Esmy had family, in fact, family she'd just discovered. Kin a lot closer than Bruce made himself out to be, that's for sure. Time for his comeuppance, I think. He's going to get the surprise of his life."

"More than one surprise, from the sound of it. I'll certainly be able to help with that."

"Gus, I'm hiring you. I have a key to a safe deposit box with some papers....." Harry told Gus the whole story. The man took down some notes, nodded, then poured Harry another coffee. This time he added a dollop of the mahogany liquor to each of their mugs.

"Don't see any problem with that. I'll take care of everything. I'll do my best to make sure this Bruce Forrest won't get a penny. You don't need to pay me either. You're helping me tie up my case, after all. Cheers, Harry."

"Maybe we'll go fishing tomorrow? It might help me deal with all this. I feel so bloody terrible."

"You staying for a bit, Harry?"

"Yeah. I'd like to paint that bit of shoreline across the road. Do what Esmy sent me down here for…."

"You paint? You know what I'd like, Harry? A nice mural in this here office. Something in keeping with the place. With pelicans. And Uncle Rod's boat tied up, looking out to sea? You know what I mean? With my uncle fishing? I have a picture of him. Live here rent free while you do it, why don't you?" Maybe Misty could pose for Harry, he thought, sunning herself on the seashore. That would be a nice touch.

"Don't see any problem with that, Gus. A good deal, for sure. Besides, it'll put another car in the parking lot, eh?" Gus smiled. Harry stopped talking to listen to the patter of Gus's fingers, tapping out a soft shoe rhythm, but this time he wasn't hypnotized by the beat. He was thinking of Esmerelda and how she'd be counting on him. He would do his best by her, especially now. He should have been there when she needed him. Damn it, he was crying again.

CHAPTER THIRTY-THREE

There is a saying in Tibetan, *"Tragedy should be utilized as a source of strength."*

Henderson was relieved to get the call from Gus. Harry's annuity would be secured now, especially with Bruce Forrest being hauled in for fraud and extortion. That had encouraged another look at Esmy's death because a second fall down the stairs was just too much of a coincidence. The investigation would be closed fairly quickly because of the lack of suspects other than the obvious – Forrest. As far as his own case went, Henderson could prove Harry hadn't exerted undue influence. Jenny had departed for parts unknown, after signing an affidavit outlining Bruce's plans for Esmerelda. In fact, it was she who first pointed the finger at Esmy's death not likely being a misadventure.

It turned out Harry had done a service, an exceptional one, in fact, restoring Esmy's son to her. A real shame the old lady had never got to meet the man face to face. Forrest had a lot to answer for in making the old woman think she was going crazy. A rotten situation, through and through. Maybe evil ran in that branch of the family? Forrest's grandmother, Esmerelda's sister Susan, had talked their father into turning young Esmy into a figure of shame. There was very little compassion on that side of the family. No wonder there had been such a rift all those years. You can't make a silk purse out of a sow's ear.

Henderson couldn't help wondering how things could have turned out. What if Esmy had kept her baby, not been railroaded by her family into giving the infant boy up for adoption? He knew Harry, his client, was having real trouble knowing he hadn't been there when Esmy needed him. To think Bruce had come back to stalk her, had in fact murdered her, was something he was going to have to live with the rest of his life. Harry told Henderson he was certainly going to do his best to make her gallery into a success. He was changing its name to *Esmy's Inspiration*. Her son was coming down for the grand opening and bringing some of his family. He'd inherited the good genes in the family, not those of Bruce and Susan. He also had donated several paintings from Esmy's art collection to Harry's gallery to be on permanent loan. He said that way the spirit of his mother would remain alive. Harry said he'd even had a dream about it with Esmy's collection right alongside his own work. Teddy had kept two for his own home, those of a mother and child, a favorite theme of Esmy. He was keeping one in trust for his daughter Carrie and hanging the other in the front hall.

Harry said he took solace from all this, but still deeply regretted he'd stopped that night at the Pelican Motel, that he hadn't traveled a day earlier, that he hadn't rushed through and got north. Fred Henderson tried to reassure him that he wouldn't have been in time. Forrest was determined. If not then, there'd likely have been an attempt later on. Still, Harry continued to berate himself. This time, though, it was Henderson who held the trump card. A letter for Harry from Esmy.

Hello Harry,

I'm a coward. I called you twice to ask your advice and then backed away both times. Instead I decided to write this letter, likely a better way. Putting my thoughts together isn't as easy as it was, certainly not on the phone. Writing them down might prove to be easier.

I am alone because the nurse Dr. Emery hired has fallen and broken her leg. Imagine that! Do you think it mean of me to say that gives me some pleasure? Eileen is a nice lady and I wish her no harm but I am so enjoying having my home back to myself. I've been doing all those things I enjoyed – birdwatching, reading a book while I dine, painting, and I'm back to my daily meditation too. It feels like the old days. I haven't felt such peace and joy since you were here.

Finding my son Teddy was a miracle, plain and simple, and it wouldn't have happened without you. It certainly shows good can come from bad. My fall down the stairs meant you came into my life. I can never thank you enough for all you've done for me.

I haven't met Teddy, yet I feel I already know him, Harry. Our communications have been amazing. Is it smug of me to say he thinks like me? Even his word choice mirrors mine. We have the same wry sense of humor. The best thing is he holds no rancor, Harry. He's taught me to forgive. Though we haven't met I've come to know my son through the wonder of modern day communications. Would it be silly of me to add that meeting in person just might be a disappointment for both of us? Right now I can imagine him as a little boy. When he tells me stories of his teen years I picture him… may I say, I picture him as a younger you? Why should he see me old and decrepit when he'll be able to watch those movies I gave you and see a vibrant, happy woman in her prime? My pride is still intact, you see. Is a get-together that important? It bears thinking about, I know, but Teddy isn't clamoring to meet either, though his youngest child Carrie feels differently.

I gave something away in that last paragraph, Harry. Our relationship, at first patient and caregiver, transformed itself, didn't it? But I don't think you know how much. From the time we started visiting galleries I began thinking of you as more than a friend. To be honest, you became my surrogate son in my mind. You could be, you know. You're about the same age and racial background. At times, I even pretended you were my long lost son. You have the same beautiful mouth that Teddy's father had. In my mind, this past year I gained two sons. My only wish is that perhaps you and Teddy shall meet one day.

Your gallery is something I think of often. I can see you, surrounded by your work, with clients dropping in to see what you've been up to lately. I hope you flourish and you gain as much peace and joy as I feel right now. I could not be happier. One day I hope Teddy and his family get to meet you. With sincere love and hope for a promising future for you,

Esmy

CHAPTER THIRTY-FOUR

The essence of all beautiful art is gratitude.

Friedrich Nietzche

"Is that your old boss?" whispered Annie.

"Yes! Can you believe it? She's actually here!" said Misty. "Huntz helped me arrange to pay her back by depositing money in her account. I already knew the numbers from when I worked for her. But he insisted I call and tell her first, though. And guess what, Annie!"

"What?"

"She wasn't that mad at me. She'd figured out I'd taken her money. She said it was not that much, that she'd been planning to give me a bonus sometime soon."

"A bonus? Five hundred dollars?" Annie's eyes widened.

"Well, not that much, of course. But when she heard me apologizing and crying on the phone she said she decided to forgive and forget. Especially when she was getting all her money back — with interest!"

"So she came down to get it?"

"No! She said she thought the money was long gone. It was like a windfall when I called and told her I'd already deposited it into her bank account. So she used it to make the trip down here. Thought it might make a nice break. And I said I really wanted her to meet Huntz. And apologize in person. I can't tell you how much better I feel, Annie."

Her old boss Marjorie was standing beside Huntz as they looked at Harry's mural of the Pelican Motel. Marjorie had spotted a figure, a pretty girl in a bikini, sitting on the shore watching the sunrise. She pointed it out and raised her eyebrows at the man.

"Yup, that's Misty. Oh! I mean Sue...."

"That's okay. Call her Misty. She's explained all that. In fact, the name suits her."

"She was thrilled to see herself in a painting. Harry's caught the way she holds her head, tilted like that."

"It's beautiful. I see it's sold."

"It's going to go up in the foyer of the motel after all the renovations are done. Gus commissioned it."

Harry couldn't help but join the two as they looked at the painting. He finally had managed to capture all the colors to his satisfaction. The pelicans were there just like that first morning he'd spent at the Pelican Motel, the day he'd drawn lines in the sand, trying to make a decision.

"Hi, Harry!" Gus patted him on the back. "Beautiful, that," he said as he gestured to the work. "You've caught the...the..... feeling that......"

"Something good's going to happen?" finished Marjorie.

"Yes! That's it. The dawn of a new day. It's perfect for The Pelican Motel's renewal."

Harry knew they were right. "I think that's what I'll call it. *Dawn of a New Day*. It may be a cliche, but it rings true for me."

"For Misty, for sure," said Marjorie.

"All of us, it seems," said Huntz.

The opening of Harry's gallery was going well. Teddy, his wife and his daughter Carrie had flown in for the first night. Harry had found that meeting bittersweet. He wished Esmy had been there. But she was, said Teddy, Esmy's son, in her work, which was part of the gallery's collection. Even more so when Harry told him he had a whole collection of movies and albums that Esmy wanted shared with the man's family. The granddaughter, Carrie, had a million questions and Harry braved his way through the young woman's interrogation. She had Esmy's eyes, Harry saw, and her spirit. When the girl went off to talk to others – she wasn't the least bit shy – Teddy told Harry more about the police's case against Bruce up north. It was ironclad, all because of the piece of gold leaf on Esmy's throat. It held the perfect thumbprint, the final nail in Bruce's conviction. Harry tried not to picture Esmy splayed out at the bottom of the cellar stairs. Teddy noticed his discomfiture. "I feel badly too. I should have insisted on a meeting."

"But Esmy wanted to arrange it in her own time," said Harry.

"Well, she thought she was losing her mind. Ironic, that. She knew I was a doctor. I could have helped her."

"But she didn't want you to remember her that way."

"I can understand, I guess. What we have to do now is make sure her wishes are carried out. Keep this gallery going and make it a success." He hesitated. "The lawyer said you had some final details that Esmerelda wanted you to tell us yourself."

"I have to hand over her films and stuff but, most of all, have a good talk with you about who Esmy really was. Not the soul who'd been terrorized by Bruce Forrest. I have a surprise for you too."

"I'm sure you have many. You have a lot to tell me about Esmerelda Graham."

"Including she's the matriarch of the Graham fortune."

"The Graham fortune?" Teddy frowned. "You don't mean... she wasn't one of those Grahams? The cookie people?"

"Yes, she was. She wanted you to know after she was gone."

"I already held her in awe. Oh, my goodness. Maybe we could set up a foundation for the arts. Something like that? Do you think she'd approve?"

Harry thought that was appropriate. "That's a good idea. She was a talented artist too, though she came to it late in life. Come here. I want to show you one picture I love." The two men moved to take in some more of the show. Misty and Annie were looking at the pictures too. They were dressed in new outfits, bought with their money from working in the salon, which had turned out to be a success. Truckers had heard of Misty's massages and learned too that she wasn't one to take liberties with. She'd decided early to not brook any advances. She was also giving hairstyling specials to customers who stayed at the motel for more than one night.

Huntz had finally paid off the debt on his mother's home. He was planning now to save a bit to bring her down for a Florida vacation, right here at the Pelican Motel. Maybe have Misty do her hair. Gus's solving of the Bruce Forrest case meant he was able to go ahead and spruce up the motel, plus he had work continually arriving from municipal and state authorities for investigation.

Harry was showing Standing Bather to Teddy. "The first conversation I had with Esmy was about that drawing."

"It's beautiful," said Teddy.

"I think from that moment we knew we'd each found a friend, though I was there to do physical therapy. It was the beginning of so much more than client and therapist."

"Well, from what your lawyer told me, that was certainly true. She wouldn't have even discovered me if it hadn't been for you."

"Instead of having this drawing as part of the permanent collection I'd like to buy it from the estate and hang it in my apartment. I hope you agree."

"Harry, Esmy was one step ahead of you. Take it down. Look at the back."

For Harry- We made a bet and you won, thank goodness!
Love, Esmy.

"Oh, she remembered! This is really something!" Harry grinned. He could see Esmy standing in her foyer saying, "I bet you that picture that you'll give up in defeat." He was glad he hadn't. Harry gripped Teddy's hands with his own until Carrie threw her arms around both men.

"Can I call you Uncle Harry? It seems friendlier, more like family."

"I think you should, Carrie," said her Dad. "Okay, Harry?"

Harry glanced at Esmy's picture, then nodded. "I'd love that."

THE END

DON'T CRY OVER SPILLED WATER

Puddles followed Dixie like water off a duck's back. The Aquatic Nature Centre paid her to feed the creatures and check the salinity and temperature of the water in the aquariums. She did it with little enthusiasm and much spillage. It was just a job, one of three, because Dixie had yet to decide what she was going to be when she grew up. Would that happen before her thirtieth birthday next month? Not likely. She also delivered mail – that bored her to tears too – and waitressed, which was more to her liking because she could chat up the customers, a captive audience, very different from home where her daughters paid her little attention. They had nothing to learn from her. The younger was already in therapy, though the doctor had determined early on it was the mother who needed treatment. Her girls took the lead from their father. In the beginning he'd been trapped by Dixie's feminine charm, but soon found it went no deeper than her make-up. His silly and selfish wife was as shallow as the puddles she left lying around at the Centre. Dixie had three jobs, not to make ends meet, but to get out of the house. She made sure she paced herself, doing the bare minimum, so she'd have energy left for nightly Bingo.

Tasks at the Centre took her a long time. Was this on purpose? Maybe so. She was smart enough to know if she finished her assignments they'd give her something else to do. She was an animal care worker, after all. Not a very good one, if truth be told. She had difficulty sorting things out, deciding what to do when, and with what. As a result, like Hansel and Gretel, Dixie's slapdash approach left a tangled trail of hoses, puddles of water and pools of pellets, much of which she ignored.

Her superior at the Centre, and a bit of a witch, Emilee Campry, couldn't control Dixie. Any reprimand went right over the long, wispy hair of the animal care worker. Campry gave up and assigned the clean-up tasks to the Centre's volunteers. Like Dixie, Campry wasn't big on co-operation either, plus she had a perverse talent for delegating her responsibilities. This didn't sit well with the volunteers but Campry didn't care. She had problems of her own, the main one being that she was in a job beyond her abilities – barely treading water, in fact – reflected by the grim set to her mouth and a penchant for clock-watching. Today she had decided to leave early as her manager wasn't on site. Campry didn't have time for another of Dixie's messes.

"Clean up that big puddle outside the aquarium room, Isabel," she told the senior citizen running the gift shop. Campry had poor people management skills too. "You'll find the mop and bucket in the janitor's closet."

The volunteer was selling nature books to tourists who'd just finished their tour of the Centre. "Pardon?"

"There's a mess in there by the big aquarium. Take care of it."

"I'm supposed to stay here. You know that." Isabel bagged the purchases, gave a pleasant farewell to her customers, then turned to face Campry. "Who left the mess? Perhaps she should see to it?" Campry grimaced. Was the woman mocking her authority? "Why don't *you* clean it up?" suggested Isabel.

It's not part of my job description, thought Campry. I'm management. "Just do it," she said.

"No." Plain and to the point, a strategy the volunteers had recently arranged among themselves. The phone rang. Isabel picked it up and turned her back to Campry. Instances of hostility like this weren't rare, but this was the first time Campry saw it for what it was, a mutiny. Disconcerted, she steered herself toward the exhibit room where Dixie was brushing her long hair- one of the few things she took pride in- before weaving it into a braid. Long hair keeps you looking young, she believed, and hadn't had a haircut in years. She'd just spent half an hour posting a sign – 'Exhibit Temporarily Clozed' – on the biggest aquarium, the size of a double horse trailer, set into one wall. Such postings were a common occurrence. As yet, no one had attributed it to the less than perfect care the animals received..

"What happened?" asked Campry, pointing to the sign. Her mouth tightened into an even thinner line as she noticed the spelling. No time to make a new one.

"Two more fish dead. And another one looks injured," muttered Dixie, intent on her hairdressing.

"Did you take them out?"

"No." Dixie hoped she wouldn't be given the job. "I don't like that rickety ladder," she said, snapping an elastic onto the end of her braid. An ancient stepladder leaned against the aquarium inside the tank room, invisible to the public gallery outside.

"Yes. Those fish have to be removed. Come along." The two women turned the corner of the aquarium, skirting the pool of water that no one would clean up. They entered the room behind the display. More water on the floor here too.

"This must be dried up," said Campry.

"I don't have time," countered Dixie.

"Nor do I!" said Campry. Neither would do it. Not their job. Campry walked as if on eggshells around the largest pool of water to get to the platform that stood high above the floor. This scaffolding was almost flush with the top of the tank. Standing on it always made Campry giddy. She grabbed a net and gingerly mounted the ladder. Up on the platform she glanced at the deep water and shivered. Then she turned to Dixie. "Well?"

"Can't you do it yourself?" asked Dixie, busily checking the length of her braid. Almost to her hips. She let go of the plait and fluffed up her bangs while Campry scooped the two dead fish out of the tank and placed them on the platform. The injured one eluded her.

"You'll have to come up. If the two of us have nets, we might be able to get this sick one," instructed Campry. Dixie shrugged, then started to mount the ladder. As usual her pace left much to be desired. "Hurry up, Dixie. I want to get out of here," snapped Campry.

Dixie muttered, "I hate heights." She was on the fourth rung when the ladder slipped on the wet floor. Dixie scurried up the last rungs – she could move fast when she wanted to – and leaped onto the scaffold. The ladder crashed to the floor, out of reach. Too late, Campry reached out to grab it. That was when her foot slipped on the dead fish on the scaffold, sending her body into a fatal spin. She was catapulted into the tank, definitely in over her head. Campry had never learned how to tread water and thrashed about in panic. The tidal wave hit Dixie. Sputtering, she used her braid to dry her eyes, then stared at the raging water. A hand shot up searching for a grasp of something – anything – and it found Dixie's hank of hair. Another hand surfaced to grip the braid too, followed by a desperate tug on the lifeline. It was enough to flip Dixie into the tank. If the women were accustomed to co-operating they might have saved themselves. Unfortunately, it was each to her own with no one the winner.

Isabel was glad Campry hadn't insisted she clean up another of Dixie's messes. The volunteers' plan to stand up for themselves had worked! It wasn't as if they didn't have enough to do, she thought. Since her conversation with Campry Isabel had folded 300 flyers, addressed just as many envelopes as well as dusted all the shelves in the gift shop. She'd taken inventory too, an extra task Campry had delegated. She was tired. Time to lock up. Moving through the exhibit hall she turned off the interactive displays and said goodnight to the terrapin. As she turned the corner to the big aquarium she saw the huge puddle of water. Why hadn't Campry cleaned it up? Or Dixie? And where were they? Once in front of the aquarium she got her answer.

Her phone call to the police confused the operator. "The first thing I saw was this huge puddle. Not that unusual. There's always spilled water around here! Always!" Isabel knew she was babbling. "All over the place. Water everywhere! That girl never cleans any- thing up. And the other one lets her get away with it." Get to the point, Isabel told herself. "But there was so much more water in the tank room. Broken wood too. I couldn't get through. I couldn't get up to the aquarium. There was no way to get there. I couldn't help them. They're there! In the aquarium! Two of them. Dead! And I don't mean fish."

THE END

AU CLAIR
DE LUNE

The invitation was printed on a blue crescent and, on opening, ballooned into a silver orb:

Announcing the moonlight nuptials of
Diana, daughter of Jane and Horace Simpson
and
Geoffrey, son of Jules & Sheona Graves
on the shores of Lake Burris, Haleyville, Ontario
at midnight, the 15th of August, in the year 2009.
Reception to follow under the stars.

That was so like Diana, overblown, the goddess. It was how Rose always thought of her. She and Diana had been friends ever since Di had stuck up for her in the seventh grade. The teacher was bullying Rose about the scratches on her arm and Di had interrupted with a plausible scenario – something about volleyball and jumps and a teammate's fingernails – shutting up the woman and earning Rose's respect. It was odd how much of her friendship with Diana had been associated with blood. The crimson scratches on Rose's arm had been nasty, matted with dried blood. She'd tried to scrape off most of it but couldn't tone down the ugly welts left behind, sparking the teacher's interrogation. Diana's explanation sent the teacher marching. Diana had never asked her about the lacerations. Rose was sure Diana knew she'd just come back from a visit with her father. Most people understood about Dad and his drinking. Rose couldn't watch over him as well as her mother had. When Mom died she tried, but it was no good. After Di's spirited defense the girls became a twosome.

Diana had calmed her down again, two years later, when the streaks of blood had appeared. She'd become quite hysterical in the school washroom, scaring the other girls until one finally ran to the office to get the principal. Diana had been her salvation then too. She'd intercepted the male principal, told him everything was under control, that she'd take Rose to the nurse as soon as she calmed down. After Diana explained what was happening, she took Rose to the nurse for supplies. The two girls marched into the office and said they'd be leaving with the principal's permission. They stayed off school the rest of the day, even went to an afternoon matinee at the Palace Theatre. It was the first time Rose had ever played hooky. Diana took her out for a 'curse' party, making jokes about the gruesome details, telling her things a mother should. They even enacted a blood sisters ceremony the same evening. Diana's qualities – her loyalty, her heightened sense of self, her zest for life – were hard to resist. Such intensity.

Nothing ever was simple with Diana, including farewells. When Rose left town to pursue her vocation she found herself in the middle of a leave-taking extravaganza with telegrams, radio announcements and a 'This is Your Life' party and the promise to never, ever lose touch. They hadn't either. In different worlds, Rose hadn't been able to do much to nurture the friendship, certainly not on Di's extravagant terms. The alliance flourished anyway. Rose always received birthday wishes from Diana through cards or quick phone calls, often accompanied by a pejorative *'Don't know why you've cut yourself off from the 21ˢᵗ century with its emails and text messaging! So convenient!'* Sometimes a newspaper clipping arrived, signed with a happy face wearing a rakish cap. *Remember him? I never thought he'd become an icon of the business community.* Or *What on earth was she thinking to wear that style dress to the gallery opening?* Rose tried to reciprocate most of the time but she wasn't much good at that side of things. It didn't seem to bother her friend, even though Diana's philosophy was absolute: If it's worth doing, it's worth doing well. No doubt, this wedding would be something to see.

She was surprised Di was actually getting married. Her friend had always been adamant about never living the 'little life', as she called marriage. Rose last saw Diana and her boyfriend a year ago. Geoff appeared to be a nice fellow, but somewhat mundane, certainly compared to Diana. During the evening he was a minor satellite of her friend, seemingly content to be eclipsed by her. They'd come to the city for a theatre event and were on their way to a follow-up party. Diana was obviously at the helm, directing the evening, surprising everyone with her inclusion of Rose, an unlikely addition to the party, even though she was a co-host for the charitable function. Di had always been an organizer, never afraid of repercussions. She cruised through life like a jet skier, unconcerned about the effect of her wake. Diana, the huntress. Some people called her wild and would have been right. Di always liked to test the boundaries, often ensnaring Rose just like that evening. One time it changed her life. Rose shivered and stopped musing.

She never had pictured Diana tying herself down, limiting herself. Why was she getting married? Why at midnight and why at the cottage? She trembled again, remembering Di's cousin and the cottage that summer when Rose turned 17. Danny. Diana had rescued her that time too. True to myth, Diana, a protector of unmarried girls. Rose had never gone back to the lake with Diana after that. Hadn't Diana realized? Was Lake Burris the best place for a wedding ceremony, anyway? Knowing her friend, the guest list was likely extensive, the plans sumptuous and the production elegant. How could all this be managed at a cottage? No doubt she'd find out.

The call came three days after she had received the invitation. "Rose? Di here. Gosh, it's hard to get hold of you in that place."

"Hello, Di. Best wishes!" Rose said.

"Bet you were a little aghast, eh?" Trust Diana to cut to the chase.

"Well..." Rose wasn't sure what to say.

"I know, I know. Marriage wasn't exactly in my DayTimer when we talked last. But you know how things happen. Geoff and I decided we'd make it official."

"Why? I thought..."

"Rose, you must know, it happens eventually to all of us," said Diana.

"Certainly not me!"

"Well, technically it did. Wouldn't you say?" asked Diana.

"Okay, okay. You and Geoff certainly seemed happy when I saw you that night six months ago, but you were pretty sure marriage wasn't in the books back then."

"But I'm not talking about the inevitability of wedlock, silly. What happens, Rose, is the urge to procreate. We've tried everything, but nothing's clicked. We're thinking we just might need some extra luck, I guess. Blessing of the church, you know. Family and friends wishing us their best. All that."

"At midnight?" Rose asked.

"That's the best part, Rose! There's a full moon on the 15ᵗʰ of August. The moon's association with fertility has been know for centuries."

Rose was dumbfounded. Did her friend think the blessing of the church came so easily? Fertility. Procreation. How could Diana talk to her of such things? Didn't she remember? How Rose's summer flirtation had gone horribly wrong? There'd been no period two weeks later, just before school started. She didn't need to have things explained to her that time. It was obvious what had happened. She was smarter then, but not smart enough. Diana had stepped in again, helping her out of her predicament. She had the contacts, the funds. There had been blood at the clinic, lots of it. Blood again. Why did her links with Diana always seem to be accompanied by blood? But by then Diana had flown to Europe for her 'victory year' after high school and couldn't have known what happened to Rose. Or the results, Rose's sterility.

"A lot of myths center around the full moon and fecundity. I've read all about it. Lots of cultures think the moon visits women and makes them pregnant. People in Greenland think the moon is a young man and no female may dare sleep lying on her back unless she wants to be with child." Diana had obviously researched the ways and means of conception.

"Really?" Rose paused at the picture in her mind. She suppressed a strangled giggle. She felt like crying.

"Lots of different tribes believe impregnation is a result of team-work between their earthly husbands and the heavenly spouse so the moonbeam, the real fertilizing agent, may enter!"

"Oh?" Rose knew Di was in full flight now.

"It's all documented. Even in childbirth. European women have always treated the moon as a midwife, calling it the 'Moistener' and the 'Dew Bringer'. They think it can lubricate the mother for an easy delivery." The picture became a little too clear for Rose. She could see Diana, legs splayed, bearing her child in the middle of a moon-speckled field. "The moon's phases help make a woman fertile, just like the fields and farms, fishing waters....everything!"

"Gee, and all this time I thought the stork did it." Rose laughed aloud, a little hysterically, if Diana had taken note.

"Even that myth comes from primitive beliefs about the moon, Rose." Rose's facetiousness was lost on Diana who was too involved in her lecture and, as usual, taking herself too seriously. No half mea-sures for Di. "In Africa they believe babies are delivered by the 'Moon Bird' sent to earth by the 'Great Moon Mother' who keeps watch over people from her lunar roost!" Diana certainly had done her homework. "A lot of the beliefs are visually-based, Rose." That was easy to see. Rose giggled. Di continued, "The moon's increase from a slender crescent to a full, rounded orb reflects the progression of a woman's pregnancy." That explained the wedding invitation. "A lot of people believe the moon causes menstruation. Bringing on the flow of blood, you know, just like it controls the tides."

It was as if Diana had read her friend's thoughts. "You never gave me that explanation when we were in the school washroom all those years ago," Rose said.

"You weren't ready for the occult, girl. This would have been all too mystical for you. My, how you've changed. Back then you would have been afraid to ever go to sleep again. You would probably have worried the moon would undo you." No, thought Rose. It was Di's handsome cousin who'd done that.

"Well, the moon has a lot to answer for, Di. Think of the deriva-tion of the word 'lunatic'." Rose's hand was clenching the phone.

"God, you're right! That should add a lot to the wedding cer-emony, wouldn't you say? I can hear our vows. *I'm crazy about you. You're the perfect antidote for what ails me. I'm nuts about you.*"

"What about *In sickness and in health, in sound mind or not...?*"

"Rose! Stop it." Di laughed. "Listen, the wedding is going to be a theme wedding..."

"I guessed that already."

"...centering round the moon and its effects – not insanity!"

"The invitation was quite ingenious, opening up from a crescent to a sphere." Rose wished she could open up. She'd shut down after that summer years ago.

"Thanks. I have so many more ideas like that, all focussing on the phases of the moon, its effects, moonbeams, and womanhood and... you get the idea."

"*Full Moons and Empty Arms...*" warbled Rose.

"Behave yourself!"

"Leave well enough alone?" countered Rose.

Since receiving the invitation Diana was in her thoughts daily. Much of the past, actually. The conversation with Di had been an 'open sesame' to a rush of memories. Her mind was a viewmaster, flashing uncomfortable shots, mostly of the street where Grandma lived, four houses down from Diana's childhood home.

Dad had finally let her stay at Grandma's full time the year she had her 10th birthday. Her attempts to take care of her father were failing anyway. She liked it at Grandma's. When her mother was alive it had been a fun place to visit. To live there was even better. Grandma would let her play out in the rain in her bathing suit and eat cherry popsicles before supper. She could have two desserts too. At night, in the big bed in Grandma's spare room she'd read as late as she wanted, all curled into a ball for warmth. On weekend mornings Grandma would let her sleep late and eat breakfast at noon. But even Grandma had her limits when nothing would change her mind, no matter how much Rose begged.

"Can I watch the coal fall, Grandma? Please?" The coal bin lurked in the far corner of the basement. At the best of times the space was filled with shiny, cragged balls of coal, heaped into a pile. As the weather got colder the black hill shrank, as if it too was drawing into itself for warmth. Then came the day when the coal truck arrived and the shrunken hill was a magnificent mound again. She longed to climb that hill. "Can I watch, Grandma? Can I go downstairs? Please?" Grandma would roll her eyes, then out would come the words.

"Leave well enough alone." That meant 'forget it'. So she'd run back outside and instead stare at the dirtiest man she had ever seen. She remembered thinking about the thick black band that would be left in the man's tub that night. She'd hate to have to clean that! It wasn't all fun and games at Grandma's. Sometimes late at night, long after she had finished reading she'd hear the neighbors. Their voices bounced against the walls with angry, butting grunts. When she saw them in the daytime they were nice, quiet people who always smiled at her and gave Rose their extra pennies.

"Why are they so loud," she'd ask, after padding into Grandma's room.

"Leave well enough alone." That time it meant 'stop being nosey'. Sometimes they would go into the kitchen and Grandma would stir chocolate brown powder into milk, not water like Dad used to, and heat it on the stove. While it warmed she'd prop open the stove door so the fire would warm Rose's knees as she sat hunched on the tallest chair. Grandma would pour the drink into a cup and sometimes she'd drop marshmallow bits into the steaming liquid. Rose would try to drink around them while they softened. The neighbors were Grandma's friends. Ewan wasn't that big but he helped Grandma do hard things, like carrying the coal scuttle upstairs. He and Doris made brushes, fastening stiff bristles into slots in flat metal paddles. The finished product would go into a carton that held 24 brushes. Their boxes filled fast. Ewan nudged the brushes together like pairs of shoes so they'd fit into rows. He had let Rose do a row once, but she was too slow. When the top row was done Ewan would seal the box and put it in a corner. You could see how long they had been working just by looking at that corner. Then one day the boxes would disappear. That night their voices would be loud again.

"Leave well enough alone," Grandma would say when Rose wondered why Ewan and Doris were up so late. This time it meant 'Don't ask'. They must have given Grandma one of their brushes because she used it to give Rose a spanking once. Rose had deserved it. It happened the day she met Diana, who was a dubious mentor even then. There had been no other kids around that November day. Despite how she felt about Grandma, Rose felt as if her Dad had dropped her into the middle of nowhere, like the last leaf drops to the ground and gets kicked aside. Grandma had sent her out to play and she had ended up just sitting hunched on the stoop, watching shadows. Diana had come down the street, a box tied around her neck. She looked like one of those girls at the movies, the kind with chocolate bars and packages of candied peanuts. People would give them some coins and the girls would hand out the treats. Diana had one of those boxes but instead of candy she had poppies. Rose could see black dots exploding in a red jumble.

"Hi," she said, stopping at the curb.

"Hi," Rose said.

"What're ya' doing?" Di asked. She flashed a smile and stared at Rose.

"Nothing much."

"Wanna sell poppies?"

"Don't know how."

"Just walk around the street. Up and down. People buy them."

"Guess so." Diana took her to an almost empty store. Someone there hung a box around Rose's neck, made the string tighter and sent them out the door. It was fun for Rose, who pretended she was in the movie theatre, handing out candy. She kept the sharp pins in her fingers so people would not prick themselves, then watched them put the flowers on their coats. They would put their money in the slot or give it to Rose to put in. She did, until Diana noticed.

"What're you doing?"

"Putting the money into the box."

"Why?"

"It's to help soldiers with no legs, isn't it?"

"Yeah, I guess so. But they don't need all that."

"Uh?" Rose didn't understand.

"Keep some of the coins. Put them in your pocket. After all, we're helping them just by walking around collecting this money, aren't we?" Leave well enough alone. Rose knew she should leave well enough alone and go back home, right then and there. But Di's words stirred some dark place inside her.

"Um... I've been putting all the money into the slot." Rose shouldn't have told her.

"You're kidding! Here, let's duck in here." With that she pulled her friend into an alley. Rose could smell pee and rotten meat. Or was that her? Diana pulled a nail file out of her pocket. After she unfastened herself from her box she pulled Rose's up and off her neck. The nail file in Di's left hand scratched Rose's ear and a warm trickle of blood made the girl squirm.

"Oh. Sorry." Had she done it on purpose? Blood then, too. Diana shoved all the poppies out onto a patch of sidewalk. Then she used the nail file to retrieve some of the coins. She didn't file the slot bigger. Instead, she made the money slide out, like kids riding down the slide at the playground. Coins splashed onto the stained pavement. Rose caught them before they bounced too far away. Diana turned the box over and listened, one ear to the slot.

"Sounds a little empty." She grabbed some coins from Rose's palm, not too many, and dropped them back into the coin box. She shook it again, nodded and replaced the poppies. "There," she said, filling Rose's pocket with coins. Do what works and do it well. Though her hard-nosed attitude fascinated Rose, she was still uneasy.

"Bu..b...bu...," Rose stuttered. Diana stared at her, not smiling, not even one of her usual quick, startled grins. Leave well enough alone, Rose thought. Somehow they finished the afternoon. Rose was sure everyone had X-ray vision and could see right into her pocket, but Diana's easy attitude swept her along. They went back to the store-front. The people took their boxes, admiring how few poppies they had left. Then they somehow opened the bottoms of the coin boxes and let the coins fall into big bowls to join more coins. They didn't even count what the girls had collected. That didn't make Rose feel any better. She felt worse. She left Diana at the corner.

"Maybe I'll see you tomorrow, eh?" Diana asked.

"Yeah. Maybe. Maybe not. I think I'm going home tomorrow." But Rose was never to go home again to stay for good.

"Oh," Di said. She nodded, turned around and marched off. The next day Grandma wanted to send Rose outside to play again but Rose said she felt sick. When Grandma made her a bowl of soup she ate it all up.

Grandma knew then. "Have you something to tell me?"

"I just want to stay here with you," Rose begged.

"Rose......" The whole story came spilling out, how Rose had stolen the money from the veterans. Rose knew about veterans. Her great-grandfather had died in the war. She used to look at his brass medallion hanging on the wall. It was all her grandmother had left of him. So Rose wasn't surprised when Grandma got Ewan's brush and gave her a spanking with the metal side.

"I won't do it again, Grandma, I won't!" When that didn't stop her Rose cried, "Leave well enough alone!" That worked. Her Grandma sat Rose right side up. Rose felt better after that. She knew it was no more than she deserved. That was another of her Grandma's sayings. But Rose never let her grandmother brush her hair again.

Her Grandma still had that brush when she died just before Rose's 17th summer. When Rose was cleaning out her grandmother's things that autumn, she was feeling very sorry for herself. That was when she found the brush in a dresser. She has kept it all these years. It is in a chest which also holds Rose's childhood scrapbook. Since that summer at Di's cousin's cottage, nothing has been added to the album. Rose had found something else in which to put her trust.

Rose filled out the reply card to the wedding invitation and slipped it into the mailbox, her mind filled with questions. Would this wedding be a contrived orgy with its focus on fertility? She could see the guests in flowing red robes, with maiden flower girls sprinkling seeds. Phallic fountains of champagne would likely flow. There would be cupids delivering condoms. Rose snorted and stopped her imaginings.

She hoped she was wrong, especially after she had agreed to officiate.

THE END

THE
ENEMY
WITHIN

H is head exploded in pain. Almost prone, he wasn't in the best position to fight back. Steve's fingernails gripped the plastic beneath his palms, soaked with sweat. A final convulsion froze his entire body. Legs locked, arms too, even his jaw, in a spasm of apprehension. Too much to bear. Could he take it?

It was all Marisa's fault. He'd found it hard to resist her entreaties to have another…and another…and another until the target hit home. She wasn't at all remorseful, or was he paranoid? The suffering muddled his thoughts, deepened his depression. He refused to eat, shied away from morning ablutions, feared sleep.

Why has she brought him here? Without a backward glance she'd dumped him inside the door. Had she been afraid to watch him take the last step to….his fate? Or just not interested? He could hear her wheels spinning as she took off, happy to be rid of him. Within moments he was taken over by attendants. He turned down an offer of help from the man and his partner in crime. A last vestige of bravado on his part? It worked. They were oblivious of his fear. Besides, he wanted to be in control, alert to their actions. The man started in on the torture. Everyday drudgery for him, I suppose, but not to me, Steve thought. Don't let on you're afraid. Brave it out.

The attack was continual. They zapped him with nuclear emissions. Probed orifices to find his frailties, then focused on them. Vibrations wracked his being. Did they stop for breathers? Didn't seem so. All he could hear, feel, was a continuous pressure. Were the pulsations echoes from a previous assault or a renewed offensive? He couldn't tell, sort out the sounds, their sources. His eardrums, his teeth, his eyeballs all hummed in protest. His mouth was immobilized. He couldn't complain if he tried. He was afraid to swallow. Where was his tongue? Had Marisa planned this attack on his person? What had he done to deserve it? Was she thinking about him, imagining his predicament, enjoying his pain? The torment became worse. How much pressure could he stand? They wanted to jerk something loose. What? He didn't want to know, tried to think of something else.

He couldn't find his peaceful place, his refuge from pain. He'd learned the technique from his daughter who was into yoga. You're too up tight, Dad. Learn to relax. She'd discounted her father's tale of suffering, told him he was delusional, exaggerating his concerns as always. She liked her stepmother, wouldn't consider his notion of assault. Deep breathe, Dad. Forget the conspiracy theory, so typical of your generation. Accidents happen, don't they, Dad? Steve didn't agree. There were no accidents. Marisa had some axes to grind. She was the first to admit it. A cutting tool whirred into action. Oh, God. He tried to imagine a stretch of beach. Snatches of blue sky skidded across his mind into an explosion of lightning. Soothing birdsong began, only to be blocked out by ripping metal and screeching sprockets. The palm tree in his mind refused to sway. Like him it was being rocketed about by a cyclone of sensations. They were using his jaw as a fulcrum for their torture. Surely it would break.

Suddenly he was jerked upright, acknowledged, asked a question. Dizziness and a dry mouth prevented a coherent answer, even after they removed the stuff from his mouth. He was allowed to spit out the blood -there was so much -before they jolted him back down again. Why didn't they give him longer to respond, to give them information? He wasn't as strong as he thought. He berated himself for his fear, then for being distracted by the sight of his own blood. He should have taken advantage of the moment but how could he have escaped? Rolled his eyes backward? Pretended to faint? Spat the blood at them, all over their cold, clinical presence? Masks hid their mouths and noses, making them hard to identify, if it came to that. Cunning. Maybe he should have tried to vomit. No, that would have been a mistake, surely. Even now, with time, he couldn't think of an effective strategy to stop the horror. The gag was shoved back into his mouth, his lip stretched out, used as part of the punishment, his head lowered even farther with a swift kick of the leg. Then the suction started.

It didn't stop there. Another person entered the room with a pestle. Steve closed his eyes and tried to pray. Desperation. Would a god undo this tragedy, be bothered to intervene? He heard a new sound, an unnerving ratchet of gears. Was there worse to come? Something pierced his eye duct and a gush of saliva filled his mouth, followed by a new salty taste. Oh, dear God, I'm crying. Big, silent, salty tears. Could anyone outside these four walls know his agony? Rush in to save him? Don't give up, he admonished himself. Don't succumb to the fear. Be strong. Think about something. Start counting backwards...by..sevens...100...93...the next? Too hard. He couldn't concentrate with all the noise of grinding gears, the gyration of the augur and the sucking tube. What was being sucked out of him? A bit of metal slid down his throat, tickling the lining of his esophagus. Don't cough. You'll pay for it.

The stuffing was pulled out of him. The pounding pestle stopped. His mouth now empty, they allowed him two short breaths, then thrust something back inside. Something worse, harder, bigger. There was no more room in there for what they had in mind but they persevered. He felt his jaw unlock as they pushed the device home. He wanted to scream but couldn't. He wanted to swallow, but wouldn't. Nothing more must go down his throat. A slimy substance oozed over his teeth, filling every available space. His tongue seemed to be hiding. He couldn't locate it. What a complicated way to achieve suffocation. Must be an easier method. A few seconds more and he'd be dead. He was sure of it.

With a slurping sound the object was yanked from his jaw. He felt as if he were being pulled inside out. Everything went blank. When he came to there was something smaller inside, as well as fingers and probes. What are they doing? Suddenly he was upright again, a headrest behind his neck. Relief. More so when they emptied his mouth of the foreign matter. They spun a small sink within spitting distance, let him get rid of the last vestiges of tooth and blood. They wiped his mouth….gently, as if they cared, then whipped off his bib. A new toothbrush and a mini vial of tooth floss and a bill were shoved into his trembling hands He was allowed to take his leave.

"You did well. I take it our future visits will be the same? Without needles or gas? As you see, it's not that bad. Much better, in fact," said the dentist.

That's what you think, thought Steve. He couldn't manage spoken words, sure his jaw was dislocated.

"No sore gums, no numb tongue, no painful thawing out process. Why, you can go home and enjoy a good meal."

I'll never eat again.

"Better stay away from your wife's walnut cookies, though. Too bad about that bit of shell that got mixed in by mistake. Amazing the damage it did."

THE END

VOLITION

"**S**he's like spartina. Willowy." His fingers motion suggestively over the fire. Its heat is creasing the air and smoking it up. Tourists all day, picking over his secondhand stuff like pensioners at the Goodwill. "And just as strong?"

His son nods. Rhoesta isn't one to give away her pleasures and Sonny won't pay the price. Move to Charleston? Take that job? Bad boys don't get reeled in like terrapins trapped in crab nets. Daddy's right, though. She's like the marsh plant, sinewy and supple. A survivor too, with deep roots. She knows what she wants and it isn't living on the barrier island where life's like the tides, up and down.

His father tosses him the keys. "Don't you go speeding. Cops hide out along these roads."

"No, sir." He's hellbent to finish things. Cops will be having siestas in their cars.

Rhoesta's home when he gets there. She's doing her laundry outside because it's hot and there's a breeze. Swaying to music from the porch radio, her hands dive into the tin tub to retrieve a slip, a bra, some panties. She shakes them to the beat, like castanets, then pegs each onto the line to flap with wild abandon. One last dive comes up empty. A slight pause, and then she reaches under her skirt to pull down a thong, brief and black. Into the tub. A wanton spin twirls her round to catch sight of Sonny standing there.

His eyes leave the swirling skirt to meet Rhoesta's gaze. Dog-tired with desire, Sonny smiles.

THE END

THE TIES
THAT BIND

N ot three steps inside the store I was accosted.

"Ma'am, could you move? You're in my way."

Ma'am? Me? Am I that old? Was he talking to me? What did this callow youth know? I'm not even married and I have no complaints about that either, no matter what you're thinking. I'm Mirabelle Mesley, on the good side of forty, free and female, or was until my mother's health started to decline. Like a ship moored at low tide, she's losing her equilibrium and is inclined to an off balance approach to life. We're all waiting for the next wave to hit her broadside, washing away another faculty. She's lost her hearing and much of her sight and memory. Judgement is running a close fourth, the most difficult to handle, at least for me. I'm afraid to leave her alone, even for a quick grocery run.

I'd gone to the store to get her favorite fig bars but had stopped at the front door with its community noticeboard. The gossip in me is always intrigued by these cries for help. *'Apartment for student, in exchange for household tasks.' 'Cocker spaniel free to good home. Owner died.' 'RV for sale. Cheap.'* I wasn't the only one with adjustment problems.

"Please?" Definitely an afterthought by the boy. I tore myself away from the tales of woe. Manners. I miss them. A simple thank you from my brother would help a lot. My living alone had made me the most likely candidate to move in with Mom, as my brother is burdened with two mortgages, a wife and kiddies. "You're in the way, ma'am." That's what Mom thinks too. 'Mabel, Why don't you go back home?' Mabel? That's what she calls me since the stroke. She can't manage my whole name anymore. Mirabelle's too much of a mouthful for her. 'Mabel, I'm okay. Leave me be, dear.' Funny, that's what my youngest niece calls me — Aunty Mabel. She has the same problem with syllables. How could I leave my mother be, when she forgets to turn off elements on the stove, or falls and cracks her forehead on the bathroom sink and doesn't remember how it happened? Our last trip to the hospital was more than embarrassing when the nurse and doctor both gave me the third degree. Believe it or not, I'd said, I'm not into battering grandmas.

The box boy's pimply chin was now in my face. A swollen pustule on his lip threatened to burst. I couldn't take my eyes off it, try as I might. I felt like puncturing it along with his arrogance. "I'm pushing these packages of pastries from the produce section over to the party place, you know. And you're in my way, ma'am." Voice raised, the pursing of his lips to produce all those P's took its toll. Pus oozed.

I wanted to turn away, but instead I asked, "Party place? In a grocery store?" When was the last party I attended? I couldn't remember. Hadn't hosted any either, not this past year with Mom. Who was in a party mood?

"Where they have the birthday cakes, you know?" he said with feigned patience. "You're in the way." Okay, okay. I know all about being in the way. 'What did you do with my jujubes, Mabel? Did you eat them all?' She doesn't remember eating the half-pound I bought her last weekend and who the hell is Mabel, anyway? 'This kitchen isn't big enough for the two of us, Mabel, and where's my toaster? You know how I like toast and cheese!' I put it up on the highest shelf when I caught you putting a hamburger patty into it, Mom, I almost told her. Besides, too much cheese constipates you. Wouldn't be so bad if you'd eat that bran I put out every morning. Her doctor refuses to give her a laxative, says to make sure she eats a half a cup of bran daily. I've taken to sprinkling it into soups and stews to get it into her. Then the complaints start. 'Why does this taste funny, Mabel? I never made vegetable soup that tasted this bad, Mabel. You using my recipe?' Can't she understand she needs help, must do what others say now and has to be watched, especially when she sets the couch afire lighting candles? She was spitting mad at me this morning when I threw all the candles away and filched her lighter. When she wasn't yelling she was crying. I just had to get out of the house.

Which aisle did I want? What was I after? Certainly not candles or birthday cakes. Doubted I'd ever celebrate one again, after that boy's comment. Maybe he was right. My memory definitely was going. He'd thrown me for a loop with his 'ma'am', an old lady's label. Much like Mabel. "My label's Mabel!" I wanted to yell. Ma'am? ME? The supermarket's speaker system crackled into action. "Special on moldy apples! Five pounds for the price of three!" Moldy apples? Surely not.

"What did he say?" I asked the young man just before he pushed his cart straight at me. I jumped back, spinning on one foot to miss the front wheel. I'm not as old as you think, young sir. Trouble was, my pirouette propelled my purse into a twirl too, smacking me in the elbow.

"What did who say, ma'am?" Enough with the ma'ams!

"The announcer!" I cringed. The purse's clunky clasp had hit my funny bone. Downright painful. "Didn't you hear what he said, young man? On the loudspeaker?" I gasped. Little boy would have been more accurate. Aren't all men little boys, expecting the women in their lives to take care of it all?

"I never listen to those announcements. I'm just here to stock shelves." The selective listening of youth. Oh, my gosh. That sounded like something my mother would say. I whimpered as I rubbed my arm. "You okay, ma'am? Need one of those motor carts? Or some oxygen?" he said, giving me another glance and not the flattering variety I'm used to. That's another thing. Mom has to check out who comes to take me out and always has a comment about every man, sometimes to his face. Only one, Bill, was unperturbed. He had laughed and sweet-talked her and said he'd come back to play Cribbage some night. I don't appreciate Mom's interest. Talk about cramping my style. I'm in pretty good shape, have the body of a woman half my age. Not a gray hair either, or a wrinkle. Well, one or two. Laugh lines. I go to the spa and gym regularly, or did, until Mom moved in. Suddenly tired, I leaned on the handlebar of my shopping cart.

"Did you hear me, ma'am? Want a motorized cart?" the youth raised his voice and spoke slowly, word by word, as I do with Mother.

"I'm fine!" I snapped, rubbing the pain out of my elbow. I headed over to the produce section to check out those apples. I'd picked a cranky cart. Just like my mother, it kept taking a direction different from the one I wanted. As I struggled with it I rummaged around in my purse for the shopping list. Big mistake. I ran into a display, collapsing a whole pyramid of packages. There I was, knee deep in adult diapers. They weren't on my list. Not yet. I tried to restack the slippery bundles but they kept sliding away. I looked over my shoulder. THE BOY stood there.

He spoke slowly. Again. "Hard.. to.. get.. a.. grip.. ma'am?" Before I could retort he waved me on. Fuming, I turned my back on him, just as Mother does when I catch her doing something stupid. Perhaps I should give her a chance to explain. Finally in the produce section, I checked my list. Moldy apples? Nope. They weren't on anyone else's list either because the place was deserted save for an old man squeezing oranges, one in each hand. He leered at me, then eyed the plums and glanced back at me. He didn't look me in the eye. Shrugging, he turned his attention back to his orange orbs.

Static preceded a trumpet fanfare from the speaker system. "Buy one block of Brie, get one tree!" One tree? What kind? Bonsai tree? Shoe tree? Couldn't be right. Buy one brie, get one.....free! Inordinately proud, I rushed over and grabbed a couple. I seemed to be running in circles today, just like my cart. Back in the produce section I grabbed some apples and one end of the roll of plastic bags, pulling hard. The roll kept spinning, leaving me standing this time in several meters of plastic. I tossed the fruit into my basket, bruises be damned. Now the old man was feeling up melons. He glanced over my way, cocked one eyebrow and smirked.

"You having trouble, ma'am?" The boy was at my elbow again, voice raised and eyebrows too. "Not my job," he grumbled, "but I better get this mess cleaned up." Not my job, brother dear. Familiar words. A fat blackhead on the end of the boy's nose distracted me. I wanted to squeeze it, just like the old man was squeezing fruit. Gad, who made me the boy's mother? Guess that proverbial hill wasn't so far off and I was on my way over it. I watched as the young man knelt down at my feet and gathered the draped plastic into his arms, a cherub all wrapped up in excelsior. Standing, he flicked his wrist and the plastic sheeting tore neatly. Looking at me he rolled his eyes heavenward. I used to do that too. I'm doing it now, in fact, to mother, all the time, acting all superior. Demeaning.

The boy strolled off – probably back to the party section. He looked like a disappointed bride, a length of plastic sheeting trailing behind him. Wet behind the ears, that boy. He still hadn't learned the value of a good scrub up with hot water. Hot water. Don't know how Mom can stand water so hot. Last night I gave her a full bath in a steaming tub and she loved it, especially the back rub. Said that was the saddest part of being a widow, not having someone touch her anymore or hug her in bed. She's so gaunt with no fleshed out bits, except for the Caesarean scar, still puckered and rough from my brother's birth. I felt sad when I saw the hollowness of her breasts, now empty bags of skin.

"Honeydew? Or is this just a dimply cantaloupe?" The old man was at my elbow. I jumped and he dropped both. They smashed on the floor. "Now, look what you done, woman! Something wrong with you? Alls I wanted was to know how to tell if these here melons was ripe." He scurried off behind the carrots and parsnips and other pointy roots. What was he planning to check out there?

"Ma'am." The boy was back. He seemed tired, older somehow, looking at the mess at my feet. "You sure are having trouble today, lady." Lady? An improvement on ma'am?

"Wasn't my fault.......I'm sorry...." I was interrupted by another trumpet fanfare, with organ music to boot. "Mesning fod de flashling in ice-cream! Buy it now. Money back carenteest!!" Mom might like some ice- cream. Maybe I'll get some frozen yogurt for me. I wheeled my cart over to the middle of the store and strolled down the frozen food aisles. More people here, two mothers with children strapped into their shopping baskets and three toddlers running around, probably to keep warm. Brrrr, certainly a cold part of the store. Must have the temperature way down, not like my place that's so hot. Mom keeps turning up the thermostat, blind as she is, because it's never warm enough for her. Frozen peas... frozen entrees... where was the ice-cream? An Arctic ice cap was pervading the freezer section. Maybe Mom feels the cold like this too. I tried to take my sweater out of the basket but it got snagged on the kiddie safety belt. Peering at the stuck button I saw the yarn was entwined with the snap closing of the belt.

"Attention! Fezzle be destimeral or you skandickity suz mush!" It wouldn't come loose. "Bashoons going to be dustceuen in cases foose and choose! Fue duel!!" blared the speakers above my head.

"Oh, shut up, for heaven's sake!" I cried to the ceiling while I fiddled with the belt. It was immovable. I was having trouble seeing the fine yarn. Where were my glasses? I was shivering — with the cold? Or exhaustion? Frustration? I started to bounce up and down to get the feeling back in my legs, while my hands twisted and turned the sweater to untangle it.

"Mommy, why is that lady strapping her sweater into the seat and dancing?"

"Shh! Don't look, sweetie."

"Special!! Mexin das trop shdurtef for thirsty kids!! Last aisle!!" Wish I had this sound system at home. Mom never hears a word I say.

"Sounds good, don't you think?" said one of the young mothers, stealing a look at me. Had she understood the announcement? I stared at her, my mouth open as I tried to put on my sweater, finally free. Too late I realized the thing was now inside out, showing all the snagged ends on the inside. I'm a terrible knitter. Maybe when I am an old lady — like next week — I'll learn to knit properly. The baby safety belt was suspended from one of my buttons and it hung down to my knees. How stupid did I look?

"You coming, Susan?" said one of the mothers. To her baby she muttered, "Let's go, sweetie. I think we need some broccoli," and walked briskly down the aisle. Huh! Wait until she gets to the fresh food section and the old guy.

"Broccopooie? Me hate brocopooie!" screamed her child. Maybe the store had infants doing their announcements? I finally found my list. Fig bars! Of course! And aspirin, bread, cheese and bran. I got them all, then added some lavender bath oil. Mom and I just might have a day at the spa too, the full works, massage and all. She'd love Andrew's hands, strong and sure. At the bins of goodies I bought two pounds of jujubes and some chocolate bonbons. Last stop was the noticeboard where I tore off the phone number for the cocker spaniel. Unconditional love. Dogs are better at that than me. They need walks too. Good exercise, that. At the till, I turned my sweater right side out. Maybe Mom could tell me what to do with all these loose ends.

THE END

THE GREAT
OUTDOORS

"Where's my beer? I can't see it in the truck."

That's because she had unpacked it, craving the aroma of pine, not the stink of alcohol. The idea popped up again, a mole in the meadow of her mind. "Don't know, Stan. Why don't we unpack? Then get out the canoe for a paddle?"

"Need a drink. I'll go into town and pick up some."

"Why not wait? It'll turn up."

"So what? It'll all get drunk."

And so will he. Stan took off while Laurie organized the kitchen things. She found a bottle of vodka, half full, somehow left from the last visit – how did that happen? – two shelves above the vermin poison. Mmmmmm, with frozen limeade and lemons, cut as slim as a scalpel? That would make one interesting cocktail. She was sitting, iced pitcher ready, when he came back.

But their neighbor was with him. "Hi, Laurie. I was telling Stan about the problems we've been having with the water. Any of your well water in that? You better pitch it."

While Laurie poured the vodka concoction down the drain, the men cracked open beers. She gathered blankets and smacked them, hard, on the porch railing. Before making the bed she dug out the electric heater to deal with the dampness. That night she suggested Stan have a nice soak in the tub. Wobbly from the afternoon's drinking, he asked her to run the bath.

"Is the heater turned on, love?" Stan couldn't stand the cold.

"Yes, I put it up on the shelf out of the way." And balanced it just so. Laurie settled into bed and turned on the lamp. Sudden blackness. A power failure.

"Laurie! Bring a flashlight! Right after the lights went out there was a big splash!" She had to hold the lantern while he finished his bath, along with more drinks for his nerves.

The next morning Laurie insisted on a canoe ride. She had to do most of the paddling but managed to get them out of sight of shore. Taking a deep breath she started rocking the boat just as jet skis came shooting out of the horizon, straight for them.

"Watch out, you guys!" yelled Stan. Teenagers hooted at the pair in the canoe, teased them like dragonflies after a mosquito, then took off. Worn out, Laurie and Stan skulked back to shore.

A close call. Time for a drink? Laurie declined and went off to the woods to sit on the bridge over the rushing river. Rolling onto her tummy, she felt the damp planks, saw the rotten wood. Insects were burrowing, weakening the structure. Interesting, that.

"A hike? Sure, Laurie, why not? We'll pack a lunch." He insisted on carrying the backpack with the wine. Nice guy.

"Why don't we split, Stan? See which way is faster to the top?"

"Okay. Meet you at the look-out?" Stan headed for the bridge while Laurie ran up the path, all the better to watch. Her husband came to the bridge, glanced down, then stopped. What on earth...? She saw him take off his clothes, toss them to the other bank, plunge into the cold water and wade across. He reached into the river to retrieve a six-pack. From last summer? Then he lay down in the sun, supping his find. Laurie moaned. What was left? Another hike, with a falling boulder? He'd bend down for a beer and have it miss him. Mosquito carrying some deadly disease? The poor bug would die of alcohol poisoning. Fall off the roof while checking the chimney? He'd land on his feet, for sure.

"How about a bike ride?" suggested Laurie the next morning. "My tires need air, though. I'll drive there with my bicycle in the truck and meet you." Perhaps his bike would slip on the gravel, landing him in the car's path. Or her cellphone could ring and she'd be distracted, run right into him. No, there'd be no record of a call. The dog could suddenly jump into her lap. Yes, that might work.

"Here, Misty," she called. "The exercise will do you good." Stan cycled off. Minutes later she and Misty turned onto Forest Road. She saw Stan riding, head down, and made straight for him. Until the dog barked. A deer – in the middle of the road! She swerved, missing the animal and her husband. Misty jumped out the window as the truck hit the mailboxes.

"Let's go back to the city," grunted Laurie.

THE END

WHAT TO DO?

E laine hasn't always been a pessimist, but cynicism has been creep-
ing up on her like mold in a damp basement. The child's words
don't surprise her.

"Mummy, I wish she was dead." The toddler is hanging onto her
sister's stroller by one hand, her feet anchored against the wheels. Her
free hand flies through the air, round and round. The carefree stance
is disturbing, a contrast to her chilling words. A cold breeze swoops
through the courtyard. Elaine shivers and pulls her sweater closed.
The library should be open by now.

"What did you say?" asks the young mother, giving a weak smile
to Elaine. Do I know you? Elaine thinks. For your information, I
don't think all children are cute.

"I don't want a baby sister. I have to take care of her. I don't like
sharing," answers the tot. Smart kid. Elaine understands. She hates her
own sister, who thinks sharing's just fine. This year she shared Elaine's
husband Larry, who didn't demur. Bastard.

"I know. But she loves you. Wouldn't you miss her?" her
Mom reasons. She hands a jacket to the girl, then reaches into
the buggy to secure a blanket around the infant. Leslie could
disappear from the face of the earth forever, as far as Elaine was

concerned. Who'd miss her? Not even Larry, who soon tired of the woman's selfishness.

The child stands up straight, thinks a moment, then shakes her head. "No, I wouldn't miss her." She struggles into her jacket, doesn't bother with the buttons.

Good for you. Sisters should be separated from birth. Or later, if necessary. Elaine had hatched several schemes. She checks her watch. Five past ten. Where is that librarian? She peeks back into the parking lot to check for the meter maid. Elaine hasn't put any money in the machine because she didn't think she'd be long. She hadn't counted on a tardy librarian.

"No more talk like that, young lady, or there'll be no dessert for supper." Now there's an incentive, thought Elaine. What would I need to forestall my own murderous intent?

"Mummy! That's not fair. I..I...don't mean...it. Not really," frowns the child, hands planted at her waist, elbows out, while she contemplates the thought of no dessert. Would it be enough to behave? She needs more facts. "What is dessert, anyway?"

"Gingerbread. With whipped cream."

It wouldn't be enough for Elaine. She's well acquainted with the urge to commit murder. She's been angry enough to kill, more than once. Her sister was the first target. Then others became possibilities. Homicide had become her hobby, though she never goes through with any of her schemes. The strategy helps her cope somehow. When she came close one time, a bad time, a few weeks ago, her therapist convinced her to quit her job. That's why she's here mid-morning, waiting for the library to open. If she gets a parking ticket she'll throttle that librarian though. It wouldn't be that hard to arrange a very serious accident. Larry had found that out.

How to murder a librarian? How hard would it be to push over a shelf brimming with books? You'd need some sort of lever. Maybe a cane, one end propped under the bottom shelf, then simply raise the other end until the whole structure topples over onto the unsuspecting woman shelving books. That would be one limp librarian, well past her due date. Discarded. Perhaps she could visit the place one evening just before closing. She'd stack some shopping in the rear window of her car. When the librarian came out she would suddenly reverse and bang! Bowling down the book lady. Surely an accident? Elaine feels better as she shoves such thoughts out of her mind. She isn't supposed to think like that anymore. Not since she came so close that time, just after she'd discovered Leslie and Larry together. Alliterative lovers...lashed lengthwise...in the lounge. Elaine giggled. The little girl stares at her. She shouldn't laugh. No parlor game, for there was no winner that day she'd discovered them together in her own bed. She couldn't believe it, but she'd just quietly shut the bedroom door and gone to work.

Not a good idea. She should have screamed, gone for a walk, left the city. But she'd just got on with things, returned to work, which wasn't the happiest place either. Sitting at her desk that afternoon Elaine saw how easily thoughts of murder can take over your heart. Her superior had been undermining her for months. Why had he chosen that very morning to steal her proposal, copy and present it as his own to the new owners? How much more could she take? She wasn't surprised at the man's lack of ethics. He'd established a pattern of keeping her unaware of developments in the merger and ignorant of instructions from higher up. Her day just kept getting worse. When the final straw came, an unwarranted accusation of questionable bookkeeping along with a demeaning reprimand, she'd left the office before the others, waited outside by her colleague's car and was that close to bashing him in the head with a tire iron. Even had it in her hand. Who'd blame her? She was being a good accountant, after all, balancing the books, evening the score. Accountants don't count, do they? She stopped just in time, hating herself for her actions. Or for not carrying it through?

The therapist told her to leave. Leave it all – the toxic working environment, the bad marriage, the sibling rivalry. You can't change events, only your reaction – always the woman's admonition. She despises the therapist's cute little phrases. Elaine doesn't much like the world anymore or what it's thrown her way, just like that little girl having to share her mother and her love. It isn't the child's fault. Evil lurks in everyone, somewhere beneath reason, a viper waiting to lash out. Human nature will always rear its ugly head. She knew she had to come to terms with Leslie's warped motives.

Elaine takes a couple of deep breaths, ends with one prolonged exhalation. The therapist had taught her that technique too, for anger management, right after Larry's car had crashed. Breathing like that only made her feel empty inside. What she needs is a good rest. Breathe again, let go. Let go of control. Another coping mantra from her therapist. She realizes she's rattling her car keys, faster and faster. The little girl is staring at Elaine's key chain as if hypnotized.

"Never mind, dear," Elaine says to the child, "sharing doesn't get any easier. But you get used to it." The tot puckers her forehead. She understands Elaine's words and doesn't like them. Elaine wants to tell her everything is supposed to get easier, like eating cauliflower, tying your shoelaces, riding your tricycle, growing up, leaving home. Getting married for better or worse, having your trust trampled, being betrayed by a deceitful boss, seeing your husband kiss your sister in that way...desertion...death. Will any of it get any easier? She notices the child has started to suck her thumb, is grabbing at her mother's skirt. She wishes she could do the same. "Remember, if you teach her to share she'll share things with you," Elaine can't help adding, bitterly. She's becoming agitated, she knows. She pauses, turns to the child's mother, but the young woman is busy with her own thoughts.

"When you get to my age, you'll find you're tired of sharing. It happens," she whispers. The mother looks at her, startled.

"You have to hope for the best," the young woman mutters. She doesn't have a clue. Do unto others as you would have them do unto you? Yeah, sure. Elaine's anger flares. She's rattling her keys again, loudly, remembering the grilling by that awful policeman. She breathes deeply. Better check the parking lot. Ten minutes, at least, she's been standing here.

"Hello, ladies," says the librarian, unlocking the door and holding it open for the mother and her children. Elaine hangs back, puts her keys into her purse. She's just seen the meter maid snap a ticket under her windshield wiper. Hostility wells up, drowning her resolve. If that librarian had been punctual! Here she is, blocking the doorway, relocating clips in her hairdo, giving an insipid smile to the toddler.

The little girl isn't fooled. Instead, she ignores the woman, kneels down and unlocks the buggy brake for her mother. As the young family heads into the building the child steps on the librarian's toes. Just like that harassment suit she'd launched against the police after she'd been exonerated and Leslie had been charged.

"Ow!" yelps the woman. Elaine bites her tongue to keep from smiling. She admires the toddler's spunk. A streak of sun pierces the entryway. Elaine feels a flutter in her chest, her mouth twitches. Is it a smile? She waits for the path to clear, then follows the family. Finally, she's able to get to the desk and gets out her library card.

"Hello, Mrs. Taverner. How are you today? Bright and early, as usual, I see."

"Hello. I'm fine, thank you. Yes, I was here at ten, when you open." Or should open! Would the stupid woman take her point? "I've lots to do today. I think you have a book for me?"

"Let me see." Elaine's words have gone right over her head. Or through it? Another librarian, the older one, comes over to see Elaine and smiles.

"Your help was invaluable last week at the sale, Mrs. Taverner." A cry comes from the children's department. She continues, in a whisper. "There's that baby crying again. Every time they come here the baby ends up whimpering. Not a very happy infant."

"If you ask me, it's the toddler's fault. I've seen her pinching her sister when her mother's not looking," says the younger clerk.

"You're kidding!" exclaims the other. "Do you know, she tromped on my foot out there? The child needs some discipline. Someone should tell the mother."

"Not me," states the young librarian.

"Did you get rid of everything? Make much money?" asks Elaine. Stop gossiping and hurry up!.

"Oh yes! It's nice to have room for new stock too." The other librarian is back, snapping off an elastic that holds a label to Elaine's book. The elastic breaks into two and part of it hits Elaine. She cries out.

"Oh dear. Sorry. Did it hit you?" Maybe her words *had* hit home. Retribution?

"No...I don't think so...no. It just startled me, I guess." Stupid woman. I should teach her a lesson. Wrap a few elastics around that crazy hairdo of hers. Doesn't she realize she looks weird with her hair like that?

"That'll be due three weeks from today, Mrs. Taverner."

"Thank you," says Elaine. If I hear her say that one more time I'll scream. Every week for how many years?

"See you," says the librarian. As Elaine walks away she hears her say, "Such a nice woman, that Mrs. Taverner." The other librarian nods. Heading out Elaine sees the young family coming to the top of the stairs from the children's section below.

"Sweetie, stop hanging on. It's hard to lift the buggy. You don't need to hold me either. Can't you see I'm busy with the baby?" Elaine can hear the little girl muttering, the infant sniffling. The woman finally has the carriage on the landing. She leans over, speaks soothingly to the infant, tucks her in and pats her until the baby quietens. Her older child, ignored, whines throughout, while trying to fit her books and videos into a little quilted book bag.

When she sees Elaine staring at her she says, "Hi."

Elaine answers, "Hello. What a nice book bag." She kneels down to the child's level. "It's nice to have something that's all yours, isn't it?" The child nods. "But some things are nice to share." The little girl frowns. "Really," says Elaine. This is a child, after all. "You'll see. Like watching one of those videos, or...or a ride on a merry-go-round. It's nice to share good times with other people, even a sister. Of course, there are things you shouldn't have to share. And won't have to."

The little girl stops sniffling, looks at her and gives a shy smile. "That's okay, I guess," she says. The mother mouths a 'thank you' to Elaine.

Back in the parking lot Elaine whips the parking ticket out from her windshield wiper, tosses it into the passenger seat, along with the library book, which lands face up. She stares at the title, another suggestion from her therapist. *The Complete Idiot's Guide to a Happy Life*. She starts to giggle, then laughs aloud. She can't stop. She feels as if she's been bungee jumping and has finally reached the end of her tether. Something is yanking her up, swift and sure. Wiping her eyes, she takes a deep breath, a real breath this time, one that soothes. Using the rear-view mirror she dries her cheeks with her scarf. She notices the windshield is streaked, sees the spring sunshine struggling to get through. Turning on the windshield washer she watches the grime run down and disappear beneath the glass. She repeats the cycle. And again. The windshield is sparkling clean now. She pauses, taking in the sun's comforting rays. Her neck, shoulders and chest relax in the heat. She clips on her sunglasses, then slips the gearshift into reverse, remembering to straighten the rear view mirror before putting her foot to the gas. Good job, too.

The young mother is leaning into the trunk of her car, rearranging parcels before placing her coat on top. Unattended, her baby's buggy is rolling across the parking lot directly into the path of Elaine's reversing car. The toddler drops her bag of books. With coat half off and one arm outstretched, she stumbles after the buggy. Managing to catch it she secures the brake, then holds up her arm, the one still in its coat sleeve, a diminutive traffic cop taking care of things, telling the world what to do.

THE END

YOU
CAN'T
TAKE IT
WITH YOU

Awakened by her cough, Jennifer reached out to David but her hand clutched only a sheet for he was long gone. David was a love 'em and leave 'em kind of guy and she'd recognized the type. Cupping her hand to her chapped nose she blew into a tissue loudly.

Echinacea – she needed some echinacea. Fumbling in the nightside table drawer she could only find a thermometer, used it and knew it was time. Gad, her throat felt awful and nausea welled. Ice chips, they should help. Jennifer shivered her way to the kitchen, changed her mind and pulled out a ginger root to gnaw on, hoping it would settle her tummy, while she removed an implement from another drawer and returned to the bedroom.

Knowing it was stupid and hating herself for it, she picked up the phone and dialed David's number, only to hear, "Leave your number after the tone. Maybe I'll call you when I get home." Not very likely, thought Jennifer. Obviously, to him, she was a one-night stand. He got what he wanted. So did she. Prophylactics are impregnable? Quality sperm from a world class athlete. Raising it to eye level she was pleased to see the condom had nearly two teaspoons of sperm. Satisfied, she took it into the bathroom. The turkey baster was the perfect tool, unless she botched it. There was a good chance this time it would take, seeing she was ovulating. Very gently, but surely, she transferred the elixir of life to where it would stay, for better or worse.

"Wonderful," she whispered as she flopped down on the bed where she stayed, her hips supported in the air by pillows. "X marks the spot, little ones," she murmured. "You can play there just as long as you stay there!"

THE END

THE LAST LAUGH

He was glad they were dead. Sharing the house with four women hadn't been easy. When Papa willed the place to all five the patriarch had had the last laugh on Thomas, the son who'd never amounted to much. As the only male heir it should have been his, especially when the daughters each had a nest egg to boot. Tom didn't have the wherewithal to buy out any of them and none would leave. Obstinate women. The four sisters were inseparable, leaving Thomas the odd man out midst their inane chatter.

It takes a patient man to play a waiting game. Only one sister left now. It's amazing what can kill off people. Falls. Bad food. Acid reflux. No one seemed even curious that the Hainsleys were dropping like houseflies. This last sister was the one Thomas liked the least. She was all sweet on the surface, but Thomas knew her hidden depths. Without the support of her womenfolk it would be an even playing field.

"Breakfast, Thomas?" Dolly asked as he shuffled into the kitchen. He knew by her raised eyebrows she didn't like his still being in pajamas and his oldest slippers, his favorite. They were worn smooth by years of use. What did he care? One against one, now.

"Yes, two eggs poached." He sat down to read the paper.

"There's an announcement in there about Father's business being sold again," said Dolly.

"Humph! They just keep making money from that mill, don't they?" And none of it ever comes to me, thought Thomas. If he'd been given a chance to run it, things would be a helluva lot different now.

"Father wouldn't believe their asking price. He'd roll over in his grave, for sure," laughed Dolly. The last girl, she'd been given that nickname and it had stuck. Her father's favorite, she was the only child of his second marriage. His doll face, he used to say. The man had a thing for women. He'd outlived two wives to marry a third. Thomas was the one offspring of wife number three, the one his father had divorced as soon as he discovered her liaisons and recovered his wits. Thomas's mother had a lot to answer for. If she'd behaved herself Thomas wouldn't be in this position.

Dolly placed the warm plate of eggs in front of him. "See, I gave you toast soldiers for dipping. The bloody woman had taken the eggs out too early. He liked his eggs solid, not runny. Thomas didn't bother to say thank you. Dolly went out the back door to get her watering can and came back to fill it at the kitchen sink.

"The water line's frozen outside, Thomas. A cold night, for sure. Will you be having a fire today?"

"Course. Have one every day." Leaving the fireplace doors open meant sparks could singe her hearth rug, That gave him lots of pleasure. It had taken her a year to hook that rug.

"I'm just going upstairs to see to the beds. I've got a chocolate cake in the oven, Thomas. Your favorite. I'll be back before it's ready to take out. Enjoy your breakfast. There's tea in the pot." Thomas liked coffee in the morning and she knew it. Bitch. He'd show her. He went over to the oven and peered inside. The cake was rising nicely. He slammed the oven door, twice. Flat as a pancake. Teach her to poach his eggs like that. Gingerbread was his favorite cake, too, not chocolate. She knew it.

Thomas ate the eggs anyway and finished off the pot of tea. He didn't bother to tidy up. Instead he pulled his cigarettes out of his pocket, lit up and smoked a couple while he finished the paper, dropping ashes onto the china plate. Some fell onto the placemat and scorched the white linen. When Dolly came back and saw what had happened to her cake she glanced at Thomas who was deep into the comics. When he heard her remove the pan from the oven with a grunt he smirked behind his paper. "How'd your cake turn out, Dolly?"

"More like a pan of brownies, for some reason. I'll just ice it and cut it up into squares. No harm done. You'll enjoy them, I'm sure. I can't have any. I've finally lost that five pounds and reached my goal. Mustn't be tempted." She proceeded to turn the disaster into a treat, then ran hot, soapy water into the sink and took Thomas's dirty plates. Within ten minutes the kitchen was clean and tidy, with a plate of vanilla iced brownies on the counter. He couldn't resist taking one when she proffered the plate to him. She saw the burns on the place-mat and rolled it up. "I might be able to mend this with some crochet cotton. It'll give me something to do."

Thomas was miffed. The woman was impossible. He went upstairs to his bedroom and was irked to see it tidy too with fresh sheets on the bed, turned down invitingly. In the bathroom he discovered a new bar of shaving soap in a pottery bowl. Grudgingly, he washed and shaved and put on a clean outfit. The damn woman had taken the clothes he'd worn all last week, likely for laundering. Who asked her? He could hear the washer running, and the vacuum too. She never did just one thing. Thomas tiptoed into Dolly's room and saw her yarns spilling out of a basket. He took her little scissors for snipping ends and did just that. He shoved the scissors into each ball as far as he could and cut, over and over. From the outside the balls looked intact. In her bathroom he turned up the scales. He stopped short of squirting some of her liquid soap into the tub. Another time, maybe. He looked out the bathroom window and saw her tidying the wood pile. Always cleaning up. He saw her pick up her watering can. 'Everything with a place and everything in its place' he sang with a sneer in his voice. Her favorite saying. His was 'You'll get yours!'

At eleven that morning they were both ready to play their TV quiz show. They'd try to say the answers before the contestants did. With only two of them Thomas finally had a chance to win. As Dolly crocheted and discovered the yarn kept coming to an end, her concentration waned and he beat her easily.

"Congratulations, Thomas. Looks like I got a bad batch of yarn. I should have rewound it when I bought it. I would have discovered it was defective. I'll have to get some more. What would you like for lunch? I should make you something special, seeing you won."

Something time-consuming. "You know, Dolly, I'd like some of that wonderful beef vegetable soup you used to make."

"That takes hours, Thomas. I'll do it for supper."

"Oh. How about some grilled cheese on rye?"

"There's no rye bread."

He knew that. "Couldn't you get some? When you go to get some yarn?" Dolly's mouth tightened, but just a little. She went to the hall closet for her coat. Thomas did the gentlemanly thing and helped her on with it. It was the least he could do.

"I won't be long, Thomas. Is there anything else you'd like while I'm out?"

He shook his head and ambled into the living room. He heard her run some more water and go outside. What was she doing out there, anyway? Watering the snow? Stupid woman. He went to the kitchen and had a few more brownies to tide him over until lunch. They were yummy and he finished off the plate. Might as well get the wood for today's fire. Dolly wasn't here to nag him about dressing properly with coat and boots. Thomas went out the back door in his worn slippers and strode quickly down the path toward the stack of logs. His feet hit a long patch of ice, groomed smooth as a skater's dream. Legs slipped out from under him. His head hit the pavement with a crack.

Amazing what can happen to people. That's what Dolly said, hours later – it had taken some time to find the right yarn –when she called the police after finding the frozen body of her brother. After they'd taken Thomas away, she put her watering can back in the summer shed where it belonged. She wouldn't be using it until spring, weeks away. That cold snap was just what she'd needed for the job. Dolly sat down in front of the fireplace for the evening, but not before she closed the glass doors. There would be no more fires in this house. Too messy. Finally, she was alone, with everything neat and clean, just the way she liked it. Daddy would have wanted it this way, for her to have the house all to herself. She was his favorite, after all.

THE END

ABOUT THE AUTHOR

Penny Gumbert pursued her desire to write after retiring from teaching. Her essays and articles have been published in Canada's national newspaper The Globe & Mail as well as in The Hamilton Spectator, North Country Business and the Port Dover Maple Leaf. Her love of nature and cottage life are shown by her published works in Muskoka Magazine, The Country Connection, Cottage Life Magazine, Vitality, Cottage Times and The Muskokan.

Her awards include being published in The Grist Mill Volume 12 after competing in the John Spencer Hill Competition, a prize in the Agnes Jamieson Gallery contest, winning the Standamar Publishing Award for best fiction during the 2002 Hamilton & Region Arts Council Literary Competition. She earned a place in Winners Circle 10 International Short Story Contest, the Writers' Federation of New Brunswick Literary Competition, Canadian Authors' Association 2001 short story contest and Muskoka Magazine's 2004 short story contest. A children's story earned her first prize in the Muskoka Storytelling Contest 2003. She has taken part in Local Literary Lapses at the Leacock Festival, and appeared in Rise up Singing, an Anthology of Women's Poetry and Prose.

CPSIA information can be obtained at www.ICGtesting.com
Printed in the USA
LVOW08s1539160716

496598LV00001B/2/P